# The shiny badge winked back at Bolan like a single mocking eye

"I've been waiting for you all my life, and here we are." The rifle didn't waver as Laurenti took a cautious step toward Bolan.

From the beginning of his private war, the Executioner had clung to certain principles. Among them was his firm refusal to drop the hammer on a cop, and his grim resolve had not been shaken by numerous encounters with corrupt detectives. He wouldn't kill Laurenti now, even if it meant his own life. Still, there might be a chance to slip beneath Laurenti's guard and grab the Colt Commando.

As if he had been able to decipher Bolan's thoughts, the gunner hesitated, although he was far enough away to stop any move to reach his weapons.

"I wanted you to know why you were dying," Laurenti grated. "When it came, I wanted you to know who pulled the trigger. I owe you that much, and I owe it to myself. I owe it to my father."

# MACK BOLAN

## The Executioner

DON PENDLETON's EXECUTIONER

# MACK BOLAN

## Eternal Triangle

A GOLD EAGLE BOOK FROM

# W⦿RLDWIDE

TORONTO • NEW YORK • LONDON • PARIS
AMSTERDAM • STOCKHOLM • HAMBURG
ATHENS • MILAN • TOKYO • SYDNEY

First edition May 1987

ISBN 0-373-61101-3

Special thanks and acknowledgment to
Mike Newton for his contribution to this work.

Printed in Canada

You must not fight too often with one enemy, or you will teach him the art of war.

—Napoleon

There is one means by which I can be sure never to see my country's ruin: I will die in the last ditch.

—William III

The last ditch may be here, in Pittsfield, and by now the enemy may know my style too well, but there are times when duty leaves no choice. Like here. Like now.

—Mack Bolan

To the victims of organized crime

## Prologue

The basement bore a musty scent of long disuse. It was several days since he had ventured down into his secret place, and now the hunter flared his nostrils, picking out the separate, familiar smells of dust and mildew, age and slow decay. He knew what lay below. The darkness held no secrets from him; it inspired no apprehension in the hunter's heart or mind. The darkness was an old and trusted friend.

Before attempting to negotiate the narrow stairs, he flicked the light switch to illuminate the basement's single naked bulb. The single naked bulb that hung from the ceiling was adequate for his requirements, and the shadows it engendered were comforting, like the cobweb haze surrounding ancient memories. The shadows blunted pain and helped the hunter focus on his prey.

A workbench stood along one basement wall, its surface stained by oils and acids, scarred by tools that hung on nails and brackets. The hunter would not work tonight. His preparations were complete, and it was time for recreation now. Before the kill, so long delayed, he needed to unwind.

He had undressed before descending to the basement, and his muscles rippled under the light. He stood erect, confident of his physique without a trace of pride, secure in himself without a hint of narcissism. He habitually came naked to the basement, shedding years and garments in the rooms upstairs, discarding all the artificial trappings of his daily life before descending the stairs to find the past that was his destiny.

The wooden chest was old. It had been a fixture in his family for years. In its time it had contained the dreams of maidens and the memories of generations gone to dust. The hunter had removed all traces of posterity save one, consigned them to the fire. In place of heirlooms, he had packed the stuff of memories to be.

He knelt before the chest, concrete unyielding, rough beneath his knees. He was unmindful of discomfort as he spun the combination dial, unlocked the chest and raised its weathered lid. At once, the smell of gun oil reached his nostrils, cutting through the scent of dust and age.

A loose-leaf scrapbook, bound in leather and secured with rawhide thongs, lay on top. The pages were irregular, rough-cut, mismatched in size and color. Some were crisp with age, their pasted clippings yellow, seamed like parchment. Others were more recent, bearing clips secured within the past few weeks or days. The hunter did not read them now. He knew each piece by heart, could have recited them from memory without referring to the faded text. His hands were steady as he laid the scrapbook carefully aside.

Neatly folded beneath was a well-worn set of camouflage fatigues. The hunter stood and slipped on the old familiar garments, his eyes already straying to the far end of the basement as he buttoned his shirt and buckled on the pistol belt of military webbing. There were boots, as well, but he ignored them, standing barefoot on the cool concrete, intent on completion of the ritual.

Beneath the clothing lay the weapons, wrapped in canvas, slick with oil and solvent. Some had been dismantled, broken down to fit the chest, while others had been small enough to pack intact. A visual inspection showed him everything secure: the guns and ammunition, extra magazines, the special items he had obtained at no small risk. Accumulating the necessary tools had taken months, years, but he was ready now. The waiting was behind him.

It was time.

He crouched before the open chest again, his fingers playing over oily steel as if enraptured by the outline of the weapons. Even in their silence they were lethal, manufactured for the single purpose of eradicating human life. No sporting weapons here, designed to ventilate a paper silhouette or drop a helpless quadruped in flight. The pieces in his private cache were manufactured for mortal combat, tested on a hundred different urban battlefields and proved in blood. The Uzi submachine gun and the smaller MAC-10 Ingram, both 9 mm weapons meant for close-up work. The Franchi SPAS 12 autoloading shotgun and the little stakeout 12-gauge pump from Ithaca, with shoulder stock removed and barrel shortened for concealment under clothing. The well-oiled Colt Commando, compact cousin of the M-16, which had surrendered size while clinging fast to the destructive capabilities of the original. The Weatherby Mark V .460 Magnum hunting rifle, fitted out with telescopic sight. The range of heavy caliber handguns, autoloaders and revolvers. The blocks of soft plastique, done up in string and oilcloth like a poor man's Christmas package.

The hunter had been circumspect in the selection of his tools, anticipating each eventuality and the reactions of his prey. The enemy would come with weapons of his own, possessed of martial skills that made him uniquely dangerous, but he was not invincible. The hunter had surprise and preparation on his side, together with the contents of his secret chest, and it would be enough.

The trailing fingers settled on a leather sheath containing half a dozen throwing knives. The hunter straightened, fastened the sheath onto his pistol belt before he took a knife in hand. The flattened steel was balanced, razor sharp, designed for accuracy, range and penetration. He had practiced with the knives dutifully, until he knew that he could kill or maim at fifty feet in daylight or in darkness.

From the corner of his eye he saw the enemy, immobile on the periphery of vision, poised to strike. A heartbeat, less, before a hostile weapon cut him down. No time for conscious thought before he made his move.

The hunter pivoted to face his enemy in profile, drew back his arm and let go before the other could react. The knife flashed once beneath the naked bulb, and then its razor tip was buried deep between Mack Bolan's eyes.

The police identisketch bore countless wounds, most clustered in the face and chest, unhealed by time. If Bolan suffered from the deep, untended scars, he gave no sign.

But soon.

His time was coming, soon, and flesh would scream where photographic prints and fiberboard had borne their wounds in stoic silence.

Soon.

The hunter smiled and reached for another knife.

# 1

On his second pass, Mack Bolan saw the sentries walking their beat outside the target warehouse. Normally there would have been a single man, but these were troubled times; Bolan knew he would have to deal with both before he made his way inside. If there were others whom he had not spotted . . . well, he would deal with that eventuality if and when it arose.

He drove the rented four-door another block and parked it in the looming shadow of a warehouse that had clearly not been used in months. He would be forced to double back on foot, but it would give him time to think and some of the combat stretch he needed to succeed in his midnight strike.

The soldier had already taped over the car's dome light, and he went EVA now without the fear of prying eyes. He shed his trench coat to reveal the jet-black skinsuit underneath. It fitted him like a second skin, with handy hidden pockets for stilettos and garrotes, a pencil flash and lock picks, other gear. The sleek Beretta 93-R, with its special silencer, was snug inside its shoulder rigging, easily accessible.

Inside the rental's trunk, he found the duffel bag that held his other gear. With practiced hands, he buckled on the military harness, fastened the web belt snugly and adjusted it until the AutoMag was comfortable on his hip. He closed his eyes and found the extra magazines, the hand grenades and slim incendiary sticks by touch, aware that in the heat of combat—if it came to that—he would not have the time to grope and guess.

He would be forced to kill the sentries, certainly, but Bolan hoped that he could end it there, without engaging any larger force. He left the Uzi and CAR-15 inside the trunk, relying on mobility and his advance reconnaissance to see him through. The play was hit-and-git; if there were any rude surprises in the warehouse, he would deal with them in turn. If it went smoothly, as he hoped, he would be that much closer to the resolution of a shooting war that had disturbed the peace and quality of life in Hartford long enough.

Connecticut's capital had a population of 140,000, give or take a few. With five distinguished colleges within a four-mile radius of the capitol dome, Hartford casually combined a sense of youth and feel for history. Mark Twain had been a native, as had Noah Webster. The town had carved itself a slice of revolution in the days when Americans were colonists, indentured to a foreign king. In those days Connecticut was the "Arsenal of the Nation," the most industrialized of the new United States. Hartford had led the way.

In Bolan's time, there was no gambling to speak of, nothing in the way of major prostitution, labor racketeering or extortion. Drugs had been the ticket for the mob in Hartford, with the student population of the seventies and eighties as a ready market for the poison organized importers could supply. The action had been run from Boston and New York till very recently, but there were signs of restlessness among the local troops, an urge to cut themselves a larger slice of pie.

The restlessness had turned to violence lately, with a string of bombings, beatings, driveby shootings and selective disappearances, as local shock troops turned upon their distant capos, then upon each other, grappling for territories, customers...the works. The Executioner hoped he could bring their present feuding to an end, so the peaceful college town could return to something like normality...for a while.

But there would be a price.

No chef could make an omelet without breaking eggs, and Bolan knew he could not eradicate the recent violence of insurgent thugs without resorting to some violence of his own. It was a law of nature, simple and immutable: the only way to stop a savage was to kill him in his tracks, or else frighten him so badly that he spent the next few weeks or months in hiding. Of the two alternatives—one permanent, one temporary—Bolan's normal choice would be elimination of the enemy, but there were other aspects to consider on the eve of war.

Connecticut was relatively free of mob contagion at the moment. Certain ranking capos made their homes around the Nutmeg State, escaping from the smog and other dangers of Manhattan, but they generally refrained from doing business there, adhering to the maxim that you don't shit where you eat. Narcotics traffic into Hartford and environs was a notable exception. If left unchecked, the rising turks among the younger mafiosi would eventually expand their local power base, extending tentacles to other towns, incorporating other rackets.

It was rare for Bolan to have an opportunity to nip a fledgling syndicate expansion in the bud; he could not afford to let the moment slip away. If he could halt the present shooting war, discourage or eliminate the chief belligerents, Hartford would survive the storm, endure and grow.

And if he played his cards right, Bolan would survive, as well.

He spent a moment staring northward, following the banks of the winding Connecticut River in the darkness. From Bolan's vantage point, he could see the runway lights of Hartford's major airport, their flashing beacons offering safe haven to travelers from near and far. There was no safety here, no haven for the Executioner, however. He had come in search of danger, courting death, and he would not be finished with his work until he spread the cleansing fire among his enemies.

He locked the car and left it, merging with the shadows as he backtracked toward his target. He would have to take the sentries first, no way around it. He could not afford to let them live, continue on their rounds and possibly discover him inside. He needed time, uninterrupted time, in which to send their boss a message from the heart.

The guards were young, their shadowed faces reminiscent of a thousand others Bolan had encountered in his war against the Mafia. Young faces with the stamp of cruel and unforgiving streets, brutality and avarice reflected in their eyes. Dead faces, for the most part, stripped of soul long before the Executioner arrived to cast his final vote.

It might seem simple to eliminate these two, but overconfidence was an insidious disease that sapped a soldier's normal caution, made him reckless, got him killed. If there were other sentries, perhaps inside the warehouse, he would have to deal with them as well, and that required a maximum of stealth, a minimum of warning to the enemy.

The final twenty yards were open ground. Bolan made it in a rush, alert to any sign that he had been observed. He found a shadowed hiding place beneath the loading dock and tugged the sleek Beretta from its armpit sheath, released the safety as he waited for his targets to complete their circuit of the warehouse. Any moment now...

He heard their voices first, and then their footsteps, slapping on the concrete of the loading dock. The sentries took no serious precautions, trusting in their guns and the invincibility of youth to see them through the boring hours of their watch. Their conversation hinged on sex and money, concepts that their minds had inextricably confused.

"You oughta see this broad, I'm tellin' ya."

"How much?"

"What is this shit, how much? I never paid her anything. A coupla presents, maybe."

"Yeah, an' that ain't payin?"

"Kiss my ass, Balducci."

"Sure, but it'll cost ya."

"Hey, tha's cute. So fuckin' funny I forgot to laugh."

They passed by Bolan without a glance into the shadows where he crouched and waited. He gave them five before he rose from cover, the Beretta braced and leveled in a double-handed grip, eyes narrowed as he sighted down the slide. At fifteen feet, the range was virtually point-blank.

He took the tallest gunner first, a single parabellum round impacting at the juncture of skull and vertebrae, obliterating life and conscious thought before the gunner realized he was dying. Bolan pivoted to take the second sentry before he could react, squeezing off a double punch that bored between his shoulder blades and pitched the young man forward on his face.

They lay together, dark blood mingling on the loading dock, as Bolan scrambled up to stand beside them. Si-

lence, except for soft, nocturnal river sounds, and in another moment Bolan knew he was alone. The way was
clear.

He dragged each hollow man in turn across the loading
dock, into the deeper shadows against the wall. Their
blood made crazy patterns on the pavement, and he
stepped around it, avoiding any footprints in the gore. It
was enough for Bolan's purpose that passing headlight
beams not illuminate the bodies. Thirty minutes after he
was gone, it would not matter who discovered them.

He found an access door and knelt before it, probing
with a slender pick until the tumblers fell consecutively into
place. He gambled that there would be a delay on the
alarm, allowing anyone who opened in the morning to
deactivate the system manually. His fingers found the cutoff switch above the doorjamb, muzzling the alarm before it could betray him.

Once inside, he used the pencil flash to find his way
around. The shipping office was a glassed-in box on Bolan's left, the warehouse proper opening before him, crates
of merchandise arranged in pyramidal rows that towered
almost to the vaulted ceiling. All or most of it was contra-
band from a string of hijacks on the coastal highway,
trucked to Hartford and allowed to cool before redistri-
bution to shady retail outlets all across New England.
There were televisions, crates of cigarettes and liquor,
clothing, appliances of every shape and size—all free of
taxes for crooked merchants anxious for a bargain, no
questions asked.

The warehouse was a gold mine for its owner, would-be
capo Larry Giulianno. Rumor billed him as the stronger of
the local warlords; his well-established trade in hijacked
merchandise kept Giulianno's war chest brimming over
while his competitor was reduced to begging loans from

other families to keep himself in men and guns. Destruction of the warehouse might not cripple Giulianno's team, but it would slow it down, and for the moment that was victory enough.

Alert to any sign that he might have overlooked another sentry in the warehouse, Bolan moved along the narrow aisles, scattering time-delay incendiaries as he went. Beginning at the far end of the building, working toward the door and loading dock, he laid a trail of fire, waiting to explode and spread among the crates of merchandise. The first incendiaries were already popping as he backed toward the door. Bolan spent a moment on the threshold, watching as the flames took hold. The sticks were built around a thermite core, designed to start a fire and keep it going in the worst of weather. Giulianno's sprinkler system would be unable to quell the blaze, and by the time a fire alarm went out, the place would be a total loss. How many stolen dollars up in smoke? Enough, for now.

Outside, the night was crisp and clear, but it would soon be smoky like the warehouse, river breezes carrying the stench of burning rubber, wood and plastic with the current, southward through the suburbs toward the sea. The stink of the fire would take a message home to Larry Giulianno. There was a slim chance that he might pull his horns in, go to ground, forget the urge to dominate a brand-new territory. But he was more likely to retaliate against his rival, Tommy Petrosina, on the theory that the fire had been an act of war.

When he moved, the Executioner would be there waiting for him.

Bolan backtracked through the shadows, still watchful for any sign of danger, any indication that he might have been observed. The risk was minimal, he knew, but carelessness could get a soldier killed; Bolan had survived this long against the odds by calculating every risk, however inconsequential it seemed.

He reached his car, popped the trunk and stripped off his harness and military hardware. At his back, through skylights of the Giulianno warehouse, the ruddy glow of flames lit up the sky with artificial dawn. A few more minutes before a watchman in some nearby warehouse saw the glow or smelled the rancid smoke and telephoned the fire department. Time for Bolan to go about his business, turning up the heat beneath his enemies until they screamed.

Larry Giulianno would be screaming this time, but before the dawn broke over Hartford, Tommy Petrosina would have felt the heat, as well. There was enough to go around, and some to spare for savages who thought they could stand and slug it out by gangland rules against the Executioner.

Bolan was not overconfident. He knew his enemies, the way they looked at life and death, their methods of responding to a challenge from outside the family. For all their ruthless power, all their street-smart ingenuity, the average mafioso ran as true to form when coping with a threat as any soldier going by the book. As for Mack Bolan, he had long since thrown the book away, inventing strategy to suit his needs, depending on the cannibals to be their own worst enemies. So far, they had not let him down.

When his gear was safely stowed, Bolan slid behind the wheel and turned the engine over, running dark until the waterfront was several blocks behind him. When he was clear, he turned the headlights on, already thinking through his next encounter with the enemy. With Tommy Petrosina.

So occupied, Bolan almost missed the tail.

When the headlights blazed to life in his rearview mirror, he thought at first the trailing motorist a hundred yards behind had pulled out of a side street, following his course by mere coincidence. A second glance showed there had been no intersection, no alleyway or parking lot from which the second car could have emerged.

The tail car had been running dark, like Bolan, and the man behind the wheel had waited precious seconds longer before turning on his headlights. Gambling, perhaps, that Bolan would not notice? Careless of the risk involved... or taking on that risk deliberately, to thumb his nose at Bolan?

Either way, Bolan had to know. He jumped the next red light, accelerating through a left turn and smoking rubber, one eye on the rearview, waiting. In his wake, the tail accelerated smoothly. It plowed through the red, narrowly avoiding impact with a station wagon, and closed fast on Bolan's car. There was power under the chase car's hood. Bolan would have difficulty shaking off the tail—if he chose to try.

All things considered, it would make more sense to take him out. Erratic streetlights showed Bolan that the tail was not a squad car, and detectives in pursuit of a suspected arsonist would have turned on their red lights by now. There was an outside chance that he had run afoul of some civilian bent upon a citizen's arrest, but it was far more likely the tail had come from Giulianno. Roving gunners touring the aspiring capo's properties, perhaps, or some relief crew that had been arriving as he left.

No time to sort the possibilities or search for pieces of the puzzle now. The tail was hanging tight on Bolan's backside, eating up the highway, blinding him with high beams when he tried to count the occupants. They had his

license number now, whatever else went down. If they were
in radio communication with Giulianno's hardsite, with
another team, then he was burned before his war got off
the ground. He would be forced to ditch the rental, find
himself another set of wheels.

Provided that he shook the tail and walked away from
it intact.

Behind him, muzzle-flashes from the driver's side eliminated any thoughts of civilian would-be heroes. The first
round rang against a fender as he swerved to take evasive
action. The chase car hung behind him, two more rounds
impacting squarely on the trunk before he caught another
intersection, gunning through the curve, his rear tires losing traction, finally digging in.

The chase car followed, closing, making up lost yard-
age on the straightaway. Bolan knew that he would have to
lose them now, or else destroy them totally, before the
driver's aim improved.

His intervention in the Giulianno-Petrosina feud was
secondary, rapidly receding in the soldier's consciousness
as survival instinct surfaced. To continue with his business in Connecticut, he had to be alive. That meant shaking off his grim pursuers while he had the chance.

Assuming that any chance remained.

## 2

Bolan caught the on-ramp for Interstate 91, rolling north toward Hartford and the airport with the river on his right. Behind him, he could feel the chase car pressing, jockeying for range, position, but the open highway gave him room to run, to let the rental's power plant unwind. The scattering of midnight traffic on the four-lane blacktop apparently inhibited the tail from potting Bolan on the open road. Bolan took advantage of the moment, standing on the gas and running serpentine between the slower vehicles, attempting to secure a lead.

The tail hung close, anticipating Bolan's moves as directional signs for downtown Hartford started sprouting overhead. Whatever else the guy might be, he was a first-class wheel, with the ability to keep his cool in hot pursuit. The Executioner could almost have admired his skill, if he had not been so intent on finding ways to kill the man.

And it was just one man—he knew that now. He had observed the tail car, backlit by the headlight beams of slower vehicles, and had marked the solitary silhouette behind the wheel. Unless the driver had a crew of midgets with him, or a backup gunner crouching on the floorboards, the chase had narrowed down to one on one. The odds were better, but a single gun could be as deadly as a firing squad. Bolan needed time to think, some combat stretch, to survive the running confrontation.

A firm ID was not required for Bolan to eradicate his enemy. The tail was no civilian; Bolan had learned that much by dodging well-placed Magnum rounds. Police were likewise out. The absence of a light or siren marked his adversary as a private gun, and that spelled *syndicate* in Bolan's mind.

Which brought him back to *how*.

How had the gunner spotted him initially?

How had he known that Bolan—anyone—was targeting the Giulianno warehouse?

If the gunner had been standing watch, a sentry somehow unobserved by Bolan, why had he permitted two of his associates to die, the warehouse to be torched? Had he been dozing at his post, awakening to find the place in flames?

It didn't play.

There wasn't anything remarkable about a sentry sleeping at his post. It happened all the time. But with the recent hostilities between the Giulianno and Petrosina forces, any button man whose negligence resulted in a million-dollar loss for his employer would be fish food. There was no room for a second chance, no margin of forgiveness when the stakes had climbed so high. If Bolan's tail was one of Giulianno's lookouts, the guy was dead already, and he knew it. Would a dead man waste his time pursuing shadows when he might have gained some precious time by heading for the hills?

Again, it didn't play, but there was no time left for mind games, a quarter mile from downtown Hartford. The soldier saved his lane change for the final instant, letting his pursuer think he would stick with Highway 91, or maybe catch the toll bridge eastward onto Highway 86. The tail hung close, prepared to play it either way.

When he was ready Bolan eased off the accelerator, saw the chase car growing in his rearview mirror while a long-haul semi closed up on his right. Split-second timing was required, or he would miss the off ramp, wind up sandwiched between his adversary and the diesel juggernaut. If he muffed it, Bolan knew, he might be ground to pulp between the semi's eighteen wheels... but he had no alternative.

He chose the moment carefully, relying on his combat instinct, *feeling* for the instant. When it came, he tromped on the accelerator, cranked the steering wheel hard right and cut across the semi's path, avoiding catastrophic impact by a whisper. Big pneumatic brakes were screeching on his flank as Bolan hit the off ramp, never braking, though reflective signs assured him he was well above the cutoff's legal safety limit. He would make the curve or he would not, but it could be his only shot. Bolan would not sacrifice slim advantage now.

Behind him, where the semi wallowed to a smoking halt across two lanes, the trailers jackknifed, Bolan's tail would be trying to recover, to continue the pursuit. Another moment to see if he had ditched the tail. Another moment now...

The headlights loomed behind him, entering the off ramp's sloping curve and following him down, accelerating. The Executioner had sacrificed some mobility by veering off the interstate, had gained no more than seconds in return. The whole maneuver had been wasted.

He could not afford to take the game downtown. Even at the midnight hour there would be too much traffic, too much risk to innocent pedestrians. He swung the rental eastward onto Brown Street, crossing Maple Avenue against the light and jogging over onto White, accelerating toward suburban Elmwood. Gradually, department stores and shopping malls gave way to convenience stores and private homes, the runway narrowing as lawns encroached on either side. And still the tail hung with him, headlights glaring at Bolan from the rearview mirror like a pair of soulless, unforgiving eyes.

They could not run indefinitely without meeting the police. Patrols might be irregular in residential areas, but they did occur. If police became involved in the pursuit...

He had to end it. The soldier started watching for a side street, any quiet lane or cul-de-sac that might serve as a killing ground. Without slowing or abandoning the search, he slid one hand beneath the driver's seat and found the Mini-Uzi nestled in its secret holster, out of sight from prying eyes. With Bolan's heavy weapons locked up in the trunk, the little stutter gun would have to do... provided he found a place to make his stand.

A smaller, lighter version of the sleek Israeli submachine gun, Bolan's choice for backup hardware surrendered nothing of the original's firepower. With a cyclic rate of 750 rounds per minute in its automatic mode, the lethal midget could unload a 32-round magazine in less than three seconds, shredding any target in its path. To raise the ante, Bolan had selected "Quad Custom" riot loads, designed to spread in flight, for better target coverage. Each cartridge seated four 52-grain projectiles, nested one atop the other like a stack of deadly Dixie cups. The stats translated into 128 separate projectiles leaving the Uzi's muzzle every 2.5 seconds, for an adjusted cyclic rate of more than 3,000 rounds per minute.

It was enough to stop a chase car and its driver. Provided Bolan could use his stutter gun at all. Provided he didn't lose it on a curve, or run afoul of uniformed patrolmen looking for a doughnut shop at half-past midnight in the suburbs. If he let the hunter get too close, a Magnum round behind the ear could bring Mack Bolan's private war to an ignominious conclusion.

As if in answer to his thoughts, the rearview mirror blossomed with reflected muzzle fire. Bolan braced himself, relaxing only slightly as the live one scored a bull's-eye on his trunk. The echo of the shot was lost behind him, swept away by speed and engine sounds, but it would not be lost upon the sleeping neighborhood that had become a battleground. One shot might be dismissed as fireworks or a backfire, but a fusillade would have the neighbors dialing 911 in droves. A SWAT team could be rolling by the time Bolan dusted off his pursuer.

Whatever Bolan planned to do, he had to do it now.

The cul-de-sac approaching on the left would have to do. Bolan gunned his mount, lengthening his lead by feet, then yards. Behind him, his pursuer matched the pace. He was closing fast when Bolan veered hard left into the cul-de-sac on smoking rubber, braking desperately as he whipped the steering wheel around, putting the rental through a tight bootlegger's turn.

He killed the lights and was EVA in time to see the chase car miss its turn, go screeching past on tires that had already given up the best part of their tread. He braced the Mini-Uzi on the driver's windowsill, secure in a double-handed grip, the safety off. If only his pursuer doubled back to finish it before the groggy neighbors groped their way to their windows, or grabbed their bedside telephones.

The numbers dragged, the soldier's pulse reverberating in his ears like cannon fire. The hunter could not possibly have missed seeing his quarry's turnoff. Bolan had seen him brake, smelled the scorching tires. He would return because he had to. He had already risked too much to let it go.

Another moment gone. Bolan visualized the worst scenario: the hunter parked in darkness just outside the cul-de-sac, waiting for him to escape. If the soldier tried to run the ambush, he would be a sitting duck. If he remained in place, police would have him soon. Too soon.

He had already wasted thirty seconds, more. Bolan was prepared to give it up, take his chances in the open, when the chase car finally crept into view. The guy was running dark, fairly begging Bolan to open fire.

Fine.

He was already shifting, bracing for the Uzi's recoil, when the hunter kicked his headlights onto high beams, surged forward on a dead collision course with a squeal of tortured rubber.

Bolan's first rounds pierced the hunter's grill and raised a cloud of steam, dark water spattering the pavement. His second burst punched through the windshield, spraying safety glass and 52-grain slugs in a lethal figure eight. Already moving, Bolan did not give his adversary time to track and fire. He emptied his Uzi on the run, ripped the sleek Beretta from its armpit sheath, held it leveled, ready, by the time he reached the driver's side.

And found the chase car empty.

Bolan double-checked in an instant, keen eyes darting from the front seat to the back, sweeping toward the entrance of the cul-de-sac. His adversary must be killing close, he knew; the headlights had not cut to high beams by themselves. He was braced to take the rounds that must be coming, when a feeling in his gut, defying logic, told him there would be no sniping fire, after all. The fleeting seconds bore him out. The opportunity for his assailant to take him had come and gone.

But Bolan knew instinctively that this one did not miss a golden opportunity by chance. If the hunter was backing off, he had his reasons. If he was waiting, it was only for the chance to strike again some other time. On some other killing ground.

Around the cul-de-sac, a few porch lights had gone on as sleepy residents responded to the reports of gunfire. Off to Bolan's left, a watchdog had begun to snap and hurl himself against a chain link fence. A few doors down, frightened voices shouted urgent questions.

He was running out of time, but he could not depart without a closer look at the hunter's abandoned car. The driver's door was not completely closed. Bolan cursed his adversary's split-second timing, picturing his scramble in the heartbeat after high beams dazzled Bolan's eyes. He would be close enough now to overtake on foot...but Bolan didn't have the time to spare.

Instead, he wrenched the door wide open, leaned inside. No blood on the upholstery, front or back, and he was certain now that his assailant had escaped intact. But not before he'd left his calling card.

Bolan almost missed it, under the pebbled safety glass shattered on the driver's seat. It took a second, closer glance to recognize a yellowed business card, worn around the edges as if from frequent handling. He picked it up and brought it to his eyes, feeling suddenly short of breath as his eyes confirmed the message flashed to his subconscious.

There was no mistake.

The card read:

TRIANGLE INDUSTRIAL FINANCE
1430 Commerce St.
Pittsfield, Mass.

**3**

It had been the turning point of Bolan's life, the grim beginning of a lonely soldier's everlasting war. He could recall the offices of TIF as clearly as the floor plan of his childhood home, the woodland paths that he had followed in his youth, a .22 repeater in his hands. He had not consciously recalled the men of TIF in years, but they were with him always, tucked away in a shadowed corner of his memory, available at need.

Triangle Industrial Finance was a savings and loan company, well-known among Pittsfield's blue-collar thousands. No one ever saved a dime with TIF, but it was big on loans, and bigger still on ''vigorish''—the weekly interest that inevitably dwarfed the principal. Commitment to a loan from TIF was tantamount to slavery, and the customer who fell behind in weekly payments could expect a visit from the company's ''collection officers.'' Such visits usually included threats of violence, and where threats were ineffective, violence followed. Beatings were routine, fractures and dislocations commonplace; if the collection process left a patron incapacitated, well, perhaps some other member of the family could be persuaded to assume his debt.

The men of Triangle were loan sharks, plain and simple, operating in conjunction with the larger syndicate that dominated vice in western Massachusetts. Sergio Frenchi was the don of that larger Family, which dabbled in narcotics, prostitution and pornography, extortion, gambling, theft and fraud. A product of the Prohibition bootleg wars, Don Sergio had risen to the upper crust of underworld society. Thanks to carefully chosen philanthropic gestures he was revered by myopic city fathers, his beginnings and his Family activities ignored or tolerated by the local law. He was a power in the Mafia—La Cosa Nostra—but command of countless rackets kept him from examining each crime in detail. Like a general at war, he could not observe each soldier on the firing line.

There was no doubt that Frenchi knew about Triangle Industrial Finance. The loan sharks were a major source of income for his Family, and he had delegated the overseeing of shylock operations to a trusted aide. The capo never knew Sam Bolan, never heard about the heart attack that kept him home from work that January, while the bills piled up, unpaid. It was an old, familiar story; illness eats away at family savings; incapacitated workers cannot raise collateral for a regular loan; hungry shylock offers "easy" terms. The customer needs no real estate, stocks or bonds. His body is the best collateral in town, and when the crunch comes down, he will do *anything* to keep that collateral intact.

Except that Samuel Bolan wouldn't crawl. He kept up his payments, until the rising vigorish made that impossible. When the collectors came to call, he bore his wounds in silence, struggling to keep the secret from his family. When, at last, the collectors stayed away, Sam Bolan thought he had beaten them, that justice had prevailed.

In his wildest nightmares, Sam could not have guessed at the arrangement that his daughter, Cindy, had accepted from TIF. Her father's health was everything to Cindy Bolan. If she could end his suffering by sacrificing a little of her pride, then the deal was cheap at half the price, and never mind the pawing hands, the sweating bodies of the men who paid to use her for an hour. Cindy Bolan's vigorish was paid in tender flesh, and Don Sergio was undoubtedly unaware that she existed.

If he watched TV or read the papers, Pittsfield's capo might have caught the Bolan name in August, when a tragic string of circumstances nearly wiped the family out. According to police and media reports, Sam Bolan, 48, had "gone berserk" without apparent provocation, gunning down his wife, his teenage son and daughter, then himself. The son alone survived, emerging from near-comatose condition after three days in intensive care. His story shed no light upon the incident, and homicide detectives were relieved to file the case away.

Until another Bolan surfaced on the streets of Pittsfield, looking for some answers of his own, attempting to make sense of the catastrophe that had destroyed his family.

On leave from Vietnam, Mack Bolan was allowed to see his brother, Johnny, and the grieving kid had poured out details never shared with homicide investigators. That steamy summer he had guessed the deal that sister Cindy had accepted from the ghouls of Triangle Finance. Some legwork proved his theory; he had tailed her to a cheap motel, observed the men who came and went in shifts, at last confronted her with evidence that she could not refute. Her answer had been tearful, but determined. She would save their father if she could, and never mind the kind of morality that allowed a decent man to suffer endlessly while thieves and savages grew fat at his expense.

In desperation, Johnny Bolan had finally approached his father, searching painfully for words to explain the situation with a minimum of damage to the family. He broke the news as gently as he could—and was completely unprepared for the explosion that ensued. In retrospect, it was possible that Sam had known subconsciously of Cindy's sacrifice, suspecting what he could never bring himself to face directly. When the proof was laid before his eyes, when there was nowhere left to hide inside his mind, the man exploded like a human bomb and took his family with him.

All but Johnny.

All but Mack.

Confronted with evidence of the criminal manipulation that had led to the destruction of his family, Mack Bolan had a choice between two grim alternatives. He could allow detectives to pursue the case, despite their frank admission that there *was* no case against the Mob, or he could move against the savages himself. No matter that one man could never hope to slay the dragon of La Cosa Nostra. Never mind that it was clearly suicide to stand against the syndicate, its armies of the night. A lone, determined warrior could extract some measure of revenge for loved ones lost, and if his action inconvenienced the Mob at large, so much the better. Knowing from the start that the situation was hopeless, Mack Bolan could not turn away and let it rest. He could not leave the debt unpaid.

A holy war must have some point of origin; for the Executioner, that point was Triangle Industrial Finance. Within a week of coming home, he knew the officers in charge, their muscle, the accountants and attorneys who were skilled at moving cash, manipulating laws. All were untouchable from every legal standpoint, but the soldier had decided on another course of action. He had recognized the enemy, a stalking predator no different, really, from the "liberators" he had gone to war against in Vietnam. They spoke one language, understood one method of communication, and it was a method that the Executioner had mastered in the Asian hellgrounds.

Frank Laurenti was the OIC—the officer in charge at TIF. His private guns were Tommy Erwin and a hulk named Vinnie Janus. Pete Rodriguez kept the books—both sets—and Eddie Brokaw "handled things" around the office, sending out collectors when the vigorish was overdue. There were others farther up the ladder, lending their support and counsel to the operation, but those five would do to start.

The soldier took them all on August 22 in a searing fusillade of rifle fire that changed the course of gangland history forever. Five rounds from a Marlin .444 and it was over for the cannibals of TIF. But it had only just begun for Bolan.

The rest was history. In the weeks to come, Don Sergio, the world at large, had come to know Mack Bolan's name. His infiltration and annihilation of the Pittsfield Family had kindled sparks across America, reminding thousands, millions, that involuntary servitude had been illegal for a century and more. It would take time before the message found its way to Washington, and in the meantime Bolan would be rolling out across the countryside, intent on carrying the fire.

He had survived that first engagement in the face of overwhelming odds; every day since Pittsfield, since the death of Don Sergio, had been another day constructed out of borrowed time. The soldier knew that death was coming, realized that he could not postpone the end indefinitely, but it was not in his nature to lie down and wait. If death was looking for him, it would find him on the firing line, still challenging his enemies and scourging them with every means at his disposal. He would hit the savages with everything he had, and when he had no more, when it was hand-to-hand, the struggle would begin in earnest.

The entire course of Bolan's life since then had flowed from Commerce Street in Pittsfield, from the blood-stained sidewalk outside TIF. Whatever else had happened, from the campaign with his Death Squad in Los Angeles, on through the death of April Rose and everything that followed, everything had begun with Bolan's summary execution of the Triangle five. Their faces were emblazoned in his memory, and he could call them up at will. Sometimes they came to him unbidden in his dreams.

From time to time, Bolan wondered what his life might have become if there had been no TIF, no heart attack to spoil his father's health, no call to stand at graveside while his family was laid to rest. If he had stayed in Vietnam, would disillusionment have sapped his strength, his will to stand against the predators?

Religion played no major part in Bolan's thinking. He was not an unbeliever, but he had observed firsthand how righteous causes could be subverted by unrighteous men, the doctrines of a loving church perverted into something hideous and deadly in the name of "liberation," "justice," even "peace." In Bolan's eyes, predestination was a poor excuse for apathy, employed by men who lacked the courage to oppose domestic predators.

And yet, if there was no predestination, that did not preclude the notion of some higher destiny. Some men were marked for greatness, some for sacrifice...and some were simply branded as the cannibals they were. It was a warrior's duty, his eternal destiny, to stand against the cannibals and beat them back or die in the attempt. From ancient times, the man of arms had borne no duty more significant, more noble, than defense of tribe and family against predators outside.

Except that the predators were *inside* now. They moved with easy grace in the upper echelons of society, accepted by politicians and philanthropists, by ministers and civic fathers. They were taken at face value while the money flowed. Few people were inclined to lift the mask, observe the rotting flesh beneath.

It took a dedicated renegade to buck the odds and strip those masks away, to lift the rocks and search out maggots underneath. It took an Executioner to carry out the self-inflicted judgment of the savages. Subverted from within, society had abrogated its responsibility to deal with the savages, but Bolan took his duty as it came and never flinched.

Duty had called him to Connecticut. He had been mopping up some unfinished business in New Jersey when the Giulianno-Petrosina feud erupted. As long as he was in the neighborhood, the Executioner could not let pass the opportunity to strike a blow against some splinter of the mob while it was still in its infancy. If he could prevent its roots from taking hold and digging deep, he would be spared the need to do it all another day, against increasing odds.

Connecticut had been a natural... until the tail appeared on Bolan's flight from Giulianno's warehouse. Now the soldier asked himself two questions: Who knew about his campaign in Hartford? What, if any, was that person's link to Triangle Industrial Finance and Pittsfield, all those bloody years ago?

The business card was no coincidence. His fusillade on Commerce Street had closed down Triangle Finance forever; any cards or other stationery from the shylock outfit were out-of-date collector's items now. And yet, for anyone to push that button so precisely, he had to know the Executioner's identity and whereabouts. It set alarm bells ringing in the soldier's mind, this sudden knowledge that he had been watched by unknown eyes. Worse still, it angered him that he had not spotted the tail until he chose to show himself.

As far as Bolan knew, there was no link between the Giulianno Mob and TIF. The would-be capo was a streetwise punk from Brooklyn, lately harboring delusions of godfatherhood. The mental mug file indicated that he had no relatives in Massachusetts and, indeed, had never visited the state except for two excursions to Boston as a third-rate errand boy for Augie Marinello's Family. Attrition above had propelled him up the ladder, but he was now just what he had been in New York, what he would always be: a third-rate hoodlum, long on mouth and short on brains.

Augie's adversary, Tommy Petrosina, was another New York product; although he had a cousin with the syndicate in Boston, nothing suggested a Pittsfield tie-in. Tommy might have welcomed Bolan's intervention against Giulianno, but he could not afford a blitz against both camps. His troops were thin and lacked the finesse required to track the Executioner.

Bolan thought about the business card. It bore no person's name, but clearly it had been preserved by someone with a link to TIF. The five who died on Commerce Street that August afternoon had all been Family men, with brothers, cousins, in-laws by the score. There had been others who survived Triangle's fall—the office staff, "collectors" who had been absorbed by other branches of the Frenchi family before it all fell out in Bolan's final blitz. Among them, there might be some who cherished thoughts of sweet revenge.

Timing was a problem. It was years since Bolan had crouched atop a roof on Commerce Street and framed his first domestic targets in the Marlin's telescopic sight. In

Bolan's experience, mafiosi were not prone to delayed reactions, preferring to strike with swift and ruthless violence while the iron was hot.

And yet there could be no denying the connection. Someone with a link to TIF had tracked him to Connecticut, observed him as he moved against the Giulianno forces and laid a skillful trap. He wasn't ready yet to ponder why the trap had not been sprung. The Executioner had been a prime target inside that cul-de-sac, the hunter armed and close at hand. A single well-placed round would have ended it there . . . and still he lived. For reasons yet unknown, his adversary had elected to prolong the game.

Bolan was gripped by an unaccustomed sense of vulnerability. The odds had been against him from day one, but this was different, infinitely worse. His advantages in the never-ending war—mobility, surprise—were being stripped away. If some anonymous assailant had the capability to track him, put him through his paces like a laboratory rat, then he was doomed. Connecticut would be the end of everything, unless he snapped the leash and put himself at liberty again.

First, he must cut his losses. He would go to ground, take stock of any errors he might have made since driving in from Jersey. If he failed to establish a connection there, he would look further back, retracing every step along the road from Newark and beyond. The Giulianno-Petrosina feud would have to evolve without him for the moment, while he found a way to shake the lethal shadow that was dogging him.

And if he failed . . . His adversary might not let another opportunity slip, might not postpone the taste of Bolan's blood another day. He must be hungry after all this time. Bolan understood that hunger well enough, he had experienced it himself from time to time, along the hellfire trail.

It was an emptiness that could be filled with death and violence, but only temporarily. In time, if it was not controlled, it must consume its victim, eat him up alive.

This time, he knew, the Executioner was on the menu.

**4**

The business card had been a stroke of genius. Never mind false modesty, it had been brilliant; the hunter only wished he had been able to observe the Executioner's reaction.

That was impossible, of course. He couldn't take the chance of Bolan spotting him—or, worse, risk an encounter with police if they found him sprinting from the scene when they arrived. The better part of valor was to save your ass, and he would have another opportunity to feast his eyes on Bolan soon enough.

So far, his plan was working like a charm. The Giulianno warehouse fire had been a bonus, and he had been pleased to grant the target time in which to finish the job. After all, it was he who had kicked off the Giulianno-Petrosina feud in the first place. Nothing difficult, some random potshots here and there, a touch of TNT, and the bastards had been off and rolling, turning on one another, wasting lives.

He had known that Bolan would not—*could* not—turn away from an impending gang war. If the bastard's history had taught him anything, it was his compulsion for one-on-one involvement. Bolan took things personally. He never missed a chance to drive a wedge between his enemies, assisting their fratricidal violence when and where he could.

The timing of the Hartford outbreak had not been co-incidental. If the Executioner had surfaced first in California, say, the hunter would have waited patiently, as he had waited oh, so many years. His time was precious, his mobility limited, and in the interests of his cover, he had been prepared to wait once more. The bastard would come east eventually, as he always had before, returning to the scene of his initial crimes. When he did, the hunter would be ready for him. Waiting.

He had elevated waiting to an art form, picking up his early lessons in the military, learning that the soldier who could watch and wait in silence was the soldier who survived the endless night. In later years, he had refined the talent, acquiring skills that would prepare him for the contest of his life. He could sit motionless for hours at a time, ignoring the insistence of his bladder, stiffness in his limbs. He could attain an almost trancelike state in which his mind remained alert, his eyes and ears missed nothing. He had trained himself to wait as if his very life depended on it . . . which it might, before he finished with the Executioner.

The hunter had no thought of failure. If he failed, then he would die; it was a simple formula with only one solution. If he failed, if Bolan lived, then all his life had been an empty waste, the futile preparation of a fool. He was not ready yet to face that judgment—not while everything was going according to plan.

The hunter knew his quarry inside out, had studied every move the bastard made since his initial strike in Pittsfield. Bolan counted on mobility, on unpredictability, on surprise, but put his movements under a microscope, and the guy was perfectly predictable. You might not know where he was going next, what guise he might assume, but over time you came to know the kinds of sit-

uations that attracted Bolan like a magnet. With fore-
thought, skill, you could *manipulate* his movements, make
up the soldier's mind for him by creating the circumstances, offering the bait that he had never yet refused.

In other circumstances, Giulianno might have been ignored, some other human bait selected for the hunter's
purpose. It would have served as well to stage an incident
in Boston, Concord, even Albany, so long as the logistics
had not become prohibitive. The hunter recognized his
limitations, knew that if he planned to tag the Executioner and make it stick, he must do it on his own home
turf.

He would not have had it any other way.

It would be poetic justice, the execution of the Executioner, conducted where he had first spilled blood. It
would have pleased the hunter to manipulate its timing,
stage the payback on an anniversary perhaps, but that was
wishful thinking. He could manage just so much, and if he
tried to push his luck beyond that point, the whole damned
scheme would blow up in his face.

Practicality and realism were the hunter's chief virtues,
after patience. He could distinguish between a working
plan and an idle pipe dream at a glance. He could follow
through, map out the necessary details logically, effectively. He could predict how Bolan would react when he
discovered the business card from TIF. He would be ahead
of his quarry all the way, prepared to cut him off if he tried
to bolt.

It was not in Bolan's makeup to run without a fight, but
this time he was facing different odds, a different kind of
threat, and anything might happen. The hunter would be
prepared at every turn: if Bolan took the bait, if he tried
to improvise, if he decided to cut and run. Whichever way
it played, the hunter would be waiting for him, ready to

head him off before his famous lightning moves could spoil the plan.

The first priority was driving Bolan out of Hartford, toward the killing ground. It would be simple, really; he was pointed in the general direction now, and one more solid shove should see him on the road. Precision timing would be necessary, but what else was new? The hunter had the target covered, knew his every move before it was made. He was certain, now, that Bolan would seek cover. Someplace safe to puzzle through the meaning of the business card. Someplace to hide.

The hunter knew Bolan's lair already, had discovered it when the quarry led him there. A firm believer in reconnaissance, the Executioner had made a point of casing Giulianno's property in Hartford, driving by the would-be capo's house, his restaurant command post, the businesses in which he held controlling interests. During one such pass, the hunter, on a stakeout of his own, had recognized his prey and given chase. Discreetly. Cautiously. Unlike this evening, when Bolan had been meant to see, that time the soldier had never guessed that he was being followed back to the safe house he had rented in suburban Newington.

The hunter knew his address now, the alias he was using in Connecticut. He could have punched up the soldier's number on any telephone and spoken to him, man-to-man. But he restrained himself, preferring stealth to amateur theatrics. He did not wish simply to kill the Executioner; he could have done that tonight, or half a dozen other times in the past three days. The hunter had a point to make. If he failed in that, then all the rest was bullshit, anyway.

He had to take the Executioner in Pittsfield, at the scene of his initial murders. He had to make it clear, to Bolan before he died and to the world, precisely who had defeated the Executioner, and why. Exposure posed no danger for him; he had given up the family name years before, when he enlisted with the Corps. Some phony paperwork acquired from friends, a lie about his age, and he was in. The war was winding down by then, with television bringing firefights to the living room and stirring up a maelstrom of dissent at home. Still time enough for action, time to blood himself; no one in the Corps had been anxious to reject an able-bodied volunteer. America's involvement in the Asian hellgrounds and his own term of service had expired within a week of each other. He had been sorry when it ended, angry at the grim necessity of coming home.

He had already conceived the general outline of his plan, but it had taken time to make the pieces fit. He had shopped around for suitable employment, something that would keep him fit, make use of his talents, while permitting him to track his quarry from a distance. The answer was simplicity itself. Settling in, the hunter strove to appear innocuous, maintaining an unremarkably average profile. If he never bungled, neither did he shine. Accepted by his peers, ignored whenever possible by his superiors, he did his job and kept his counsel.

The Corps had taught him patience, endless hours squatting in the jungle darkness, staking out a game trail, never moving while the worms and vipers twined around the ankles, insects scuttled into sleeves and collars, poked their bristly feelers into ears and nostrils. Later, on the job, he honed those jungle skills, adapted them to the urban jungle and prepared himself for the contest of his life.

The final confrontation had been long in coming. He had tracked his quarry through the media, through channels open only to his own profession. For a time, he had felt desperate, cheated, by the news of Bolan's fiery death in Central Park, but hope had been revived by subsequent announcement of his enemy's survival. He suspected that the soldier had been "sanitized," absorbed by the establishment. Then the Executioner had finally emerged from limbo, shoring up the hunter's belief that there was still a chance, still time.

The face had changed, of course, but not since Texas. There had been mug shots, leaked and published by the media, descriptions circulated by the FBI and Texas Rangers. Plastic surgery was possible, of course, but with the syndicate after him, stripped of government support, it stood to reason the Executioner would hesitate to put his faith in hospitals, entrust his life to any surgeon's hands.

The hunter's stakeout had confirmed his first impression. Bolan had not changed since Texas. Oh, his hair was longer, and his tan had faded, but he was still the same in every critical respect. Before his first full day in Hartford had elapsed, the soldier had been made.

There was a world of difference, though, between identifying Bolan in the field and running him to earth. The first required only perseverance and an eye for detail; the latter would demand a great deal more. Courage, though the hunter did not think himself exceptionally brave. His move against the Executioner was *necessary*; he could no more shirk that duty than he could deliberately cease to breathe. Extraordinary skill would be required, and here he cast false modesty aside. For years he had been training, exercising martial skills against the day when he would face his enemy in mortal combat. When the moment came, the hunter knew he would be worthy of the contest.

It wouldn't hurt him any, though, if his prey's confidence was shaken in the interim. Step one had been the business card, a subtle thorn beneath the Bolan hide. Step two was coming, and the hunter felt his bowels constricting in anticipation, gooseflesh rising on his arms. The sudden sense of power was erotic in its swift intensity. He was forced to calm himself, to remember that tonight was only the prelude, edging Bolan closer to the final killing ground.

If Bolan died tonight, the hunter would have failed, disgraced himself and his mission. He needed every ounce of concentration to ensure the right effect, elicit the desired reaction from his quarry. If the soldier balked and stood his ground, or broke and ran for any point except the designated battleground, the hunger would have wasted years—his life—in the pursuit of empty shadows.

It was all or nothing tonight; if he failed, the hunter knew he would not be going home alive.

The morbid thoughts had drained away his brief elation of a moment past, and now the hunter sought to recapture equilibrium. Depression might be every bit as lethal to his plans as manic overconfidence; extremes of any sort betrayed a soldier in the field. Stoic silence was his only friend; his enemy was the only other living man on earth. Later, when they were finished, he would be alone. Alone and free.

Logistics had been a problem for the hunter. Transportation and the like—two cars in Hartford, plus the other special items—had already eaten up a large part of his budget. But it would be worth the cost when he had the thing behind him. The hunter would have gladly mortgaged his remaining days, leased out his vital organs one by one to see his duty through.

He felt the beginning of a headache behind his eyes, and swallowed two Excedrin tablets. The sour flavor helped him focus, bring his mind to crystal clarity. Mere moments now, and he would see the second phase of his campaign completed.

He had picked a car at random near the cul-de-sac where Bolan had disabled his first set of wheels, had used a special set of master keys designed for repo men and had driven clear before police arrived. The move had cost him time, but there had been no way around it. He could never have predicted the direction of his quarry's flight from Giulianno's warehouse. Accordingly he had parked his backup rental at a central point designed for easy access. Luck was with him, and the quarter hour that elapsed before he took up his position at the secondary target was acceptable, though tight.

The groundwork had been taken care of earlier that afternoon, while Bolan ran a final recon of the Giulianno properties that he had selected for attention. Confident that he could keep the soldier on his leash, the hunter had spent an hour in the safe house, breathing Bolan's air and soaking up his essence from the sparsely furnished living quarters. He had stood in Bolan's bedroom, urinated in his toilet, seen his own reflection in the soldier's bathroom mirror. For a moment, he felt he had stepped inside Mack Bolan's mind and peered out through his eyes to face a hostile world.

A world that Bolan would be leaving soon.

When he was certain that he knew the Executioner as well as any man could know another, he had done his job and slipped away, careful to leave nothing of himself behind. An expert at invading privacy, he knew the soldier's sanctuary bore no telltale signs of penetration. Bolan would return when he was finished with his recon, gird himself for war by night and sortie out again, completely unaware that hostile eyes had scrutinized his very soul.

The hunter's calculations had allowed for no mistakes, and there had been none up to now. His plan was operating with a slick precision that was gratifying, clockwork ticking down the heartbeats toward extinction for the Executioner.

The quarry was approaching; he could feel it in his bones, inside his vitals. One step closer, and another, each stride tangling him more securely in the hunter's snare. When Bolan split from Hartford, rolling north in search of answers, there would be a lethal shadow running with him, clinging to his heels. When he was safely in the killing zone, aware that he had been manipulated, suckered, that would be the shadow's time to strike.

Not yet. But soon.

He felt the quarry's presence microseconds before his headlights appeared at the end of the darkened residential street. The soldier was predictable in some things, anyway. It would be the death of him, in time.

For now, an object lesson would be satisfactory.

Another piece of bait, and nestled in its midst, a deadly hook.

The hunter settled back in darkness, waiting for his prey.

**5**

Bolan followed Hartford Avenue until it canted south and changed its name to Main Street, running smoothly into downtown Newington. He spent another fifteen minutes cruising aimlessly, until he was sure that he had not been followed, finally homing on his safe house when he felt secure. The hideout was a four-room crackerbox removed from other, larger houses on the block by wide expanses of lawn that had gone to weeds from neglect. Perpetually for rent, the house would never be a showplace, but was not yet an eyesore that the neighbors openly lamented. Here, the soldier knew, he would be comfortably ignored.

The neighborhood was dark as Bolan entered from the east, a porch light here and there providing sparse illumination, leaving predawn shadows undisturbed. Alert, he made one pass around the block to check for tails, another to observe the empty vehicles at curbside, keen eyes scanning for lookouts near the drop. He kept the Mini-Uzi cocked and loaded on the seat beside him just in case, but saw no sign of a stakeout. On his third pass, from the west this time, he pulled into the shaded driveway of the safe house, shutting down his lights and engine, coasting toward the one-car garage in back.

If anyone was waiting for him, he knew, they would hit him while he was trapped inside the car. A single burst of automatic fire would do the job, and he would never know the difference if they timed it right. He had no reason to believe that anyone knew about his safe house, that anyone had traced him, but still . . .

The nagging apprehension had been with him since ne discovered the business card for TIF. Against all odds, it was apparent that some enemy *had* traced him into Hartford, following his movements well enough to pick him up at Giulianno's warehouse and pursue him from there. Discovery of the safe house was unlikely, true, but not impossible. For the remainder of his stay in Hartford—if he stayed at all—the soldier would be forced to watch his back at every turn.

As always...but with a twist. He had been hunted by his enemies for years, and some of them had very nearly done the job, but none had ever touched the hidden nerve that this opponent had found with such unerring accuracy. Unseen, unknown, his adversary knew precisely how to jerk the soldier's chain. Bolan knew he would have to be on guard against the psychological effects of being hunted like an animal. Whoever his assailant was, the guy was still at large. He had not staged the production back in Elmwood solely for his own amusement. He was not about to fade away and leave the Executioner in peace.

No problem there. He wanted one more chance to face his enemy, identify him and settle it between them one-on-one. And if the enemy turned out to be a crew, an army...well, so be it. He had played against the odds before, and would again...provided he survived this strange Connecticut campaign.

It had been simple going in, a hit and run designed to leave the fledgling syndicate in disarray, but it was turning into something else entirely. Something dark and dangerous, beyond the soldier's understanding.

He parked the rental, set the brake and picked the Mini-Uzi off the seat beside him. He was ready if they tried to take him here, at least as ready as a man could be for death. If they were waiting for him, he would play it as it came, and damn the consequences. No one lived forever. The Executioner had long resigned himself to the fact that he was spinning out his life, his war, on borrowed time.

The predawn chill invaded Bolan's body as he locked the car and stood in darkness for a moment under the drooping branches of a tree. His clothing could not keep out the cold entirely, and an involuntary shiver raced along his spine. If he had been a superstitious man, he might have seen the physical reaction as an omen of impending doom. But Bolan had no time for imaginary fears.

He circled warily around the car, the Mini-Uzi held against his leg, invisible in shadow. Checking out the garage would take only a moment, and it was the sort of detail that a savvy warrior never leaves to chance. The little clapboard structure seemed secure, but Bolan walked the circuit anyway, applied his pencil flash to grimy windows, satisfied himself that only roaches lurked within.

No danger there. Bolan relaxed a fraction, though he knew it was premature. The house would be his adversary's preference for a trap. It would be easier to take him inside, away from prying eyes. Of course, his nemesis was not exactly shy; the Elmwood set had been a public free-for-all.

As he finished checking out the small garage, Bolan thought about the bullet-punctured rental. He would have to ditch it now, secure new wheels. A minor inconvenience, taken by itself, but each compulsory exposure put the Executioner at risk, a fact his unknown enemy was doubtless counting on.

He scanned the trees that stood like sentries, guarding the perimeter of his rented hideaway. No movement in the darkness there, no shadow out of place. If anyone was watching him, he was inside the house.

Bolan crossed the driveway, overgrown with grass and weeds, and angled across the lawn to enter through the kitchen, at the rear. Two steps up, and he was standing on the narrow porch outside the kitchen door. The drapes were drawn on windows to his right and left, and Bolan half expected the dusty panes to shatter with gunfire as he fished inside his pocket for the key.

Not yet. Outside, he would be a moving target, initial rounds deflected by the window glass and screens. If the hunter played his hand too soon Bolan might escape completely. But once inside the kitchen...

Of course, he had no alternative. It would be folly to desert the safe house now without a look inside. If the enemy had not discovered the hideout, he was safe tonight. If he decided a move was necessary, it could wait for daylight, when the rental offices were open. But if the nest was blown...

Then he might not be moving anywhere. If they were waiting for him in the darkened safe house, it could be all over, here and now.

Enough.

He turned the key. Alert for any sound of movement from within, he stooped forward, one ear pressed to the door. No sound at all. He straightened.

The door swung open at his touch. Bolan paused on the threshold, realizing that his silhouette made a perfect target from within. When the silent darkness did not blossom into gunfire, he let his pent-up breath escape between clenched teeth. Too early to relax, but he could feel the tension easing slightly. Later, after he had checked the rooms and found them empty, peered beneath beds and inside closets, he would pour himself a drink and offer up a toast to paranoia.

But it wasn't paranoid to watch your back when enemies were out to kill you. After one close brush with death tonight, the soldier knew his caution was entirely justified. As long as one of Bolan's enemies survived, as long as there was a price on his head, a healthy paranoia would be his best defense.

Bolan stepped inside, his Mini-Uzi still directed toward the floor. The empty kitchen mocked him silently, moonlight reflecting off stainless steel and porcelain. The inexpensive dining table with its brace of chairs was planted in the center of the room, the spindly legs affording no concealment for a crouching enemy.

The Executioner was alone.

The living room and bedroom next, the bathroom with its curtained shower saved for last. Relief had sparked a sudden pressure in his bladder, and the soldier would be glad when he finished checking out the house. A wasted effort, all his fears in vain.

The sound alerted Bolan as he stepped stealthily across the kitchen. From the living room came a thin, metallic ratchet sound, barely audible, as if some tiny clock was winding down.

Bolan recognized the sound from grim experience. Without a second thought or backward glance he sprinted for the door. Split seconds left, if there was any time at all, and Bolan knew he was racing for his life against the clock.

The *timer*.

He cleared the doorway, running with his head hunched between his shoulders, like a fighter braced to take the blow that will bring him down. Another stride and he would clear the porch, find refuge in the darkness of the lawn. A few more yards...

Too late.

Behind him, Bolan felt the shock wave microseconds before it arrived. He was diving forward when the awesome *crack* of the explosion tore the night apart, the heavy fist of its concussion slamming square between his shoulders. Airborne, tumbling, he caught a quick, inverted glimpse of the disintegrating safe house, walls bowed outward, roof in flames and canted crazily. Instinctively he closed his eyes against the spray of shattered glass and plaster.

Peppered by debris, he hit the grass and rolled with arms and legs tucked in against his body, like a fetus violently expelled from some explosive womb. A smoking strip of lumber shot overhead and speared the wall of the garage, protruding like an outsize javelin. Around him, bits and pieces of the crackerbox rained down, the shingles drifting lazily like embers, snagging in trees and setting boughs alight like torches.

For a moment Bolan lay immobile on the grass, his empty lungs straining for air. At last a gasp of breath passed the tight constriction of his throat, and he thought he might live. The roaring in his ears was Niagara amplified ten thousand times; even if his eardrums had escaped concussion damage he would not hear normally for hours. He was vulnerable, nearly helpless, yet the soldier knew he must move if he was to survive.

Gingerly he unfolded, rolling onto hands and knees. Eyes open, he could see the firelight, even feel its heat. Sudden nausea racked his body, and he vomited, a greasy puddle in the spiky grass. He fought to keep his arms and legs from trembling.

Bolan staggered to his feet, maintained his balance on the second try and lurched in the direction of his rental car. The dark sedan was chalky now with dust and ash, like some relic from Pompeii. A blackened two-by-four lay square across the hood, and Bolan raked it off before he climbed behind the wheel. The Mini-Uzi lay behind him somewhere in the darkness, but he did not have time to pursue it now.

As Bolan turned the rental's engine over, the house was crumbling in upon itself, charcoal beams protruding skyward, swathed in flames. From the direction of the street, a babble rose as frightened neighbors stumbled from their homes in bathrobes and pajamas and gingerly walked in little groups toward the scene of the explosion. None of them had known the crackerbox's latest resident, few of them had even seen him, but they had gathered in the firelit darkness now to watch him burn.

Mack Bolan had no fear that they would catch his license number. It was dark, their attention was focused on the fire, and he did not intend to dawdle. As the first neighbor appeared around the hedge, Bolan dropped the shift into reverse and stood on the accelerator. The wheels dug furrows in the grassy driveway as he powered backward, putting ground between himself and the inferno of the safe house. Faces looked startled, sunburned in the cherry glow of taillights, figures dodged awkwardly when Bolan did not brake. He hit the pavement, smoking rubber in the turn, then kicked the headlights onto high beams, blinding the onlookers before they had a chance to focus on the auto or his face.

Even in his haste, despite his shaken state, Bolan watched the rearview, straining to detect a tail. When he had covered half a dozen blocks without a glimpse of headlights on his backtrack, he slowed down to the posted limit, cruised north and west until he found an all-night filling station with rest rooms at the back.

He parked the rental close against the curb and sat behind the wheel for several moments, waiting for the solitary clerk to show himself. As Bolan hoped, the guy remained secure inside his cage, uninterested in challenging the motives of a man who needed privacy at 2:00 a.m. As long as Bolan did not try to rip the fixtures out by hand, he would be undisturbed.

The trunk gave up a first-aid kit that Bolan always carried. It was adequate for most emergencies, excluding broken bones, and Bolan knew already that the aching and throbbing of his limbs and rib cage were caused by bruising rather than by fractures.

Still, there might be some internal injury. Once inside the rest room Bolan urinated painfully, alert for any sign of blood. His stream was clear. He spent another moment probing his abdomen, his groin and kidneys with the fingers of a medic educated on the field of battle. Satisfied finally that nothing had been punctured, torn or twisted, he stripped off the dusty, tattered clothes and stood before the grimy mirror naked.

Wooden splinters, bits of masonry and glass had peppered Bolan's body, urban shrapnel clinging to his clothes and sifting down around him as he stripped. His skin was torn in half a dozen places, and his back was mottled with bruises in a camouflage pattern that would linger for days. His face, too, was bruised, a smudge beneath one eye would not wipe away, and his eyebrows had been singed. From head to foot, he smelled of fire and smoke. Slowly he set about cleaning up and ministering to his wounds.

First he washed, the powdered soap like grit against his smarting flesh. When he was finished, standing in a puddle on the dirty tile floor, he dried himself with paper towels that could have been used to sand furniture. Hydrogen peroxide next, cool liquid tingling on his skin, foaming energetically on contact with open wounds. He let the antiseptic do its work, then gritted his teeth against the burning as he daubed on merthiolate.

Finished at last, Bolan stowed the first-aid gear and shook out his dusty clothes. A change would have felt even better, but all his other clothes had gone up with the house, and he would be forced to do some shopping in the morning. Thankful for the caution that made him keep a hoard of cash and weapons in the car, the soldier knew he was not disabled yet, by any means. The immediate problem was mobility, a set of wheels without battle scars to draw attention from police. Then there would be time to replace the gear that had been lost.

The next problem, Bolan knew, was to discover who had wired the safe house, who had trailed him from the Giulianno strike, who had left behind the business card from TIF. The enemy—or enemies—had charted Bolan's every move, had traced him to his den and wired the place for doomsday in his absence, very nearly finishing his war in one fell swoop. An adversary who could do it once would try again, as soon as he found that the snare back in Newington was empty.

A swift solution to the mystery took top priority in Bolan's mind. The Giulianno-Petrosina feud was an amusing sideshow by comparison. If his security had failed—and obviously it had—then Bolan's war, his very life, was hanging by a slender thread. He could not risk another move against the local syndicate until he knew who was tracking him, and why.

Reluctantly, the soldier came to grips with the solution—or part of it, at any rate. He could not name his enemy, not yet, but he knew where he must look to find the answers. The information did not lie in Hartford; he must seek it out on more familiar ground. Bolan knew exactly where he had to go and what he had to do, had known it from the moment he saw the yellowed business card.

The Executioner was going home.

6

The hunter followed Interstate 91 north out of Hartford toward the Massachusetts border, the roseate dawn just breaking to the east. Another hour would see him home, but there was time enough to think about the day that he had planned for himself. The sweet anticipation could be dangerous, he knew, but he would temper it with caution when he took the field. For now, alone and cruising, he was able to indulge himself.

The hunter was driving his own car now. He had returned the second rental to an airport parking lot attendant, left the keys and settled his bill with stolen plastic, walked the hundred yards to another lot where he had stashed his private wheels upon arrival in Connecticut. The Camaro was waiting for him, safe and sound, the theft alarm still primed to shriek at any unfamiliar touch. He deactivated the screamer, paid another lot attendant a usurious seven bucks a day and put the airport sprawl behind him, rolling north.

The darkness had been comforting, but he loved the sunrise best. It put his plan in perspective, banished shadows so he could see the fine points clearly. He knew, beyond the slightest doubt, that his plan would run like clockwork. He had thought of everything, and nothing short of death could stop him now.

The Newington surprise had been a beauty, timed to sheer perfection, executed with a master's eye for detail. He had been watching, nestled motionless on the lower branch of an ancient oak, when the Executioner arrived. He could easily have taken out his quarry on the spot, but he was not inclined to take the easy out when he could wait a few more hours—days, at most—and have it all. With final absolution only inches from his fingertips, the hunter stolidly refused to go for any shortcuts, turn the contest into something base and primitive.

Leaving nothing to chance, the hunter had secured his rental wheels a block from Bolan's house and locked the car at the curb outside a patently deserted home. He made a show of doubling back in the direction of the house next door, in case some busybody was watching, then went through darkened yards that he had previously learned were free of dogs. A brisk ten minutes saw him at his station, and he had been waiting only moments when the Executioner made his first cautious pass.

The set had been ridiculously simple. He had wired the "safe house" on his first inspection, using just enough C-4 to turn the little four-room inside out and upside down. He didn't want a holocaust, just sound and fury adequate to speed Mack Bolan on his way.

The timing had been critical, of course. Judging that his quarry would enter from the rear, the hunter had secured his explosive in a tiny living room closet. Close enough to foster the illusion of reality, and at the same time far enough away to give his prey a running chance. The detonator had been chosen for its noise potential, an early model that had fallen out of favor for its tendency to warn a target seconds before detonation. Few professionals used the obsolete devices anymore, but they were still around. The hunter had his sources. He knew that Bolan would recognize the detonator's whirring sound, a warning as distinctive as a rattlesnake's for anyone with expertise in demolitions.

And the soldier had that skill, in spades.

There was potential danger, even with the hunter watching from his crow's nest, finger on the radio-remote control that he had afterward discarded in a Dumpster, miles away. He could not really *see* his quarry after Bolan crossed the kitchen threshold. He had had to estimate his progress, calculate his stride, incorporating all the hesitation that a hunted man must feel on realizing he might be walking straight into a trap. If he had muffed the calculations, let the soldier cross that tiny kitchen, enter the living room, then it would have been over, finished. He would have had to kill his quarry then, or else abort the strike and miss his chance of driving Bolan north.

Anxiety had made him punch the button early, but it had worked out fine. The soldier had reacted like a pro, escaping from the crackerbox with microseconds to spare before it blew up behind him. The hunter stood his ground to verify there was no disabling injury, was satisfied when Bolan gunned his rental four-door through a straggling crowd of sleepy neighbors and away.

He knew precisely where the Executioner was going, where he *had* to go. The soldier would be desperate for answers now, aware that someone had him pegged, cleverly anticipated his movements. Robbed of alternatives, deprived of sanctuary, he would have to move, and all the answers lay in Pittsfield. Bolan would pursue them there, and there the hunter would be waiting for him.

Highway 91 would take him north to Springfield, Massachusetts. From there he would turn westward, on Interstate 90, following the four-lane blacktop into Berkshire county. North again then, through rolling hills, immune to beauty after all the pain he had witnessed, all the blood he had spilled. And into Pittsfield. Home.

Anticipation made the hunter bear down on the Camaro's accelerator, but he held it to the posted limit. Speed patrols were unlikely this early in the morning, but he could not ignore the risk; it would be disastrous if official records placed him so close to Hartford, in the wake of Bolan's brief, abortive war. The others, back at home in Pittsfield, thought he was in Rhode Island. They were not expecting him until tomorrow morning, and though they would have no reason to connect him with events already starting to unfold, the hunter wanted no loose ends.

From the beginning, he had counted on perfection, demanded nothing less of his equipment, of himself. The game was worth it, certainly, and worth the risks that were the flip side of the coin. Death was the reward for bungling a crucial play, and in the last analysis every play was crucial. The least mistake, the smallest error could snowball. It was the hunter's task to see that there were no mistakes, no wrinkles in his plan.

How long had Bolan run against the odds, defying all the numbers with sheer bravado? Long enough. But there was more than nerve involved, the hunter knew, a great deal more than cast-iron balls and nerves of stainless steel. The Executioner was still alive because whenever possible he planned ahead, refusing to be buffeted by circumstance, confounded by coincidence. Undoubtedly, there had been times when he had played a set by ear, but then his battlefield experience had seen him through. The hunter's slim advantage now was Bolan's disorientation at the swift disruption of his plans in Hartford. Any way you sliced it, he was running in the dark, without sufficient clues to name his enemy or plot effective action at the other end. It was inevitable that he visit Pittsfield, but beyond that point, the Executioner was flying blind.

No matter. He would get the message soon enough, and when he read the bloody writing on the wall, it would be too late. The hunter had a hot reception waiting for his prey in Pittsfield. He hoped that Bolan would appreciate the gesture.

A few miles south of Springfield, with the morning sun a hazy searchlight lost in drifting clouds, the hunter pulled the car into an all-night diner's empty parking lot. He was not hungry, but the outdoor telephone provided an opportunity to put the wheels in motion.

He dropped the necessary coins and punched up a number from memory, relaxed with an eye on the highway as he waited through the rings. A sleepy voice responded. He left the message, carefully repeating it and waiting while the person gave it back to him verbatim. Satisfied, he hung up on the sudden rush of questions, smiling to himself.

Before the second call, he drew a boxlike object from his pocket, fitted it around the mouthpiece of the telephone, and tried the on-off switch. More coins, another Pittsfield number. A switchboard operator took it this time, alert despite the hour.

"Pittsfield Police Department."

"Captain Pappas, please." It never hurt to be polite.

"The captain won't be in till eight o'clock. If I could take a message..."

"Patch me through to Pappas. Wake him if you have to." No more time for courtesy. "And tell him it's important."

"Sir, if you could give me some idea—"

"Mack Bolan," he responded, trusting the box to make his normal tone a snarling guttural. "Is that idea enough? The goddamned Executioner is back in town."

THE FORD SEDAN WAS NONDESCRIPT, a midsize with sufficient power under the hood to meet Mack Bolan's needs. His weapons and other gear were safely locked away in the trunk, an Ingram MAC-10 submachine gun tucked beneath the raincoat folded on the seat beside him. Stiff and aching after the explosion that had turned his safe house into kindling, the soldier was taking no chances on the road.

Preferring privacy to speed, he was avoiding the interstates. Traffic would be thinner on the two-lane state highways, a pursuit car easier to recognize. If Bolan's enemies were short on personnel, they were unlikely to have eyes along the secondary routes, and at the moment, any edge was comforting. The time he spent driving extra miles would be a good investment if it helped recapture the advantage of surprise.

His route would follow Highway 6 due west to Thomaston, there turning on the northbound Highway 8 for Massachusetts. In the rolling Berkshire Hills, he would forsake the back roads, homing in on U.S. Highway 7 for the final run to Pittsfield and the killing ground. With any luck at all, he might evade the eyes that would be waiting, watching for him.

But the soldier's luck was running thin already, and he had no reason to believe that it would change. Within an hour he had been bested twice by enemies unknown; only providence or some plan beyond his grasp had saved Mack Bolan's life. His war had never been defensive, he had never waited for the enemy to capture the initiative and seek him out, but now the Executioner felt an urge to burrow in, go underground until he understood his latest adversary.

Clearly, there was more at stake than Hartford and the petty Giulianno-Petrosina feud. The more he thought about it, Bolan was sure that Hartford had been window dressing, even coincidence. The enemy who stalked him now had no more interest in Connecticut than Bolan had in Chinese checkers. He—or they—had seen an opportunity to reach the Executioner and had seized the time. If not in Hartford, they might as easily have made the touch in Jersey, in New York—or in Los Angeles, for all he knew. Without ID he could not judge his adversary's strength, mobility or reach, but Bolan's nemesis was two-for-two so far.

Except that Bolan lived.

He had already hashed the problem over in his mind, determined that his survival of the Elmwood confrontation had been calculated in advance. The faceless gunner could have taken him at any time, but opted to withdraw instead, postponing the conclusion of their death game. As for Newington and the destruction of the safe house, evidence was inconclusive. The house had been invaded, wired by a professional with goop enough to do the job, and then some . . . but it was possible that he had been intended to survive. He did not relish playing cat-and-mouse, but as it seemed to be the only game in town, he felt compelled to see it through.

From the beginning it had been obvious that someone wanted him in Pittsfield. The question now was, why? What made the setting special, other than his own familial connection to the town, its role as the initial battleground in his private war against the Mafia?

The answer: nothing.

Bolan had returned to Pittsfield once before, when dapper Dave Eritrea was reaching for the moon and Augie Marinello's vacant throne had been his launching pad. The mafioso had abducted Leo Turrin's wife, sweet Angelina, from their Pittsfield home, and Bolan had retrieved her from captivity. His strike had been the grim beginning of the end for the Manhattan mob as it was constituted then, but as in Bolan's first campaign, the guns had spoken first in Pittsfield.

Still, there seemed to be no connection. Augie Marinello and his bastard son, Ernesto, were safely in their graves. Likewise Barney Matilda and his lethal offspring, the Talifero twins. As for Eritrea, he had become a songbird for the federal protected witness program, buried under layers of bogus documents supplied by Washington, observed around the clock by federal marshals sworn to keep him healthy, keep him talking while he still had stories to tell.

No enemies remained from Bolan's second Pittsfield strike...and none had been connected with TIF, in any case. No matter how he laid it out, whatever his angle of approach, the riddle brought him back to the beginning of his war. Square one.

An ancient pickup truck had fallen in behind him. He scrutinized the driver for a moment in his rearview mirror, finally deciding that the guy was what he seemed to be, a farmer on his way to town. The guy had worry written on his weathered face, but he would still be going home alive, no matter what his business in the city. Mack Bolan could not with any certainty say the same about himself.

He did not relish going home. No family left outside the Catholic cemetery, his childhood memories soured, tainted with the smell of blood and death. His brother was in San Diego, managing the double life of holding down their strongbase and working with a storefront law firm. Sweet Val Querente—Valentina Gray, these days—had married, moved away and built herself a life removed from the incessant threat of violent death. Why not? Who chose the path of everlasting war except a soldier who had nothing left to lose?

Even Leo Turrin, Bolan's closest ally in his holy war against the Mafia, had pulled up stakes and settled in Washington as part of Hal Brognola's special strike force team. As Leonard Justice, he was riding an important desk in Wonderland, affiliated with the revamped Phoenix project, keeping tabs on all the inside moves and funneling selected information back to Bolan as the need arose. Turrin was not in Pittsfield now.

So many gone. Bolan wondered whether he would recognize the old hometown. No matter, really; someone was waiting for him who would recognize the Executioner. Survival was the game, and if the rules decreed that the game be played on old, familiar ground, he was ready to oblige. Selection of the battleground might be his unseen adversary's first mistake, and one mistake could end it all.

The Executioner had made his peace with death long years before in Vietnam. Resigned to the inevitable, he was able to plot strategy that other men, intimidated by their mortality, would never dare to contemplate. He had gradually collected others like himself, the "borning dead" who forged a living legend out of fire and steel on both sides of the DMZ.

The war had followed Bolan home—or rather, it had been there waiting for him all the time—and once again his cool rapport with death had dazzled lesser men. A legend in the making, Bolan had been somewhat staggered by the spread of his mystique among Americans who had been too long starved for heroes. In his own opinion, Bolan was

a soldier who had seen his duty, recognized his obligation
to society and done what any other fighting man might do.
The legend was a thing apart. It was no more part of Bolan's war than any other myth was part of day-to-day
reality. From time to time, the legend was helpful psycho-
logically against the enemy, but Bolan sensed that this time
in Pittsfield, he would have more need of steel than smoke.

He was going home to fight, perhaps to die, and Bolan
did not even know his enemy. It was something he would
have to learn, and soon. The soldier had no hope of living
through a war with shadows, especially with shadows that
foresaw his every move.

There were still a few moves that the shadows might not
recognize, a few refinements on the game of cat-and-
mouse that had been written by a master. He was not ready
yet to fold his hand and slavishly admit defeat.

Anything his adversaries wanted from him, they would
have to take. Mack Bolan was not giving anything away.

7

Morning was Al Weatherbee's favorite time of day. The world seemed new, full of light and hope, and a fresh day's possibilities seemed endless. Sunrises held promises for Weatherbee; by afternoon he knew the promises were empty lies, and sometimes in the night he wondered how a man dared hope at all.

This morning, Weatherbee had risen early, more from habit than from need. He had no place to go, no errand more demanding than a round trip to the hardware store, and the young flower plants out back would never know if he slept an extra hour. Weatherbee would know, however; he clung to the routine that had been his for a quarter century. The process of decline was cumulative—in a man or in society—and Weatherbee believed the process could be stalled, postponed indefinitely, if you took decisive action going in.

Of course, the police brass had disagreed, however diplomatically. They had talked about the need for new blood, fresh faces on the firing line. A quarter century was nothing when you took the long view, but the brass were interested in here and now. A man who makes life-and-death decisions should be fresh and energetic, youthful. Never mind the years of street experience, the knowledge gained through butting heads with generations of barbarians. Experience and wisdom had become passé. Technology was everything, and if they couldn't print it on a micro-chip it was already obsolete.

He could have fought the bastards, dragged them through the courts until they sickened at the sight of him and paid him off. But, if the truth were known, Al Weatherbee had soured on the job before that all-important birthday rolled around. He had grown weary of office politics and bargained pleas, of the manacles and blinders that had come to be part of every street cop's uniform, as much a part of each detective and patrolman as his badge or gun. Retirement had been welcome, a relief. . . or so he had told himself.

But he had been wrong, at least in part.

He missed the squad room, with its fragrance derived in equal parts from perspiration, cigarettes and fear. He missed the familiar weight of handcuffs and revolver in his belt, the flashing lights and screaming siren when the team rolled out on a homicide. He didn't miss the double shifts, the stifling odor of a stiff gone rotten inside a two-room walk-up, the numbing terror of a midnight foot pursuit through twisting streets and alleyways.

The job had been a pain, all things considered, a hem-orrhoid with pay. He should be thankful they had put him out to pasture, grateful for the mercy they had shown him.

Still . . .

He smelled the eggs and bacon when he left the shower, groping for a towel as hunger growled in his stomach. Glancing in the direction of the bathroom scales, he decided it was pointless, shrugged and padded naked into the master bedroom. His usual outfit of slacks, sport shirt and moccasins made Alice gibe sometimes that he still dressed in uniform. Today he had selected blue jeans, faded with the years but clean and neatly pressed. As for the rest, his "uniform" would be the same.

The former homicide detective knew he was a creature of habit. Decades of the law enforcement regimen had left their mark. Good detectives were automatically suspicious of change. A man who altered his schedule suddenly might be hiding something, planning something. Sudden variations in appearance, appetite, opinion—all were suspect. A man was most vulnerable when he broke his normal stride, his life off balance. Thus were victims snared and savages undone.

He finished dressing, slipped the moccasins on bare, size-thirteen feet and headed for the stairs. The years had scarcely touched his catlike grace, the vigor and coordination that had saved his life on more than one occasion. True, he couldn't run the mile so well these days, but he could hold his own. No more than six months earlier, a would-be mugger had selected Weatherbee for easy pickings as he left a downtown liquor store. The confrontation had been brief, ending with the mugger on his back waiting for a black-and-white to make the scene. It had reminded Weatherbee of good old times.

It had reminded him, as well, that he was getting old.

The fight had taken more away from him than it had given, left him winded and, above all else, embarrassed. Nobody was paying him to duke it out with misfits anymore. He had no stake in going head-to-head with low-lifes—not, at any rate, until they sought him out and made it personal.

The food cooking in the kitchen smelled heavenly. Weatherbee lingered in the doorway for a moment, watching Alice as she worked. The only woman he had ever loved, she stood before him now as if untouched by hostile time. The salt-and-pepper hair was not a sign of age, but rather of maturity and grace. Time had softly, subtly altered the girlish figure, but looking at her now, Al

Weatherbee was stricken with a longing more intense than any he had felt in years.

"Good morning."

Alice glanced across her shoulder, graced her husband with the kind of smile that made a day complete. "Sleep well?"

"Uh-huh."

In fact, his sleep had been disturbed by restless dreams that had left him feeling empty, almost apprehensive, as he woke. He could recall nothing of their content—just impressions of chaotic action, blood, bitter loss—and maybe it was just as well. Recurring nightmares were a deviation from routine, a signal that the old machinery was on the verge of breaking down.

Recurring? Nightmares?

Yes.

If truth be told, his sleep had been disrupted three nights running by a formless dream that he could not recall. In daylight, all Weatherbee retained was a vague impression of someone, something familiar, a wisp of grim nostalgia coming back to haunt him. He did not believe in premonitions, but the dreams were starting to disturb him, all the same.

"Eggs are almost ready," Alice said.

Weatherbee was drifting toward the dining table when the telephone intruded on his reverie. "I'll get it."

He moved languidly, half hoping that the caller would give up. Slowly he lifted the receiver. "Hello?"

"Good morning, Al. John Pappas."

"John."

He felt Alice's disapproving glare boring through his skull and did not have to turn around to know what she was thinking. Pappas was one of those who had offered his condolences when Weatherbee retired, suggesting they get together soon and often, keep in touch for old times' sake. It was eighteen months since they'd had a really good talk, and their last encounter had been accidental, in a supermarket checkout line.

"How are you, Al?"

"I'm fine."

He held no grudge against John Pappas. Hell, John had enough to do between his family and the job. Weatherbee could still recall his own reaction to the grizzled former cops who sometimes hung around the station house, intent on talking shop and leeching off the soldiers they had left behind. It got so you could almost smell them coming, and they smelled like failure. Some of them had smelled like death.

Who needed that shit, anyway? And so he said, "I'm fine. What can I do you for?"

"We got a call this morning, Al. It made me think of you."

Weatherbee grinned. "A breather? Better get your number changed, or he'll be keeping you awake down there."

"I wish it was a breather, Al." Pappas waited for a moment, finally dropped the other shoe. "It's Bolan."

"Ah."

Just that, but Weatherbee could feel his stomach turning over, writhing into knots.

"We got a tip that he was coming into town. It could be bullshit, but you never know."

"That's right. You never do."

"We thought—*I* thought—it might be useful to have the benefit of your experience."

And there it was.

"My old reports are in the files."

"They're on my desk," the man from homicide responded. "And I know damned well there's only so much information you can put on paper."

"Well..."

"You were the Bolan expert, Al. You knew the bastard when he was still wet behind the ears."

"That one was never wet behind the ears."

"You had him pegged from the beginning."

"And it didn't do a frigging bit of good."

Behind him, silence. Alice would be watching, waiting.

"I need to see you, Al. We need to talk."

"You may have noticed I'm retired."

"That so?"

"I've got a thank-you letter from the mayor to prove it."

"We can't afford another shitstorm, Al."

"What makes you think I can head it off?"

"You're all I've got."

"I'd say you're up shit creek."

"Not yet. Not if you let me pick your brain awhile."

The former homicide commander closed his eyes, then opened them again abruptly. He was frightened by the images unfolding on the viewing screen of memory.

"What time?"

"Let's say eleven, shall we? We can talk a bit, go out and grab a bite of lunch on the department. Hell, you pick the restaurant."

"I will."

"Eleven, then?"

"Why not?"

"I owe you one."

"You owe me more than one."

He cradled the receiver, slowly turned to face his wife of thirty years.

"John Pappas."

"Oh?"

He sensed the disapproval in her voice. "We're having lunch around eleven."

"Why?"

"He's got a case he wants to talk about."

She pinned him with a glance that spoke of dark suspicions, hidden fears, and then she turned away without another word to serve their breakfast.

"Hell, I don't mind talking to him." Weatherbee was angry at himself, dismayed by the compulsion to explain a meeting with his friend and former colleague. "Anyway, he's buying."

Alice didn't laugh or otherwise acknowledge the remark. Against his better instincts, Weatherbee decided to tell her everything.

"John thinks Bolan's coming back to town."

She stiffened for an instant. Before the moment broke, the rigor passed, he could have sworn that she was trembling.

"So? What's that to you? John knows that you're retired."

She spoke the final word as if it were distasteful, and that saddened Weatherbee. She realized how much he missed the job, and recognized the grudge he bore against the men who had forced him out.

He thought about his answer for a moment, tried to make it reasonable. In the end, he knew that he was searching for excuses, grasping at straws.

"I'm the only one in town who ever met the guy. John knows I used to follow different aspects of the case. He wants some input. Simple."

"Simple."

She was having trouble serving the eggs. He moved to stand beside her, slid one strong arm around her shoulders. Tears were already welling in her eyes.

"What is it, Alice?"

"Pappas. The department. Dammit, Al, they bundled up your years of service, your experience, and threw them all away. You don't owe them a goddamned thing."

He blinked, amazed more by the vehemence of her reaction than by the language she used. Mild-mannered for the most part, Alice generally took more time to build a head of steam.

"He's asking for opinions, hon, that's all. A little conversation in a public place."

"Oh, sure. And then what? I can hear it now: 'Hey, Al, we need the benefit of your experience.' Or, 'Say, we've got a little situation here we thought maybe you could help us with.' And, 'Say, can you identify this body for us, Al?'"

The tears were streaming down her cheeks now.

"It won't be like that, Alice. Honestly."

She shifted slightly, shrugged her arm away and turned to face him squarely. The former homicide detective knew that she could look right through him, pierce his petty lies and small evasions with her intuition like a knife through gauze. And he was suddenly ashamed.

"Do what you like," she said, and turned away.

"Well, wait a second . . . what about your breakfast?"

"I'm not hungry anymore."

And she was gone.

He watched the empty kitchen doorway for a moment, hoping she would return. Then the rich aroma of the cooling eggs and bacon took control. In spite of everything—the argument, his nervousness about the lunch date with Pappas—Weatherbee was suddenly ravenous. He recognized the signs: a hunter prepping for action, stoking energy reserves against the hours when he would be forced to run on nerves and guts alone. It was the stake-out syndrome, sure, and he had felt the pangs a thousand times before.

But this was different, dammit. Weatherbee was not a hunter anymore. The game belonged to Pappas, and he wasn't doing anybody any good by spinning elaborate fantasies inside his head. The former sergeant—captain now, and well deserving—wasn't looking for a partner on the Bolan case. Provided there even *was* a case. Pappas needed background information, something that would let him "feel" his prey in case the Executioner surfaced once again in Pittsfield. And Weatherbee had been the local "Bolan expert" for as long as anyone could recollect.

It was an honor Weatherbee would happily have traded off for damned near anything except a dose of clap. He hadn't started out to make the hellfire warrior his career, but it had happened somehow. Of course, chance had been involved; it had been Weatherbee's report that "closed" the murder-suicide that wiped out Bolan's family. As captain of detectives working homicide, he'd known about the elder Bolan's loans from Triangle Finance, the pressure that collectors sometimes brought to bear on clients who were slow paying back the vigorish. But there was nothing he could do without sufficient evidence, nothing he could tell a grieving soldier home from one war, looking for another in the streets.

Assignment to the massacre at TIF had been a logical follow-up of the Bolan family homicides. Of course, the Bolan case was closed, but Weatherbee was no believer in coincidence. The presence of a vengeful son, an expert sniper with ninety-odd kills to his credit in Asia, had spelled *vendetta* in bloody letters ten feet tall. It was Weatherbee who had pulled the soldier in for questioning. He had laid it on the line in no uncertain terms: evidence was nonexistent, either way, and Bolan could walk, provided he let it lie. The soldier's debt was paid, and no one on the force was weeping bitter tears or pulling voluntary overtime to break the TIF assassinations, anyway. Good riddance was the party line, though not for publication, of course.

Weatherbee had known somehow that Bolan wouldn't buy it. He had recognized the courage in the man and had realized the syndicate would never let the matter drop. The mafiosi would be bound to find their man and claim his head for "honor's" sake. He understood the twisted logic, realized that an illicit brotherhood that runs on terror cannot afford to have its people terrorized.

The soldier's refusal to be scared off, his grim determination to proceed with what could only be a losing war, had frightened Weatherbee as much as they had angered him. He pictured streets awash in blood, as Bolan threw his martial skills against the legions of the underworld. As a believer in the odds, he knew Bolan didn't stand a chance in hell of walking out of that one-sided war alive.

But he was wrong.

The soldier had not only walked, he had been charging ever since, from coast to coast and God knows where—all overseas. The nervy bastard had not only wrestled victory from sure defeat in Pittsfield, but he had survived against the syndicate's shock troops in a series of campaigns that had left La Cosa Nostra reeling.

From the first, when it was clear that Bolan had escaped from Pittsfield and was carrying his war abroad, police in other jurisdictions had been drawn to Weatherbee like moths to flame. They called, and sometimes flew cross-country, to pick his brains, absorb his impressions of the man they would never see. In Pittsfield, Bolan had been flesh and blood. Throughout the rest of it—New York, Chicago, on and on—the legend had run interference for him on both sides of the law. He was accused of crimes committed simultaneously, states apart, and every lawman with a "Bolan case" before him had sought initial guidance from the "Bolan expert."

Some, he knew, had wanted to learn why Weatherbee had failed. They had searched his face, his files, for some discrepancy, some weakness that they would take care to avoid themselves. If any of the visitors had found his error, they had kept it secret through the years, and they had been no more successful than the Pittsfield team. No one had searched more ardently for errors of omission or commission than Al Weatherbee himself, and in the end he was compelled to accept that nothing had gone wrong with the investigation.

Bolan had eluded Weatherbee's detectives as he had evaded teams of mafiosi, through his ability to strike then fade away. The sense of shame, of professional embarrassment that Weatherbee had carried with him in the wake of Bolan's Pittsfield war had long since faded into dusty memory. The brass, no doubt, still held him personally responsible for Bolan's getaway. Successive chiefs had clearly been annoyed by their force's exemplifying what not to do for lawmen all across the country. It wasn't fair, to Pittsfield or to Weatherbee, but someone had to take the heat, and shit had always run downhill.

But now they needed Weatherbee again. He could imagine all the arguments Pappas must have used to sell the brass on his idea . . . or was he taking this one on himself, without informing his superiors? If anyone got wise, it could be passed off as a lunch with a friend, for old times' sake.

It didn't play. Weatherbee was certain Pappas would have cleared his move with someone higher up. The crowned heads would have shaken ruefully before they finally nodded and gave the go-ahead. The taste of crow was nothing in comparison to the god-awful stink that would be stirred up by another Bolan war in Pittsfield.

Weatherbee would have no official status. No salary. The brass would never risk involving him directly in the conduct of the case. He smiled at the idea of butting heads against the city fathers over something like a twisted ankle on the job, for instance. Their insurance carriers would hit the roof, and heads would roll.

He chuckled to himself and shook his head. John Pappas was only looking for advice, no more, no less. A glance inside the soldier's mind, to see what made him tick.

But Weatherbee could not provide that information. Not after all the years that had elapsed, the changes in Bolan's life, and in his own. He no more understood the Executioner today than he might understand a foreign head of state. America's most wanted fugitive bore small resemblance to the soldier who had faced Al Weatherbee across a littered desk at Homicide so long ago.

Things change. And people, too. Or do they?

Weatherbee had aged—the mirror told him that much every morning, every night—but his basic beliefs were still as firm as they had been when he first pinned on the badge. A certain cynicism had been added, but he still believed in right and wrong, the difference between good and evil. Black and white existed for him still, despite the modern tendency to think in shades of gray.

Bolan, he suspected, just might feel the same.

The soldier might not be so very different, after all.

It would be worth a look, in any case, and if they froze him out when they were finished picking through his memories, so be it. There were other ways to see a problem through.

Enough of that, he told himself, refusing to pursue that train of thought. John Pappas wanted information. Fine. It was ridiculous to think in terms of a personal involvement in the case. There might not even *be* a case, and if there was, Pappas was capable of dealing with it on his own.

Like hell.

You didn't "deal" with Bolan, you *experienced* the guy, the way you might experience an earthquake or a hurricane. For now, the brass were counting on Al Weatherbee to give them some vicarious experience up front, and he was happy to comply.

For all the good that it would do them.

He wished the bastards luck.

## 8

Home is where the heart is, so they say, and part of Bolan's heart would always be in Pittsfield. Where he had been born and raised. Where it had all begun. The old, familiar streets inspired a mixture of emotions for the Executioner: nostalgia for childhood pleasures, the pain of loss all mingled into something he could not easily define. The western Massachusetts city had its share of ghosts, and Bolan knew he would have to search among them, face them down, to solve the riddle that had drawn him home.

There had been progress during the years of Bolan's war, dramatic changes in the face of certain neighborhoods, expansion of the city limits, but he recognized the areas that mattered to him easily enough. The Bolan family home was gone, together with its neighbors. Condominiums had been erected on the site. Bolan didn't like the change—it smacked of corporate profits at the expense of individuals. He wondered if the architects and wrecking crew had known the story of what happened here, the grim destruction of a loving family that sparked a worldwide struggle to the death.

A few blocks from his former homesite, Bolan found the park and playground still intact. Against his better judgment, he stopped the rental Ford and got out to stretch his legs, wandering around the swings and teeter-totter, the simple steel merry-go-round that was driven by kid power, the slides and monkey bars. All was silent now, this early in the morning, but he could hear the distant voices, feel the darting shapes around him as he stopped to listen.

His first encounter with aggression had been acted out right here. An inconsequential battleground in retrospect, but at the time, it had been everything to Bolan and his playmates from the neighborhood. They had relied on the playground and adjacent park, had exercised their bodies and their boyhood fantasies there; they had embarked on safaris through the hedgerows, waged ruthless war against one another with water pistols, staked out the so-familiar Martian landscape in the name of Mother Earth. Until the bully came.

His name was Richie Latham. Having repeated two grades, he was bigger than his classmates, and by the time he was twelve his size and willingness to throw a punch intimidated kids his own age and younger. What he lacked in intelligence, Richie compensated for in cunning and in cruelty. By the middle of his sixth-grade year, he had conceived a plan to claim the park and playground as his own preserve, allowing other children to use the facilities on payment of a small fee.

It was a risky business, with the specter of parental intervention glaring over Richie's shoulder, but he shrewdly shaved the odds by leaving girls alone and concentrating on the smaller boys. Most sixth-grade boys would rather face a beating from their peers than run to Mom and Dad for help, a fact that Richie used to his advantage. He was careful not to overcharge—a nickel here and there, with discount rates for groups when he felt benevolent. Those who couldn't ante up took a sad walk home, before or after sampling a knuckle sandwich à la Richie.

Mack Bolan first met Richie Latham on a Saturday in spring, when he stopped by the park with friends. They might have played a game of war, or simply ridden on the creaking carousel . . . but Richie had appeared, demanding tribute. Mack Bolan watched, amazed, as his friends surrendered nickels, pennies, turned out their empty pockets to appease the bully. Bolan had a quarter in his pocket, but when Richie stood before him, waiting, he had stubbornly refused to produce it.

"No pay, no play," the bully had informed him, angling a thumb behind him toward the street. "Take off."

"I've got a right to be here," Bolan had responded. "You don't own the park."

Surprise had been supplanted on the bully's face by anger. "Oh, yeah? We got a tough guy here."

The bully feinted with his left, a sucker punch, and as Bolan responded, Richie's right exploded in his face. The ground rushed up to meet him, and Richie's laughter rang in his ears.

It was a long walk home. When his father asked about the shiner, Bolan had responded, haltingly, embarrassed. Papa Sam had listened sympathetically, then delivered the advice that had stayed with his son through adolescence into manhood.

"No matter where you go in life," he said, "there's always gonna be a Richie Latham, pushing people, taking anything that he can get. Avoid their kind if you can, but never—I mean *never*—be afraid to fight for what you know is right, for what's yours. The bullies in this world only understand one thing."

Papa Sam had raised one hand, the fingers curling, closing slowly until they formed a fist. "Go play," the elder Bolan told his son. "It's Saturday."

Back at the park Richie Latham waited for Mack, lounging on a swing. He did not rise as Bolan walked over and stood in front of him.

"The tough guy." Richie bared yellow teeth in a grin. "So where's my money?"

"You don't own the park," Mack Bolan told him softly. "I don't owe you anything."

"I thought we settled that."

Before the bully got to his feet Bolan punched the freckled nose with his fist. Then he swung both arms like a windmill, missing more than he connected, but riding Richie to the ground. The larger boy fought back, but weakly, startled by the ferocity of his intended victim. When a second blow connected with his nose and a third rebounded from his jaw, he folded, bleating for his parents.

Bolan staggered to his feet and backed away, only then noticing the crowd that had gathered to watch the fight. The faces ringing Richie Latham reflected new emotions; no longer fear but satisfaction, confidence, contempt for the bully. They knew he could be beaten now. They were not afraid of Richie anymore.

"Go home," Mack Bolan told the battered bully. "Go home, and don't come back."

But Richie Latham kept on coming back over the years, wearing other faces, seeking other forms of tribute. Bolan had been running into bullies all his life—in high school, in the Asian hellgrounds, on the home front when a telegram had summoned him to stand before three open graves. The war was everywhere, the bullies all around him, and it seemed appropriate somehow that this time Bolan's war had brought him home.

He left the playground, drove the rental north past Franklin High where he had graduated years before. Franklin's campus summoned up nostalgic memories of homework, football, dating and early exploratory sexual encounters. He drove the memories away and put the place behind him, rolling on in search of answers to the puzzle that had brought him here.

If Bolan planned on walking out of this one, he had to concentrate on the beginning of his war, the origin of his crusade.

And it came back to TIF.

He drove the rental Ford down Commerce Street and past the storefront office that had served Triangle Finance in its salad days. Faded For Rent signs hung on the door and in dirty windows that had been painted over to discourage vandalism. Had any business prospered at 1430 Commerce Street since he'd put the loan sharks out of business, Bolan wondered. Had his retribution jinxed any new tenants of the building?

Someone bore a grudge from Bolan's campaign. Someone still remembered, the hardmen who had been cut down outside TIF. Or was the business card a ruse, a lure to draw the Executioner home to Pittsfield? What enemy knew Bolan well enough to push those ancient buttons? Who remembered Bolan's first campaign? Who cared?

Somebody.

Bolan dared not underestimate his adversary. The destruction of his safe house in Connecticut, following the encounter in the cul-de-sac, had demonstrated that the Executioner was dealing with a pro. His own response would have to be professional, if he was to emerge victorious.

And if he failed... what then? Was his war destined to end here, where it began?

The soldier rejected pessimism, drove the fatalistic visions from his mind. If fate demand Bolan's death in Pittsfield, it could damned well come and get him. It would find him on the firing line.

From Commerce Street, Bolan cruised the Liberty district, passed the apartment house where he had lived while working to infiltrate the local Mafia. The mob had tumbled to his game and sent a pair of heavies out to cancel Bolan's ticket there, but they had failed, the first of many paid exterminators dispatched to bring him down. All dead now. Dead and gone.

He passed the former home of Leo Turrin, where he had been wounded in their first encounter, passed the tract house where he had been taken in by Val Querente in his time of need. Val had adopted brother Johnny, nurtured him to manhood, remarried, sure, and moved away, the smartest move she ever made. The soldier had been grateful for her love, her understanding and her sanctuary.

Inevitably, Bolan's tour took him to South Hills, where the final bloodbath had been staged. The Pittsfield capo, Sergio Frenchi, had been a resident there. Confronted by Bolan's war, the aging don had drawn his troops around him, gone to ground on his walled estate. But Frenchi had failed to learn from Bolan's early moves in Pittsfield. The Executioner had found him in his lair, annihilated him and his troops as if they were cutout figures in a shooting gallery.

Now Bolan parked the rental on a grassy knoll and locked it, followed a narrow footpath through the trees. The woods were rich and ripe on this bright spring day, so different now from the summer darkness of that night so long ago.

Fifty yards from his car, the footpath disappeared and Bolan was surrounded by trees. He made his way unerringly across the sloping hillside, following a course that had been etched on his memory on a night of fire and blood. The clearing was overgrown with ferns and creepers, but he recognized it at once and stood a moment with his eyes closed, listening to echoes from the past. The booming of a big-game rifle, the *crump* of mortar fire, the *whup-whup-whup* of a helicopter gunship closing fast.

And nothing.

Bolan turned to stare across the wooded gorge, toward old Don Sergio's deserted ruin. It had been a palace in its day, but the corruption and decay on which it was founded had inevitably consumed it. The Executioner had helped the course of nature—and the firemen had arrived too late for Frenchi or the manor house. They saved the forest, though. That was all that mattered in the end.

For a moment it seemed to Bolan as if the years had telescoped. For an instant, he felt he had never left his hometown, had never put the hurt behind him in pursuit of duty.

There was some truth in that. The pain could never be absolutely wiped away. His loss was with him always—on the firing line and when he went to sleep at night. The soldier had not let old memories, old wounds, impede his progress. In the Special Forces, he had been taught to fight despite hostile weather, fatigue, injury or pain. He had learned to curb desire, control emotions, bodily reactions—to a point.

For there was pain in coming home, and he could not deny the fact. Some wounds never healed completely. Bolan knew that he would miss his family as long as he survived. Underneath the cool, professional facade, Mack Bolan's war was personal.

It always had been, always would be, intensely personal.

He stood another moment on the sunlit hillside, silently reflecting on his war against the savages. The Executioner had learned early that his opponents had many different names, wore different faces; but whether they were Communists or neofascists, terrorists or racist vigilantes, they all were sculpted from the same malignant slime.

This time, the war had chosen Bolan rather than the other way around. His enemy was nameless, faceless, but it didn't matter in the end. It was still Mack Bolan going up against the cannibals, against the odds.

As always, sure.

There were no answers here. Bolan turned his back on the echoes of the past. The answers would be found in Pittsfield proper, not among the ashes of Don Sergio's estate. If TIF turned out to be the key, as Bolan half suspected, then the threat would come from living men, not from ghosts of campaigns past. His war was among the living and the soon to die.

If Bolan was one of the latter, he was ready, had been ready since the beginning of his everlasting war. He did not choose to die in Pittsfield, but the choice might not be his to make.

He set his sights on survival and performance of his duty. If the two were incompatible, he would go with duty. The soldier had no choice.

No choice at all.

## 9

The hunter parked his two-door Camaro in his driveway and locked it, circled back to get his luggage from the trunk. There was no crime to speak of in the neighborhood, but he had taken time to set the tamper-proof alarm. Precautions made good sense.

He had survived in Vietnam and afterward by nurturing a healthy distrust of fellow men. In Nam, if you allowed the other guy to handle your security precautions, you could get your ass shot off; so far it had been the same at home.

Inside, he locked the door behind himself and checked out the interior of the house. The living room and kitchen, visible from the door, were all secure, but he checked the windows, anyway. In the bathroom, he removed a thread that he had tucked beneath the second layer of toilet tissue on the roll, and scanned the edges of the medicine cabinet mirror for fingerprints. None.

Two bedrooms, one unfurnished. Why bother? No one stayed overnight, he knew of no living relatives, and there would be no wife, no children. Once he had resigned himself to perpetual bachelorhood, a vasectomy had seemed advisable. No accidents that way, no grasping female turning up with babe in arms. When he required a woman, he paid for sex, anonymously, safely. No entanglements, no mornings after, no recriminations when he couldn't summon up the emotions women expected.

At an early age, the hunter's obsession with revenge had swallowed up all his other feelings. From observation, he was able to simulate the moods and attitudes required for civilized encounters, but inside himself, the man felt cold and dead. Except when he was focused on the image of his enemy. The thought of Bolan could kindle fire inside him, thaw the glacier of his mind. At mention of the name, his pulse would hammer double time. A glimpse of Bolan in the flesh, as he had learned last night, could make him almost giddy with the hunger for revenge.

The bedrooms were, of course, secure.

Satisfied, he brought his luggage from the living room and left it on the bed. Undressing swiftly, he stuffed his soiled clothing in the laundry hamper and turned on the taps in the shower. When the water was hot enough to wash his weariness away, he slipped behind the curtain.

For several moments the hunter allowed the stinging spray to strike him, turning slowly until his hair was plastered to his skull and steaming rivulets ran down his chest, his back, his flanks. Finally, he picked up the bar of Safeguard and, soaping first his face then his body with energetic thoroughness, he washed away the smell of perspiration and anticipation, smoke and cordite, hours on the road. He could not wash away the memories, and that was fine. They warmed him better than the shower ever could.

He saw Mack Bolan crouching by his bullet-punctured car in the cul-de-sac, waiting for sudden death to strike him from the shadows. And again, the soldier airborne, somersaulting clear of the explosion that destroyed his safe house. Bolan had trembled as he rose, from shock. From fear? Was it too much to hope for that the Executioner, however briefly, had been afraid?

The hunter felt arousal stir in his groin and turned to face the shower head, eyes closed. When every trace of lather had been washed away, he turned off the hot water faucet and stood beneath an icy waterfall, teeth clenched, gooseflesh rising on his chest and shoulders. The warm tumescence in his loins subsided, but he remained immobile, punishing himself with the icy needles on his skin.

By slow degrees, he turned his back against the spray, enduring the Arctic river coursing down his spine, between clenched buttocks. Shivering, he counted down another thirty seconds before he turned again to shut off the water. He pulled a bath towel from the rack and dried himself with almost brutal strokes that left his flesh a livid pink, then hung the towel across the shower rod to dry.

He stood before a full-length mirror mounted on the inside of the bathroom door, examining his body with a critic's eye. Stomach flat, well muscled at an age when his contemporaries had begun to spread. A runner's legs, rounded thighs and supple calves, with strength and stamina enough to see him through a marathon. He could have used more beef around the chest and shoulders, but karate exercises kept him limber, swift and deadly in the clinches.

He could hold his own. If the Executioner was taller, heavier, the guy was also older. Granted he had a lifetime of experience behind him, countless tricks stored in the corners of his mind, still, living on the run for more than a decade had to take its toll. Bolan had been living on the edge so long that he should be ready for a shove to send him over.

Not that the hunter cherished illusions that Bolan was frightened yet. His quarry would be curious, disturbed at the most. But fear would follow once Bolan recognized the odds against him, realized the situation was already beyond his control. The bastard was a take-charge guy, by all accounts, but he would not be taking charge in Pittsfield. His pursuer knew the moves by heart, had been rehearsing them as long as he could remember.

He had shaken Bolan's confidence twice already, alerting him to the fact that he was not invincible. He could be found and followed, cornered, killed. It was a lesson that would bear repeating here on more familiar ground.

If Bolan's war had roots in Pittsfield, so, appropriately, did his downfall. By returning to the scene of his initial crime, the bastard had made the classic error singled out in every mystery and penny-dreadful since invention of the printing press. He had returned, and so had become ensnared.

The hunter combed his hair straight back, eschewing fashion. Still damp, it lay against his skull like seaweed, offering no balance to his ruddy, squarish face. Beginning with that face, he took an inventory of his scars.

The nose, twice broken during fistfights, canted slightly to the left so that his face appeared uneven on the rare occasions when he smiled. Below the jawline, on the right, a hairline scar from his nearest brush with death. (The punk had stumbled, missed his thrust, and there had been no time for second chances with the slim stiletto.) A bullet graze above the hip, which could have been a mortal wound except that his assailant—a Vietnamese "assassin" scarcely twelve years old—had panicked at the final instant, flinched away from killing face-to-face. Another souvenir from Nam, the ragged scarring on one calf where he had taken pungi stakes while on a night patrol.

The hunter's body was a road map of his violent life, but all the scars that mattered were inside. No X ray could reveal the wounds to soul and psyche, wounds that had been devilishly slow to heal.

The hunter left the bathroom, padded naked through the bedroom, across the living room and kitchen to the closet that concealed the basement stairs. His fingers found the light switch, brought the single bulb to life below, and he descended swiftly to his shadowed sanctuary. It was cooler there, enough to make him shiver, but his eyes had locked with Bolan's on the far side of the room, and for a moment he was unaware of his surroundings.

"Looking good," he told the silent, knife-scarred face and laughed out loud.

The bastard would look even better soon.

He did not open the trunk this time. Turning toward the workbench on the opposite wall, he found what he was looking for, wrapped neatly in a blanket stained with oil.

The Marlin Model 444 was awesome, with its twenty-four-inch barrel and the twenty-power telescopic sight that he had mounted personally, to take the guesswork out of long-range shots. A big-game rifle in the true sense of the word, it could hurl 240 grains of death downrange at 2,440 feet per second, exploding with 3,070 foot-pounds of raw killing energy. The heavy slug would lose 600 feet per second at 100 yards, but no one on the grim receiving end would ever know the difference.

Years before, a rifle such as this one had destroyed his life and stripped him of his childhood. Selection of the Marlin to complete the hunter's private arsenal had been no accident. He had practiced with it faithfully, on solitary "hunting trips" where human silhouettes replaced elusive bucks, until he knew that he could handle anything the big gun had to offer.

He would not be practicing today, not here. Still he picked up the Marlin, excited when he cradled it and ran one hand along the polished stock. It smelled of oil and solvent, the familiar fragrances of military hardware that could conjure up so many memories of basic training, Vietnam, the aftermath of war.

He pivoted and raised the Marlin to his shoulder, framing Bolan's knife-scarred face inside the twenty-power's field of vision. He could almost count the bastard's pores. He worked the lever action smoothly, chambered an imaginary round and smiled with satisfaction as his aim held steady on the target. Casually, he hooked an index finger through the trigger guard, inhaling deeply as he did so, swallowing to lock the stabilizing breath inside his lungs. The squeeze was slow, meticulous, precise.

The Marlin's hammer fell with a resounding *snap* against the firing pin. He repeated the procedure, dry-firing through a magazine of six imaginary rounds. One slug would take his target's head off, certainly, but he owed Bolan so much more.

Disturbing images of men in uniform flashed through the hunter's mind like color slides on some mental viewing screen. The first ones he saw wore badges on their blue serge tunics, and they stood with hats in hand, explaining something to his mother while she trembled, weeping, building up to a scream. The others were dressed in olive drab or camouflage, and he was one of them as they pushed off into hostile jungle darkness, searching for the faceless enemy.

Unlike so many others, he had enjoyed his tours in Vietnam. The steaming jungle was a classroom where the lessons learned in basic training were made practical to fit his needs. Already dedicated to the task that would become his obsession, he knew raw hate was not enough to see him through.

Nam had given him the skill, the grim experience he needed for his war at home. On grueling night patrols, he took the point whenever possible, determined to overcome any fear of darkness or the unknown. He had earned a reputation for ferocity in combat that left older, more experienced soldiers muttering about his "hero complex." They never understood the burning urgency that drove him on.

One night, in Bien Hoa province, he had known that he was ready.

The war was in its final weeks, with Nixon promising withdrawal, avidly collecting votes as interest on the promise. The hunter had been shaken, saddened by the news that left his comrades cheering. They were going home, and soon, but he still had so much to learn.

He volunteered for mission after mission, seeking out danger, confronting it at every turn. Within a week he slaughtered twenty-seven enemy soldiers, and when he was offered three days R&R in Adelaide he turned it down, refusing to explain. His place was in the jungle, and he could not tear himself away. When Operation Boomerang was devised to sweep the VC out of Bien Hoa province, he had been among the first to volunteer for duty.

The village was called Thai Hiep. It had sheltered VC sappers from the beginning of American involvement in the war, and relocation drives had never been successful. The CIA's assassination of selected traitors only seemed to stiffen the resolve of a rebellious people, deepening their commitment to the revolution.

They had approached Thai Hiep by night, faces blackened, gear secured with tape and Velcro to prevent any sound from giving them away. He took the point, alert for booby traps or hostile movement in the undergrowth. In retrospect, he wondered why a die-hard VC village had no lookouts posted, but at the time he had not questioned his good luck.

The people of Thai Hiep were asleep when men in camouflage fell upon them—kicking in doors and shouting into groggy faces, herding children, women and men toward the center of the village, slapping those who moved too slowly or seemed about to offer some resistance. Huts were ransacked, sleeping mats torn up in search of tunnels where arms and fugitives might be secured. The sweep was nearly finished when it happened . . . and his life was forever changed.

The woman appeared from nowhere, closing on him from his flank, a long machete raised above her head, its razor edge already slicing toward his face. He spun and fired instinctively, the short precision burst of 5.56 mm manglers lifting her completely off her feet and blowing her away.

For just a heartbeat, there was silence in the village. Then the other M-16s opened up in grim, reflexive fire. The troops were wired, some of them frightened, and the peasant woman's suicidal play triggered something in their minds that turned loose a homicidal fury. He watched the villagers collapsing, folding upon themselves as they were torn apart by tumbling projectiles. He watched . . . and held his fire.

Within that fraction of a second, he had known that Vietnam had nothing left to teach him. He had seen it all, and he was getting out before he lost control.

Control had always been the key to Bolan's war, and it was crucial to the hunter, as well. Control and caution were the watchwords of his vendetta with the Executioner. He had worked too long, too hard to blow it now.

But there were steps to follow, if the plan was to succeed. If Bolan's death had been the solitary focus of his scheme, he could have killed the soldier in Connecticut. A bullet in the cul-de-sac, a moment longer in the safe house… But the hunter's exercise in retribution was more subtle, more refined. Before he finished with his quarry, Bolan would be stripped of all his hero's trappings. He would lose the covert legion of admirers who had followed his campaigns with bated breath, applauding all the way. When Bolan paid the final tab in blood, he would recognize the hunter's motives, know his identity—and he would understand the kind of terror a fifteen-year-old boy is forced to live with from the moment that his father is assassinated on the street.

Before he punched Mack Bolan's ticket, finally, forever, he would take the time to spell it out and let the bastard know precisely why he had to die. The hunter didn't mind explaining it at all.

In fact, he was looking forward to it.

## 10

Al Weatherbee had picked the restaurant, a small place known for its New England decor, decent food and lavish prices. With Pappas picking up the tab, he saw no reason to be frugal. They were greeted by a hostess dressed like a scullery maid and shown to a secluded booth. A real flint-lock pistol had been mounted on the wall above their table, and the waiter who arrived to take their order could have passed for Paul Revere, with knee pants, buckled shoes and phony pigtail jutting from underneath his tri-cornered hat.

Splurging, Weatherbee decided on the surf 'n' turf. He didn't need the added poundage, but it did him good to see John Pappas flinch, his own eyes homing on the thrifty "Revolution Burgers." It occurred to Weatherbee that Pappas might be paying for their lunch out of his own pocket, but his sense of guilt was fleeting. When they were left alone, the newest chief of homicide put on a friendly smile and settled back in his padded seat.

"You're looking good," he said.

"I feel okay."

He was expecting more—some bullshit like *retirement must agree with you*—but Pappas deftly stepped around the snare and took him by surprise.

"So how was Texas?"

"It was . . . interesting."

"I'll bet it was. I talked to Andy Foster, from L.A. He seemed to think you were on active duty at the time."

"That's his mistake. I never flashed the tin at anybody."

"So give me your impressions."

Easily said. Al Weatherbee had flown to Texas at his own expense, on receiving word of Bolan's capture in McLary County. He had been charged with murder, which was no surprise, but it was the murder of a common prostitute; her body, mutilated after death, had been discovered in the soldier's motel room. A tip had led the raiders straight to Bolan, enabled them to take him with his guard down, momentarily...but it had been too slick, too pat for Weatherbee to swallow. If the stiff had been a pusher or a pimp, a local mafioso...maybe. But a hooker? No, it wouldn't wash, and he had said as much to anyone who would listen. Andy Foster from L.A., Brognola out of Washington, the whole damned crew of Bolan watchers who had flocked to Texas like vultures circling a carcass, waiting for their turn.

The guy had foxed them all, however, with a little help from friends and some stupendous bungling by the opposition. Someone—odds were heavy on a mob-connected rancher by the name of Peck—had tried to make a hit on Bolan in the courtroom, and the goddamned guy had wriggled through their net. But while his day in court had lasted...

"Nothing much to tell. In my opinion, he was framed, set up for execution by the Mob."

"I thought the charges sounded lame. You see him fly the coop?"

"I did."

"They tell me he had help. Somebody in the audience?"

"The press box," Weatherbee corrected him, remembering the young man's dash to intercept the nearest gunner as he rose, the automatic weapons sliding out from under his coat. There had been something in the young fellow's face, something familiar...but no, it wouldn't come. Not yet.

"Some deal." Their food arrived, and Pappas waited for the waiter to retreat before he leaned across his burger, frowning. "Were you glad he got away?"

If Pappas expected a reaction, Weatherbee decided, he could wait until his goddamned revolutionary burger turned to fossil fuel.

"I haven't thought about it, John."

A lie, but it would have to do. He didn't know the answer yet, himself, but he had thought about it since McLary County. Endlessly.

The chief of homicide was clearly skeptical. "I think you're glad," he said at last. "I think it tickled you no end when Bolan pulled his disappearing act."

"You may be right."

And having voiced the words, Weatherbee could no longer hide their import from himself. He would be forced to deal with attitudes that ran counter to everything he had ever said and done as a policeman. He was not certain he could live with that . . . or that he wanted to.

"I told you, John, the charges sounded bogus. Even Bolan has the right to an impartial trial."

Across from Weatherbee, his former second in command was grinning, nodding.

"That's exactly why I want you in on this. You *like* the guy."

"That's bullshit, John."

"Okay, okay. Let's say you've got a feeling for him. Hell, the guy was yours before he took his show on tour."

"The guy was *ours*, John. Ours. I didn't let him get away all by myself."

"I know that, Al. The whole department knows it. No one's pointing any fingers here."

"Let's cut the hearts and flowers, shall we? Tell me what you want before my steak gets cold."

"We got a tip that Bolan's back in town, or will be soon."

"You told me that already. Was the tip anonymous?"

"What else?"

"Male voice?"

"As far as we can tell. It was disguised, of course."

"You're working on the voiceprints?"

"Slow but sure."

"You're biting on the tip?"

"We're standing ready. Bolan was in Hartford, raising hell last night. It's not that far."

Al Weatherbee allowed himself a mild expression of surprise. He had not known that Bolan was so near. A swing by home might strike the soldier's fancy, or he might have business here, in Pittsfield, where it all began.

"What was the action in Connecticut?"

"Apparently some falling-out between enforcers. Local boys are working on it now. They've confirmed that Bolan was involved."

"That doesn't mean he'll run for home. There's nothing for him here."

"We can't afford to take the chance."

They ate awhile in silence, each man busy with his private thoughts. It was Weatherbee who finally broke the spell of char-broiled beef and lobster dipped in melted butter.

"What exactly do you want from me?" he asked.

"Advice. The benefit of all your knowledge. Pointers, if you see us veering off the beam."

"That's lame. You've got my files, my notes. You've got some others who were on the case—hell, *you* were on that yourself."

John Pappas put his mangled burger down and stared across the table, looking glum.

"I haven't got your feeling for the guy," he said. "I know that. *Every*body knows it."

Weatherbee was tempted to inquire if Pappas had been taking heat, but he dismissed the thought. The current chief of homicide had made his bed, and if it wasn't comfortable now... well, that **was too** damned bad.

"I'm retired," Weatherbee said, and he made no attempt to filter out the bitterness that stained his voice.

"I know you're smarting over that," John Pappas said. "There's nothing I can do about it. But you're still a cop, in here—" he jabbed a thumb against his chest, above the heart "—and you know what we're up against better than anybody else alive."

"I don't know that you're up against a goddamned thing," he snapped. "You get a call that Bolan's back in town, or that he *might* be coming back, and now the brass is breathing down your neck."

"We can't afford a replay of what happened with Don Sergio."

"No problem," Weatherbee replied. "Unless there's been a drastic change since I 'decided' to retire, the mob is pretty well washed up in Pittsfield. All the action's handled out of Boston now, with strong connections to New York. If Bolan wants the capos, he'll be smart enough to take his business there."

"And if he doesn't? If he wants to kick some ass right here, around his own hometown, for old times' sake?"

The smile felt good on Weatherbee. "Then you've got problems," he replied.

"Damned right. Which brings us back to you."

"I'm out. Kaput. Finis. You may have noticed that I haven't been around the office lately."

"Al, you know as well as I do the reasoning behind their move."

"I do," the former chief of homicide agreed. "The force was looking old around the edges. Someone safe upstairs was reaching for the Grecian Formula and covering his ass."

"You've got a perfect right to be pissed off."

"Don't stroke me, John. It doesn't work, and I've been stroked by experts."

"Fine. So will you help me out or not?"

"Who dreamed this up?"

"You're looking at him, buddy. From the minute I took that call, I knew you were the only man to save my bacon if the Executioner is back in town."

"You took the call?"

"What? Oh . . . well, yeah, the caller asked for me."

"By name?"

John Pappas hesitated, frowning. "Yeah, he did. What is it, Al?"

"Oh, nothing. I just wondered how he knew you, John."

"Well . . . shit, I didn't think about it at the time. I figured something in the paper, maybe on the tube."

"I haven't seen you in the papers lately, John. Not since that business with D'Antoni—what? Six months ago? Now I'm not much up on television, but . . ."

"All right, don't rub it in. I know I'm not exactly Andy Rooney."

"Someone's got a decent memory, or else . . ."

"Go on."

"Or else they know you well enough to ask for you by name."

"I know a lot of people, Al."

"I guess."

"You're getting spooky on me now."

"Don't mean to. Sorry."

"Well?"

"Well, what?"

"Goddamn it, will you help me out?"

"You haven't told me what I'd have to do."

"Officially you won't do anything." Pappas hesitated, sensing that he might be on the verge of blowing it and hastened to explain. "Of course you'd take a look at any crime scenes, if they smell like Bolan. You could eyeball any suspects, if we get a lucky break."

"You'll never bag him, John."

"Don't be so pessimistic, Al. It happens."

"Texas was a fluke. A setup. You could wait a million years and never have another chance to put the cuffs on Bolan."

"I'll be satisfied to see him out of town without a trail of bodies left behind."

"Good luck. If Bolan's coming home, he's got a reason."

Pappas made a sour face. "It damned sure can't be family."

"There was a brother...."

"Jimmy? Jerry?"

"John."

"Oh, yeah."

"Whatever happened to him?"

Pappas shrugged and spread his hands. "He was adopted, someone in the government. They moved away. It's ancient history."

"I guess."

But Weatherbee was thinking of a young man, dark and agile, hurdling the wooden railing in a Texas courtroom, closing on the gunner who was poised to kill Mack Bolan. Poised to kill his brother?

"Can we check him out?"

"Check who?"

"The brother."

Pappas mulled it over, shrugged again. "I'll try, but it's a long shot. Those adoption records, minors . . . all that damned red tape. It's murder."

"That's your business, John."

"Hey, don't remind me."

Silence stretched between them for a moment, growing strained, and Pappas was the first to speak.

"I need you, Al. The city needs you. Bolan on the rampage is a cop's worst nightmare—any cop. If you can help us take him off the streets, you owe it to the city. Hell, you owe it to yourself."

When Weatherbee responded, he could feel the ticking of a tightly wound internal clock beginning in his skull, as if there had never been an interruption. As if he was back in uniform, back in harness, taking to the streets again. The former chief of homicide immediately swallowed the familiar feelings, consciously suppressed his excitement at the mere suggestion of a manhunt. Lurking under the surge of his adrenaline was another, less pleasant feeling. Something else . . .

"I'll make myself available," he said at last. "In case you have a squeal that looks like Bolan's work." He raised a hand before Pappas could thank him. "There are two conditions. First, you keep the newshounds off my back. If anybody prints my name, or even whispers it in public, I'll be gone before you have a chance to start up the apology machine.''

"Agreed. What else?''

"If there's some kind of miracle, if Bolan suddenly goes senile and lets your men corner him, I want to be there.''

Pappas hesitated, thinking fast. He could almost hear the objections from the brass. Weatherbee was a mere civilian now—an *old* civilian, by their own account—and he could take them to the cleaners if he got injured. The chief of homicide was silent for another moment, finally decided he could pull it off.

"You're on.''

"All right. So how about dessert?''

They wanted him—Weatherbee knew that much. Somewhere up the ladder of command, they had convinced themselves they needed him. It wasn't true—at least he didn't think it was—but Weatherbee was tickled at the thought of the brass in uproar, chewing on their polished nails and searching for a lure to bring him back, part-time, in spite of all that had been said and done when he departed. When he was *evicted*.

The idea to consult Weatherbee had not come from John, of course, although it would have pleased him. The present chief of homicide had never turned his back on Weatherbee; if anything, he thought, it was the other way around. Throughout the whole fiasco, Pappas was supportive, caring—or at least as much as he could be and still survive in the department. Weatherbee himself had turned against his former friends and lumped them all with the men who drove him from his desk. He had been killing the messenger because he didn't like the news, and it was time to get a firm grip on reality before he lost it all.

The search for Bolan might be therapeutic, in its way. He would not be returning to active duty, would not have an office or a desk to call his own, but he would still be doing something... *if* the soldier came to town.

The timing bothered Weatherbee. He was even more concerned about the call to Pappas from a tipster who had called the chief of homicide by name. Of course there were mobsters on the street who knew John Pappas by reputation, snitches who had worked with Pappas on his cases through the years. A host of possibilities... and none of them rang true. A caller should have left his whispered message with the operator, cut and run in the erroneous belief that calls received by the police could be immediately traced. Unless...

Unless the caller knew John Pappas, knew he would take the Bolan lure and run with it for all he was worth. Unless he dialed the station house and asked for John by name, as the first step in some devious plan.

He didn't like the possibilities suggested by that line of speculation, so he turned to other thoughts. Of Texas, and the slender, dark young man there who had rescued Bolan, snatched him from the brink of execution by a mercenary firing squad. Of Bolan's face, so different after plastic surgery, yet immediately recognizable to anyone who had ever looked into those graveyard eyes.

The man could change his face, his hair, his clothing, sure. But he could never change his soul.

And that was problem number one for Weatherbee.

The former chief of homicide was not entirely sure, these days, that Bolan *should* be taken off the streets. Since his forced retirement, even before that, he had been questioning the values he had carried with him through his long career behind the badge. His dedication to the law had not faltered, but he had begun to recognize the system's defects. If the courts were not revolving doors, they were at least deficient in performing their primary task—enforcing the law, dispensing justice. Clogged with frivolous lawsuits, overdedicated to the rights of criminals at the expense of injured victims, at its worst the system obstructed justice. There was cause enough for righteous anger in a man like Weatherbee...and he had lost no members of his family to the predators. Not yet.

Whenever he explored this ground, the former chief of homicide stopped short of granting Bolan his approval. Vigilante justice had no place within the system, but he understood the soldier's feelings. In Bolan's place, would Weatherbee have acted differently?

No answer.

If the victim was Alice, or one of the children—all grown now, and gone—would he stand back and wait for justice from a system he knew to be impotent? What did it take for disgust with the courts and police to turn to a personal quest for revenge? Was Bolan's method better, after all?

Again, no answer.

From the start, Weatherbee had nursed a sneaking admiration for the soldier. You couldn't help but respect the soldier for his rigid code of honor. Bolan never dropped the hammer on a cop, no matter how corrupt. He never harmed an innocent civilian. His war had damaged untold millions' worth of property, but for the most part it was the property of savages, which the system would have confiscated, anyway, if it had been operating as it should.

The soldier was a menace, Weatherbee supposed. The fact that he never fired on innocent civilians didn't mean his next round might not ricochet to kill a child. The conduct of his war was reckless. The guy was gambling with lives every time he hit the streets, and someday, somewhere, he was bound to lose.

The news of Bolan's death in Central Park, so long ago, had filled Al Weatherbee with mixed relief and sadness. At a conscious level, he had been glad to see the last of Bolan's bloody, doomed crusade. But he had felt a sense of loss, as well, a wistful sadness when he realized there might be no one left to stand alone against the savages.

One evening, five or six days after Bolan's "death," Weatherbee had been drinking beer with Pappas and another homicide detective when the sudden thought of taking over Bolan's role had come to Weatherbee. It would be simple. Drive to Boston, use the addresses that he knew by heart and work his way right through the ranking mafiosi till they cut him down or he exhausted all his targets. It was the whiskey, he supposed. Before he got farther than the parking lot, John Pappas had collared him and driven him home.... But still, *the thought was there.*

What might a young Al Weatherbee have done, completely sober, if his family had been annihilated by savages? What might he do today, if confronted with the opportunity to bring Mack Bolan down or let him walk?

The shock of Bolan's public "resurrection" had recalled those mingled feelings of distress and relief. The former chief of homicide had been like a sleeper who awakes to find his nightmare all around him, unabated in daylight. Anguish, yet it was tempered by the knowledge that a champion survived, that there was someone out there who wasn't afraid to face the cannibals and drive them back into the jungle.

Weatherbee would provide John Pappas with the benefit of all his hard-won expertise because police work was his life. But he had no wish to harm the Executioner. Alive, Mack Bolan was the single greatest crime deterrent

Weatherbee had ever seen. Bolan's death, he thought, would be a loss to society.

And it would have to be his death this time. The soldier would not let himself be caged again. The experience in Texas had been a fluke, that could never be repeated. Bolan had survived his brief captivity—in spite of two determined efforts to assassinate him—but he could not expect to duplicate the feat in Massachusetts. He would have to know that, going in. Weatherbee suspected the soldier was prepared to die resisting arrest, thereby avoiding slow death in a cage.

Can't say I blame him, Weatherbee decided, sipping his coffee, letting Pappas carry the conversation. Can't say I blame the guy for anything.

The former chief of homicide could not predict his reaction if he met Mack Bolan on the street. It rattled him, as always, to realize that youthful concepts of black and white had changed, with time, to subtle shades of gray.

God help him if he had to face the Executioner.

God help them both.

## 11

Gino Girrardi was pissed. When his profits declined, when business fell off and he had to explain the red ink to his sponsors, the man from Manhattan got angry. When angry, Girrardi might drink, take it out on some whore or just get in his Caddy and drive. The Caddy was power unleashed, a magnificent juggernaut throbbing with life of its own, taking Gino as fast and as far as he wanted to go.

Like to Boston.

The thought brought him down, made him angry again. In a week he was due to report to the capos who had given him his break. The old men expected progress, profits, and Gino was not looking forward to disappointing them. They would look at each other and frown, finally staring at him as if picking the flesh from his bones with their eyes. If Girrardi was lucky, that was *all* they would do.

The posting to Pittsfield had been a test, Gino knew. They were giving him rope and the time he needed to tie up the town—or to string himself up. It could go either way. The capos would sit in their boardrooms in Boston, snug and secure with their profits, or else they would send someone else to succeed where Girrardi had failed. As for Gino, a failure in Pittsfield would mark him for life as a loser—*if* the capos allowed him to live. He would never advance through the ranks, never ride in a stretch limousine of his own, never sit by the pool in his mansion with

babes in bikinis to bring him scotch on the rocks. He
would never be anything more than a soldier if Pittsfield
blew up in his face, and he knew it.

So Gino Girrardi was pissed. And with reason.

For one thing, the frigging economy hadn't played along
with his plans. As the interest rates fell, the consumer price
index declined, fewer factory workers came begging for
loans from his shylocks. His money was dead on the
streets, and most of his regular customers were paying their
loans back on time.

Still, if more prosperous times were bad for loan sharks,
they were good for some of Gino's other lucrative side-
lines. For workers with money in their hands, and their
children and neighbors, he offered a full line of chemicals, from grass to cocaine and the hard stuff. If romance
was lacking in anyone's life, he could rent the illusion of
love at affordable hourly rates. For the timid, who steered
clear of warm, living flesh, there were video, film, magazines. Whether the customer was white or black, straight
or gay or somewhere in between, Gino Girrardi offered
satisfaction at rates the youngest and the poorest could
afford.

But lately, there were problems. Agents for the DEA
were drying up supplies of heroin from Mexico and Asia,
sending prices through the roof when there was any skag
to sell at all. The goddamned bikers had their meth labs
cooking speed around the clock and driving prices *down*—
forget about the quality—and if you tried to reason with
them, cut a deal, they started shooting like Wild West
psychos on parade. For all that, however, Gino preferred
to deal with bikers any day rather than mess with the Colombians—and that was where the business was disappearing, bet your ass. The Indians controlled cocaine in the
United States, or near enough, and with their Cuban run-

ners and their bottomless supply of flake they were cutting deeply into Family business. No sooner did the Feds attack Miami than it started snowing in Los Angeles, Las Vegas, Tucson, even Atlanta. While it had taken a little longer for the Colombians to discover Massachusetts, they were already strong enough there to present Girrardi with some major problems.

Squaring off with the Colombians and bikers over junk was bad enough, but now the blacks were cutting Gino out of numbers, shylock operations, even girls. It seemed like no one feared the families anymore. They tested boundaries, stepped across at every opportunity and challenged the *amici* to defend their old preserves. As soon as one smart bastard got away with something, a dozen more popped up to follow his example, and a hundred after that.

When Gino thought about it—which was constantly—his memory coughed up something he had read in school about the Roman Empire. The Romans once had owned the goddamned *world*, from one end to the other, but they had got soft and fat, while their borders went to hell. Savages had risen up against them in the sticks, and the Romans were too lazy, too preoccupied with orgies to stop and kick some ass. The savages got closer, eating up the territory Rome had held for centuries, until finally there was no more Rome, just a bunch of greasy barbarians pretending they were civilized, kicking back to watch the world go by.

Girrardi was a firm believer in the lessons taught by history. If you substituted Mafia for Rome, you had the Pittsfield problem in a nutshell. The families had got soft, allowing half-assed savages and greasy foreigners to operate in areas that used to be secure. One day, the capos would look around and find the savages had picked them clean.

For Gino's money, you could date the brotherhood's decline from the appearance of one Mack the Bastard Bolan. Busting old Don Sergio the way he did, and rolling on to shake the families from coast to coast. Forget about the way he scorched their asses overseas. The guy was gangbusters, in the flesh, and his success had been the downfall of the syndicate. Once the Cubans and Colombians and all the rest had seen how one determined man could beat the odds, they figured, hey, why not? The families united can't eliminate *one man*, what can they do against a hundred men? A thousand?

There was still a chance to save it, turn it all around, if they moved in time. Pittsfield was the perfect place to take a stand and get some recognition from the capos. But he had to make sure that everything ran smoothly. There were different kinds of recognition, and he didn't need the kind that went to losers.

The losses in Pittsfield could be useful, in their way. When he asked the capos for troops to whip the savages in line, declining profits were the lever he could use to get the sluggish bastards off their butts. Greed would motivate his sponsors to come through with the troops and guns he needed to reclaim western Massachusetts for the brotherhood. Provided that he played his cards right, sure.

Some of the capos might prefer to dump him outright, place another overseer at the head of an invading army ordered to purge the barbarians. It would be Gino's task to sell himself to the doubters, to convince them of his familiarity with the problems and people of Pittsfield, to make himself sound indispensable. It was a tactic fraught with perils, for if Gino shouldered the responsibility alone, there would be no one to share the blame for any failure. But his mind would not accept the possibility of defeat.

When he finished mopping up in Pittsfield, there were other worlds to conquer. He would be a man to reckon with, commander of an army that had been tested on the streets. The soldiers would belong to others at the start, but he would win them over, promise them the moon—or, anyway, a piece of Mother Earth—to plant their loyalties firmly in his pocket. After Pittsfield, he would take another ride to Boston, and the capos would listen this time.

But first, he needed troops, munitions. He had to go before the board with hat in hand, suggesting rather than demanding, making them believe that it was all their idea. If he had to kiss some ass to earn his one big break, then Gino was prepared to pucker with the best. The time would come when they would stand in line to kiss *his* ass, and thank their lucky stars for the opportunity.

He locked the office, squinting into sunlight for a moment, fumbling with his shades before he got them on. Late afternoon, and spring was lengthening the days. So warm a spring promised a hot summer, a record breaker. The thought made Gino smile as he strutted toward his cherry-red El Dorado in the parking lot. Ready for a turn behind the wheel, he whistled as he walked, the keys in his hand.

Girrardi never heard the tail fall into step behind him, never felt him there until his key was in the lock, the muzzle of a pistol jammed against his kidney. Nimble fingers found the .38 beneath his arm and whisked it away.

"Get in and slide across."

The voice was calm and businesslike. It made Girrardi's hair stand on end.

"You're making a mistake," he said, embarrassed when his voice cracked.

No answer, but the pistol dug in deeper. He braced himself for the explosion that would drop him where he stood. Another heartbeat, and he got the message, clammed up and followed instructions. Huddled in the shotgun seat, he averted his eyes as his captor slid behind the wheel.

The El Dorado came to life, and Gino risked a glance in the direction of the gunner. Tall and muscular, the chiseled features deadpan, automatic leveled in his left hand while he used the right to drive.

For twenty minutes they drove westward, out of town, until they were surrounded by evergreens and rolling countryside. When he was satisfied with the degree of isolation, Bolan nosed the El Dorado down a narrow, rutted track between the trees. He could sense Girrardi's nervousness beside him.

"We oughta talk about this deal," Gino said, as Bolan brought the car to a halt and killed the engine.

Bolan looked him over, the Beretta angled casually in the direction of Girrardi's face. "So talk."

The mobster looked surprised, but actual relief was premature. Behind narrowed eyes, his mind was racing, desperate to cut a deal.

"You tell me what'll make you happy, an' you got it, man. If I ain't got it, I can put my finger on it for you, quick as shit."

The soldier smiled. "I'm glad to hear that, Gino."

Bolan knew about the problems of the Pittsfield mob. He kept himself informed. The syndicates had been in decline in western Massachusetts since the elimination of Don Sergio. Orders came from Boston now, some said from New York, as greedy capos quarreled over territory that was up for grabs. Girrardi had been sent to pacify an area in revolt, eliminate competition and recapture the illicit profits that were flowing into the pockets of the mob's chaotic rivals. After nearly six months on the job, the new enforcer's gains were minimal. His employers back in Beantown would be looking at replacements, if he didn't cut the mustard soon.

"I'm after information, Gino."

Girrardi swallowed hard and glanced around, as if he feared the brooding evergreens might overhear.

"Oh, yeah?"

"I figure you can help me, Gino. Anything I want, remember?"

"Yeah...well, sure. Why not? What do you wanna know?"

"A name."

"I'm listening."

"Somebody called me home. He didn't leave a name, but I'm interested in making contact. Follow me so far?"

"Uh...not exactly."

"Maybe this will help."

He fished inside the pocket of his coat and watched Girrardi flinch despite the fact that he was already staring down the barrel of a gun. Bolan found the yellowed TIF business card and passed it over. When he had read it, Gino shook his head.

"I don't know anything about this outfit. Are they new in town?"

The guy was drawing blanks, and Bolan didn't read it as a stall. He knew Girrardi's background, Bronx to Boston. There was no reason why he should recognize the card...unless he was behind the man who dropped it, back in Hartford.

"Maybe you've seen this before?"

The hand went into the pocket again, and Girrardi flinched once more. The marksman's medal rested coolly on the outstretched palm.

"Aw, shit."

Gino was with him now, and reading Bolan's message loud and clear.

"Somebody called me home," Bolan said again. "I want to touch base as soon as possible. If you know anything at all..."

Girrardi wore a mask of total incredulity. "You crazy, man? I mean...hey, no offense, okay? This is crazy. Why would anybody from the Families want you back in Pittsfield? Why would anybody from the Families want you *any*where? You're poison, man. Let's face it, everything you touch turns into shit for the *amici.*"

Bolan heard him out, alert for any hint of falsehood... but there was nothing. Fear, oh yes. A lifetime's worth of nervousness. And something else—a sharp, almost indignant tone, as if the mobster's intelligence had been insulted.

"How solid are your communications, Gino?"

"What? My... Oh, yeah, I get you." Momentary hesitation, as the mafioso pondered what he could afford to give away. "I've got ears out, dig it? Hey, I wouldn't shit you...it could be better, right? But I've got eyes and ears on the Colombians, the biker trash. You name it."

"No. *You* name it, Gino."

"Huh?"

"I'm looking for a name. You give, you live."

"Well, Jesus...if I had the name you're looking for, you think I'd keep it to myself? I told you, this ain't Family business, man. I got no stake in this, nobody to protect. *I just don't know!*"

Desperation in the narrow eyes. Girrardi wasn't lying, at least no more than necessary for the preservation of his twisted self-respect. He would have sold his mother to save himself from death.

"All right. Get out."

"What?" Girrardi couldn't keep the sudden panic from his voice.

"I said, get out."

"Hey, man, I leveled with you, swear to God."

"And I believe you, Gino."

"Huh? Well, what the hell—"

"You've got a long walk home. I'll drop the Caddy where I found it."

"Walk? That's it? I mean, you wouldn't . . ." Gino couldn't bring himself to voice the thought, plant deadly seeds in Bolan's mind.

"Relax," the soldier said. "White flag."

"I don't suppose you could drop me near a phone?"

"Don't push it, Gino."

"Right."

He scrambled clear and closed the door, ducked to face his adversary through the open window. "Listen, if I run across that name you're lookin' for . . ."

"I'll be in touch," the Executioner assured him.

Bolan put the El Dorado in reverse and backed down the hundred yards of rutted, unpaved road until he reached the shoulder of the highway. He could just make out Girrardi's silhouette among the longer shadows of the trees, already trudging toward the highway where he would thumb a ride. He wished the mafioso luck and powered out of there. Toward Pittsfield.

Bolan was convinced that Girrardi had no useful information. The guy's reaction had been convincing. Gino had been horrified to think that any member of the family would lure Bolan into town deliberately, inviting grim disaster when the territory was already in disarray. But if the Mafia was not responsible . . .

He considered the other possibilities. Revenge, of course, still topped the list—but there would have to be a syndicate connection even so, and Girrardi would be sniffing after that one. A rival mob might be responsible—the bikers or Colombians Girrardi had referred to, or some unexpected clique of players. Anyone could study ancient news on microfilm, discover Bolan's links to TIF in Pittsfield. It would take a strategist of some sophistication to devise the final plan, but mafiosi had no corner on intelligence.

Which put the soldier back where he had started. Except that now his eyes and ears were multiplied by the number of Girrardi soldiers on the street. Before he made it back to town, the syndicate enforcer would be faced with an unpleasant choice: he could report to Boston or New York, wherever, that the Executioner was back in town, or he could keep the news to himself awhile and play the game with Bolan, using every means at his disposal to uncover Bolan's adversary. With any luck at all, his men might turn up the name, and he might offer it to Bolan as a sacrifice, anything at all to get him out of town and off his back.

He didn't like to use the syndicate. He felt more comfortable pursuing them than working hand in glove, but time was of the essence now. Whoever had designed the plan that lured him to Pittsfield, he would not be sitting on his hands.

A hunter all his life, Mack Bolan knew a snare awaited him in Pittsfield, but he could not turn away to save himself. His destiny was here, entangled with his roots. If he had to use the syndicate to find that destiny, so be it.

Bolan had already bitten on the lure, was hooked and waiting for the fisherman to reel him in. There might be some surprises, though, before his faceless adversary had him safely on the dock. The fisherman might find that he had hooked a monster that he couldn't handle. And the fisherman might become the fish food, if he wasn't careful.

Smiling to himself, Mack Bolan let the El Dorado's power plant take him home.

## 12

"Sit down, Frank. Take a load off."

Captain Pappas closed the office door and circled back around his desk, then relaxed in the padded swivel chair. Across the desk, Sergeant Frank Lawrence settled stiffly in a straight-backed chair. With eight years on the force and two of those in Homicide, the younger officer was one of Pappas's trusted aides. He had been summoned to discuss strategy for dealing with the Executioner's possible visit to Pittsfield.

"What's the word?" Frank Lawrence asked.

"He'll play," the chief of homicide responded. "Claims he won't be much help, but even so..."

"Might be the truth. He's rusty, out of touch."

Pappas was surprised to feel the sudden heat of irritation rising in his cheeks. "He's as sharp as anybody on the force today. Hell, *I* should be so rusty."

Lawrence seemed surprised by the vehement response. Grinning sheepishly, the sergeant shrugged. "No offense," he said. "I didn't know you two were all that tight."

"None taken," Pappas told him, embarrassed by his gut reaction to the criticism of a friend. "He brought me up from foot patrol and taught me everything there is to know on homicide. He partnered with me when I was a rookie, wet behind the ears. Our third night out, he saved my life. I'd say that we were tight."

*Except the past year or two. Where were you then, Big John?*

The sergeant looked Pappas square in the eye and said, "Okay."

As if to cover for the show of sentiment, Pappas felt compelled to say, "He won't be taking any active role in the investigation. Purely advisory, nowhere near the firing line."

"We don't have an active case for him to work on, anyway. For all we know, that call was bullshit."

Pappas frowned. "I've thought about that," he said. "Whichever way it cuts, we can't afford to take a chance. I'd rather be unnecessarily prepared than have a firefight take us by surprise. Nobody knows our boy like Weatherbee."

"He missed our boy the first time out."

"*We* missed him, all of us. It wasn't Al's mistake. He focused in on Bolan from the first, but there was nothing we could hang a case on. Then, one day, we had the goods to send him up forever, and we couldn't find the bastard. He was here and there and everywhere...and he was gone."

"Tough break."

"The toughest. No one ever said a thing—at least they never did where I could hear them—but I think Al's been feeling guilty ever since."

The sergeant frowned in sympathy and kept his personal opinions to himself. "So what's the action?"

"Only one way we can play the game. That's watch and wait. Increase surveillance on the likely targets, and be ready with backup if and when he hits."

"Defensive posture?" Lawrence sounded disappointed. More, there was a trace of disgust in his tone.

"For now," the captain answered, nodding slowly. "Till we have confirmation, anyway. Some kind of fix on a potential target."

"By the time we get our fix, it'll be too damned late. The way this bastard moves, we'll always be two steps behind him, eating dust."

Surprised by Lawrence's intensity, the chief of homicide leaned back and cocked an eyebrow at his young subordinate. "I'm open to suggestions, Frank."

"All right, sir, since you ask. I'd like to see a more aggressive attitude on this. Go after those potential targets you mentioned, drive them underground and make our boy go hunting for them, knock him off his stride. While he's chasing shadows, we can take him on his blind side."

"Two problems," Pappas told him wearily. "The first is that we can't harass 'law-abiding citizens' without due cause. I'd have a flock of high-priced lawyers crawling up my ass with flashlights by the time you got the first bunch into booking. We'd be sifting through injunctions and restraining orders till the cows come home."

He hesitated, reading his subordinate's expression, conscious of the fact that he had seen it staring back at him from mirrors countless times before.

"The second thing you should remember is we're here in Pittsfield, not in Vietnam." Before the sergeant could respond, he raised a warning hand. "All this blind-side talk is strictly borderline, and you should know that. You have a plan for locking Bolan up, I'll talk about it with you all night long. But I have never run a firing-squad division, and I never will."

"You'll never get the cuffs on Bolan."

"I gave up telling fortunes, Frank. You may be right, but it's been done before. Our boy's a citizen like anybody else, and he's got rights that we are obligated to respect within the limits of the law."

A short, derisive snort from Lawrence. "*Citizen?* This guy's a one-man crime wave. He's a goddamned national disgrace! Desertion from the Army. Homicides too numerous to tabulate. A list of felonies you'd need a week to read. He's been shoot on sight with CIA and FBI for years."

The chief of homicide made an effort to refrain from snapping back at Lawrence. "What the federals do is their concern, and none of ours until they cross the line. We're running a police department here, and we're operating by the book. If you're looking for search and destroy, you're in the wrong place."

Lawrence sobered, the angry color draining from his cheeks. He sat back in his chair, as if attempting to relax, but he still struck Pappas as uncomfortable, unbending.

"Bolan held this whole department up to ridicule. He made this force a laughingstock."

John Pappas cocked his head, as if intent on listening to something while his eyes bored into Lawrence. "You hear anybody laughing, Sergeant? I don't. Bolan is top priority with this department. He's top priority with me. That doesn't—I repeat, does *not*—eliminate our duty to obey the laws that we enforce. If one of our men pops the cap on Bolan, I'll be looking at the details, just like any other shooting on the street."

"Yes, sir."

The chief of homicide relaxed a little, offering Lawrence a cigarette, lighting one himself when the sergeant shook his head.

"What is it, Frank?"

"I beg your pardon, sir?"

"You're wired about this Bolan thing. It's getting under your skin. I want to know what's eating at you."

Lawrence mulled over the question for a moment, frowning as he tried to pin down vague, half-formed ideas. When he responded, craning forward in his uncomfortable chair, he spoke slowly, anxious to be clearly understood.

"Maybe I see some of Bolan in myself," he said. "I did the tour in Vietnam, saw things—*did* things—I wouldn't tell my priest about to save my soul. But I came back. I made it, just like umpteen thousand other guys. We've got our problems, sure, but we're home. This Bolan, he's still out there somewhere in the jungle, way to hell and gone beyond the DMZ. I think about him making sweeps like he was still on active duty, and sometimes I think I know the way he feels.

"The first months back from Nam, I used to jump at shadows, couldn't sleep at night unless I had a pallet on the floor, my back against the wall. But I got over it. Bolan…he's still out there living it, day in, day out. He's out of touch with everything except the war that's going on inside his head. You can't negotiate surrender with the guy is all I'm saying, sir. You've got to put him down."

The well ran dry, and Lawrence blinked, sat back as if embarrassed by the speech he had made. He seemed about to offer an apology when Pappas cut him off.

"You may be right," he said. "But if you are, and if we have to smoke him, then we do it by the book."

"Yes, sir."

"What say we take you off this awhile, pass it on to Bartolucci? We've got cases backlogged up the ying-yang if you need a change of scene."

"No, sir. I've got it covered. Really."

Pappas scoured the sergeant's face, his eyes, but found no window on his soul.

"All right. Coordinate surveillance of potential targets with our people on the street. Around the clock on majors, business hours for the rest. I'm canceling all leaves for the duration." Pappas stubbed out his cigarette in the ashtray on his desk. "We might get lucky. Maybe it's a false alarm, some whipdick looking for publicity."

"I hope so." Lawrence hesitated in the doorway, turned to face the chief of homicide again. "One thing," he said, and raised an index finger to his temple, tapping softly. "Where he lives, in here, destruction is a way of life. You're going in with one hand tied behind your back. This guy has thrown the book away."

"We'll help him find it," Pappas answered.

The sergeant nodded glumly, unconvinced, closed the door behind him and was gone.

Alone, the captain propped his feet up on the desk and ran the conversation through his mind again. Was the sergeant right? Was Bolan too far gone for rational negotiations? Had he slipped across the line since Texas, losing the discipline that told him cops were untouchable? If he was cornered here in Pittsfield, would he turn on the badges like a wounded animal at bay?

The sergeant had proposed some valid questions. But his attitude had raised some questions too... about himself. The line about department honor, his vehemence where Bolan was concerned, his angry indignation over incidents that occurred while he was still in high school. Lawrence had no family members on the force, as far as Pappas could remember. He made a mental note to check that out. The sergeant's disregard for Weatherbee, his righteous anger over Bolan's getaway the first time out had

sounded almost personal. His explanation dating back to
Vietnam had been convincing, on the face of it, but still…

The chief of homicide had other things to think about
besides his sergeant. After all, Lawrence knew his job, and
he would do it as he always had in the past. If Pappas
noted signs of strain, there would be time enough to bench
him down the road.

Mack Bolan was the problem now. Dammit, Pappas
thought, he didn't know if Bolan was back in town already or en route, or even if the tip phoned in had been
some stupid-assed charade. He mulled over what facts he
knew, and heard the muffled voice on the telephone again:
*"Bolan's coming back. Today."* Just that, then dial tone,
droning in his ear.

The call had been untraceable, of course. If the whole
thing proved to be a hoax, he wouldn't know for days.
Leaves canceled, overtime approved, the whole department in a goddamned uproar over the prediction of one
man's arrival in his own hometown. Except that Bolan
wasn't *any* man. He was the king of all the "public enemies" who ever staked out space in headlines. The very
mention of his name was guaranteed to double circulation
for the dailies, give the local mob a catastrophic case of
nerves and turn the heat up under a certain chief of homicide.

If Bolan was in town or on his way, then Pappas had to
try to get inside his mind, before the guns went off. He
might be homesick, anxious for a quiet look around familiar streets, a peaceful visit to the family plot. That
thought reminded Pappas that he had not ordered surveillance of the Bolan graves and he made a note. Or Bolan might be in Pittsfield to keep tabs on local mob activity
for old times' sake, reminding the survivors that they were
not forgotten.

Or he might be hunting.

That was the worst scenario, and therefore uppermost in the detective's mind. The mob in Pittsfield was a withered vestige of its former self, but there were still enough targets for the Executioner to stage a blitz. A shooting war was one thing Pappas definitely didn't need, and it would suit him fine if the call turned out to be a hoax.

And yet the apprehension gnawing at his gut felt genuine, the way a trick knee throbs before the first real snow of winter. Pappas wasn't psychic, had no flair for precognition, but at the moment he could swear he *felt* the Executioner close by. He would have given almost anything to prove the feeling wrong.

Frank Lawrence had been right, to some extent, about the drubbing the department's image had endured when Bolan had slipped away the first time, leaving bodies stacked in the county morgue like cord wood. It was preposterous, a single man, however skilled, outrunning mafiosi and police alike for weeks on end. If Bolan surfaced, if the syndicate did not eliminate him, the next department down the road should have been sure to sweep him up like yesterday's discarded litter.

But they didn't sweep him up. Not in Los Angeles, Chicago, San Francisco or New York. They let him slip the net in Dallas, in New Orleans and Detroit, in Cleveland and Miami and Seattle. In Las Vegas, Bolan had outmaneuvered federal marshals *and* the local law, together with the toughest shock troops the syndicate could muster. Within a few short months, the laughter directed at Pittsfield had died away. The officers of larger, more sophisticated agencies had learned what the cops in Pittsfield knew already: the Executioner did not conform to any preconceived, computerized profiles of criminal behavior. He broke every rule, rewriting guidelines as he went along.

The chief of homicide in Pittsfield meant to take him by the book. Pappas couldn't fault Frank Lawrence for his skepticism, his desire to tackle Bolan on the soldier's terms, with no holds barred. Despite the difference in their ages, Bolan and the sergeant were alike in many ways, both products of the Asian crucible where boys became men and were tested in the fire before they were allowed to vote. Both, in their separate ways, had taken stands against the savages. In other circumstances, Pappas thought, it might have been Mack Bolan carrying the badge and making plans to bring Frank Lawrence down.

There were differences, of course, between the battle-tested veterans. Lawrence trusted in the system, striving to make it work, while the Executioner had stepped outside to wage one-man war against his enemies. A world of difference lay between the two...and yet, Pappas could see those similarities that made them look like brothers under the skin.

Al Weatherbee's involvement in the case presented Pappas with another bushel of potential problems. Pappas had bristled when the sergeant voiced his reservations over Weatherbee, but Lawrence had raised some valid points. The former chief of homicide *was* out of touch, and his participation, however unofficial, was bound to spark resentment among the regulars. Would Weatherbee's undeniable expertise make him an asset or a liability? And once he was part of the team, could he be controlled?

The Bolan case was personal for Weatherbee, no doubt about it. He was not exactly raking in the money, but the guy had cared enough to travel to Texas when the deputies had taken Bolan in McLary County. Al had been in the courtroom when the roof fell in. When they had spoken of it, briefly, over their lunch, there had been something in

Weatherbee's manner that raised a host of questions for
the homicide chief. Was it possible Weatherbee had been
relieved when the Executioner escaped? Had he been
chasing Bolan all this time, living with the memories for so
damned long, that he was on the soldier's side?

And how would Pappas himself answer, if someone
posed those questions now to him?

He stood four-square for law and order, certainly,
but . . . there was something undeniably seductive about a
solitary hero, battling against the odds. If you were careless, if you let the propaganda get to you, it was easy to
envision Bolan as a kind of modern Robin Hood. You
could forget about the gutted buildings and the shattered
corpses if you tried, or at least transform them into something else, the symbols of a bold crusade. St. George
against a different dragon, in the here and now.

Except it wouldn't wash.

John Pappas had been tracking Bolan from the start, as
long as Weatherbee, in fact. But up to now there had never
been any question in his mind concerning Bolan's role. At
best, the Executioner was a self-appointed vigilante,
threatening the peace of any city where he waged his solitary war. At worst, he was a predator, no different from
the animals he hunted through the streets.

There *was* a difference, though, and Pappas knew that
it was this difference that made the man so dangerous. He
had become a living legend, elevated to heroic status in the
media, until the populace was rooting for him, actively
obstructing the investigations of police and federal agents
sworn to track him down. The Bolan myth had intertwined with grim reality until the two became damned near
inseparable in the public consciousness. From the captain's point of view, it was a deadly situation, and one he
intended to correct.

But by the book.

He would not be reduced to playing Bolan's game, to abandoning the rules of civilized procedure. Lawrence might be itching for a high-noon confrontation, but the chief of homicide could handle his subordinate. Al Weatherbee might want a larger piece of the investigation, but he would be sadly disappointed. John Pappas was in charge. Pappas knew his job, and he would do it if it killed him.

Which it might, he realized. It might, at that.

**13**

It was cool and almost quiet on the hotel rooftop. Street sounds, drifting up seven stories, were no distraction for the hunter as he went about his preparations. Nimble fingers sheathed in latex moved with swift precision born of practice. He could have done it blind, but seeing it was half the fun.

The Marlin lay across his lap, the duffel bag that had concealed it crumpled at his side. No witnesses were likely to disturb him here, so far above the street, but he had to admit to himself that the danger of discovery probably heightened his excitement, set his nerves on edge. If someone, anyone, happened on him now...

Then he would deal with them, of course. He could permit no interruptions, no disturbance of the plans he had set in motion. It was time to turn up the heat, get the pot boiling, and the hunter was prepared. For anything.

He weighed the heavy cartridges in one cupped palm, then fed them slowly, almost lovingly, into the loading gate. Four rounds into the magazine, before he had to work the lever action, chambering a live one, then he eased the hammer down and topped the load off with a fifth. The cartridges had been meticulously wiped to remove fingerprints before he packed the duffel, and the latex gloves prevented him from leaving any trace of his identity now. When he was finished, there would be no need to crawl on hands and knees collecting brass. He could afford to leave the empty shells behind.

In fact, doing so was essential to his plan.

Without the brass, there might have been some doubt about the weapon used this night. The slugs would be deformed on impact, useless for ballistics studies. He was using hollow-points, and there might even be some doubt about the caliber, once they were mushroomed, mangled by their brief, explosive passage into flesh and bone. No lab on earth could trace the slugs to one specific weapon, but the cartridges could identify the *type*, and that was all the hunter needed.

Finished with his preparations for the moment, he stood up and leaned across the parapet, his elbows resting on the masonry. He did not possess a night scope, but the street below was bright with neon, turning darkness into artificial day. There would be enough light for his purpose, and darkness would assist in his retreat.

It was the kind of neighborhood that every city has, but none is proud of. Tacky bars were jammed together, cheek by jowl with seedy pool halls, pawn shops, porno theaters, a tattoo artist's unhygienic-looking storefront studio. By day, the streets were drab and dirty, sidewalks sparsely decorated with the slouching forms of derelicts, some sleeping, others wishing they could sleep. By night, the streets came alive in brilliant colors, tawdry signs enticing customers. The sidewalks were jammed with pushers, pimps and prostitutes, their customers, vice cops on the prowl. Within a three-block radius, discriminating shoppers could fulfill every fantasy, obtaining sex of all persuasions, or chemicals to put their brains in orbit and to bring them down again. Even those on a tight budget could have a beer and shoot some pool.

It was no accident that brought the hunter to this rooftop. Below him and directly opposite, a bank of neon scrollwork advertised The Pleasure Chest, a bar where hookers—gay and straight—were known to ply their trade. The owner and proprietor, one Manny Ingenito, encouraged prostitutes because they lured in other customers; tricks were often nervous, therefore thirsty, as they searched inside themselves for nerve to make a deal. When critics pointed out that Manny had a record of convictions for procuring, suggested that his interest in the working girls—and boys—might be financial, Ingenito forced a weary smile and shook his head. How was a man supposed to mend his ways, escape his past mistakes, if bible-thumping busybodies never gave him a moment's peace?

As he watched Ingenito's doorway, the hunter smiled benignly. Manny could expect some peace tonight, and evermore. Amen.

The hunter knew his target well, had selected him with loving care. The Pleasure Chest's proprietor was second-generation Mafia, a transplant from Chicago. His Family had backed the losing side in one of those perennial upheavals that have made the Windy City famous for its body count. New England offered sanctuary of a sort; Manny had enlisted with the Boston clan of Harold Sicilia, running numbers, running girls, whatever helped ends meet. It was a sweet arrangement until Sicilia got ambitious, nurturing delusions of his own invincibility. Sicilia's son was a classmate of a kid named Johnny Bolan, younger brother of the Executioner himself. It didn't take the mafioso long to see that he was sitting on a gold mine. He could suck the bastard into range, delude him into wiping out the Beantown opposition and then cement his own status as a hero by eliminating Bolan personally.

Simple.

Except the plan had blown up in Harold's face, and Manny found himself without a sponsor once again. He had been lucky, even so; most of Harold Sicilia's troops had bought the farm on that one. Lucky Manny had looked around for shelter, had found himself another capo—granted, the guy was no Sicilia—and he had started over, rising through the ranks and kissing ass where necessary, until he was in position to suggest his own assignment. Sick and tired of fighting for survival in the urban jungles, Manny shopped for someplace nice and peaceful, where a man could turn a dollar and be left alone. Someplace like Pittsfield.

Smiling again at the irony of Ingenito's choice, the hunter checked his watch. Another twenty minutes before the target showed himself, if he was running on his normal schedule.

From Manny's point of view, the choice of Pittsfield was inspired. The Bolan plague had started there, and everybody knew that lightning never hit the same spot twice. Besides, the Pittsfield syndicate was in a shambles, nothing to fight about, and lots of room for enterprising guys like Ingenito to expand. Somebody else could play enforcer, whip the peasants into shape if he was so inclined. Let Manny earn his daily bread in peace—with just a little gravy on the side—and he was satisfied.

The hunter had selected Manny Ingenito mainly because he was accessible. There were a dozen higher-ranking mafiosi in the city, but their very rank demanded the trappings of imperial security. With Ingenito, it would be in and out, the kind of score that made a splash without incurring a substantial risk. Manny was a pawn, no more, but his removal from the game should get things rolling.

Midnight. The Pleasure Chest's proprietor emerged on cue, his bodyguard-chauffeur one step behind him. Manny's briefcase held the day's receipts, two-thirds already banded for the night depository at his bank, the rest—the skim—intended for the safe built into his bedroom floor. Saloons were perfect for the kind of cash-and-carry skimming operation Ingenito specialized in. His capo might not even know the size of Manny's private slice, and then again...

The hunter crouched, retrieved his Marlin, raised it smoothly to his shoulder, forward elbow resting on the parapet. Inside the twenty-power's field of vision, Ingenito sprang to life in giant size, his flabby cheeks turned pink and purple by garish neon signs. You could count the wrinkles on his forehead as he glanced to either side, scowled at the low-lifes who were paying for his house, his car, the suit he wore. He moved among them with the fine contempt of one who has risen from the gutter on his own and has forgotten its odor on the way.

The hunter shifted, sighted in on Manny's squat companion, finger curling easily around the Marlin's trigger. He would take the shooter first, of course. As a convicted felon, Manny Ingenito was prohibited from carrying a firearm. His bodyguard would be the only source of opposition here tonight. The hunter could have shot Manny first, allowed the gunner to survive, but the hit would not have been complete.

It would not have had the Bolan touch.

The shooter waited for his boss to fall in step. They moved out together, marching north until they reached an alleyway that flanked the Pleasure Chest. The hunter could have taken them at any time, but he was in no hurry now. He knew where they were going, and he could afford to wait.

The alley was a dead-end box, providing access to a tiny parking lot behind the Pleasure Chest. Surrounded on all sides by buildings, like an asphalt afterthought, the lot was big enough for Ingenito's Cadillac and the vehicles of two or three employees. Anyone who parked in the protected lot had to leave as he had entered, through the narrow alley fronting on the hunter's rooftop vantage point.

And he could wait for Manny Ingenito.

He watched the tandem figures disappear into the alley, lost in shadow for a time. He could not hear the Caddy's engine turning over, but he saw the headlights when the driver turned them on, and he was ready, waiting, when the target rumbled into view. With a bit of caution, the big car could squeeze through the narrow alley, but once it entered the alley, the Caddy's doors could not be opened far enough for either man to wriggle free. The hunter had them boxed—provided he could stall the tank, for openers.

He zeroed on the grill. His finger tightened around the trigger as he drew a breath and held it, swallowed to lock the air inside his lungs. Precision timing was required; if he muffed the shot, they would be away before he could correct his error. Calling on the hours of practice, years of waiting for this moment, concentrating on his target to the exclusion of the whole damned world outside, he said a silent prayer and squeezed.

The Marlin bucked against his shoulder, bruising, but the slug was on its way before he felt the recoil, slamming in on target through the Caddy's unprotected grill, releasing radiator steam and oily smoke that told him he had cracked the engine block. Another round for safety's sake. Smoke poured out from under the hood, partially obscuring his view.

Below him, people on the sidewalks were reacting to the gunfire, a few seeking cover with the instincts of embattled veterans, the rest still gawking skyward, searching for the source of man-made thunder. He ignored them all and concentrated on his targets in the Cadillac, while he could see them through the smoke.

The wheelman had a pistol in his hand, although he had to know it wouldn't do him any good while he was stuck inside the car. Instinctively the guy tried the driver's door and banged it hard against the brickwork on his left, apparently surprised the ancient wall was there. The shooter slammed his open palm against the steering wheel and cursed. The hunter might have read his lips through the twenty-power, had he taken the time.

Instead he blew the guy away, 240 grains of death exploding through the windshield, flattened by the impact, tumbling already when the slug struck his face. The scowling head snapped back, one side disintegrating before the hunter's eyes. Blood and mutilated flesh sprayed directly in Manny Ingenito's face.

Manny seemed to go insane. Before the hunter could react, his secondary target rose and rolled, feet braced against the dashboard, wallowing across the seat and disappearing down in back. Still sane enough to think in terms of dollars, Manny took the leather briefcase with him. Natch.

No matter. If he couldn't drill the pig, then he would roast him where he sat. The hunter spent a precious moment reloading the Marlin's tubular magazine. He scanned the street below him for any sign of police response to the shooting. There was none, which vindicated his selection of this neighborhood. Its regulars would rather burn in hell than call the law, and casual visitors, out slumming, would have no idea where to turn for help.

He sighted through the twenty-power scope again, the cross hairs centered on the Caddy's smoking hood. He tried to estimate the carburetor's placement beneath the flimsy sheet of metal, finally zeroing in on an imaginary circle.

All right.

Methodically the hunter emptied the rifle's magazine, striving for precision rather than speed. His third round made the hot spot, but he used up the others to make sure. Before he lifted off, the Cadillac was burning brightly, tongues of flame licking along the underbelly, searching out the gas tank.

When the gas blew, the hunter thought he might have heard a strangled scream from Ingenito, caught up in all that fire and twisted steel, but he was never sure. It didn't matter either way. The bastard was a statistic now. They would have to cut him out of there with torches, and the syndicate could kiss that cash goodbye.

The hunter was almost finished. Moving swiftly now, he stowed the Marlin in the duffel bag, depositing the extra ammunition from his pocket in a zippered outer pouch. He straightened, the stench of burning oil and rubber in his nostrils, fished inside a different pocket for the marksman's medal, left it on the parapet. Together with the Marlin cartridges and the choice of target, Homicide would be sure to find the Bolan signature on Manny Ingenito's smoky exit.

Let them doubt the soldier's presence in their city now. The mob would never doubt it, that was certain. They would have gunners on the street before the night was out. The police could not ignore them, as they had ignored the Executioner before, allowing him to trample roughshod over law and order, murdering at will. The widows of his war, their orphaned children, would have justice, finally.

And if it came too late for some, at least the rest would know and understand.

He met no interference on the stairs. If occupants of the cheap hotel had heard the shooting, seen or heard the explosions on the street, they had already taken their curiosity outside. Most tenants would have been drunk or drugged by midnight, anyway, too far gone to recognize an alien invasion if the UFOs crash landed through their open bedroom windows. Once again, the hunter's preparations had paid off.

He used the back door, avoiding the hotel lobby where the night clerk would be dry enough to make his face, the bag he carried. The route was shorter this way, too. Two more minutes saw the hunter safely to his car, the Marlin stowed inside the trunk.

He had performed a service for the city here tonight. *Two* services, in fact. He had eliminated Manny Ingenito, cauterizing one of several open sores on the inner city's face, and he had sounded the alarm to Bolan's presence in Pittsfield. They would be forced to listen now—the lawmen, politicians, prosecutors, journalists who had been negligent before. They would be watching for the bastard now.

They would be watching when he died.

The Executioner would have an audience to cheer him on his way, and they would thank the hunter in the end. For saving them. For seeing justice done.

For evening the score.

It was a good night's work, all right, and he was satisfied. For now.

The hunter drove directly home, and was asleep within the hour. He did not dream.

## 14

The neighborhood was posh, by Pittsfield standards. South Hills would never pose a challenge to Rodeo Drive, but stately homes sat square on roomy lots, serene behind rolling lawns and security fences. Primarily professionals, the residents took precautions against theft, but thought vice and violent crime occurred in another world altogether. Narcotics? Prostitution? Child pornography? They were the problems of a blighted inner city, far removed from the routine of country clubs and cocktail parties that the better half enjoyed. Few, if any, South Hill residents would recognize the predators among their own neighbors . . . but predators were among them, all the same.

The Executioner came seeking predators in South Hill on his second night in Pittsfield. The previous day he had leased a base of operations, paying the first and last months' rent although he didn't plan to be in town past Friday morning. With the drop secure, he had gone to ground for twenty-four hours and waited—for Girrardi's troops to make a move, for something, *anything*, to happen.

He had not had long to wait.

By sunrise on Bolan's second day in Pittsfield, press reports were naming him as the sniper who had taken out the local "vice lord." Homicide detectives had found a marksman's medal and a dozen cartridges from a Marlin

.444 at the scene of the shooting. They had put two and two together... but their math was wrong.

The Ingenito strike had been a smoke screen and a frame. No one knew it yet, except for Bolan and the man—or men—behind the Marlin. For now he was satisfied to let detectives pursue their empty leads, but that did not mean he was going to let it rest.

The Ingenito shooting and Bolan's interrogation of Girrardi had started the pot boiling, but now the soldier needed to turn the heat up higher. Someone meant to force his hand, and Bolan was happy to oblige. That someone did not—could not—know where he would appear next, and from the fireworks at the Pleasure Chest, his adversary was expecting Bolan to begin his cleanup in the gutter. Cruising slowly through the tree-lined streets of South Hill, Bolan wondered what would happen to his adversary's plans if he began to rattle cages at the top.

He passed Girrardi's minimansion, marked the soldier's on the gate and kept on driving. Gino had a white flag, for the moment. He would be working overtime to finger the demented idiot who planned a reenactment of the Bolan blitz in Pittsfield. Gino's job, and possibly his life, were on the line, and Bolan trusted him to leave no stone unturned.

He trusted Gino as far as he could drop-kick City Hall.

Though he was convinced Girrardi knew nothing about the violence in Connecticut, or the lure back to Pittsfield, Bolan still could not rule out a syndicate involvement. Someone in the ranks might view the Executioner's return as a heaven-sent chance to winnow out the chaff, create some vacancies for rising young executives. There might be treachery within Girrardi's camp or from some rival family. With the shifting ethnic makeup of the underworld these days, the adversary might not be a bloodline mafioso, after all. The Executioner would have to wait and see.

And while he waited, he could rattle cages. Remind his ancient enemies that psychological warfare was a two-edged sword that could cut both ways.

His target for the evening was Girrardi's number two, a recently promoted veteran shooter named Ernie "Spider" Tarantella. Like his namesake in the insect world, he was a hairy brute who spoke and moved with slow deliberation until the time was ripe to strike against his enemies. In combat—on the streets of Brooklyn as a youth, and later from behind a desk, with soldiers of his own—the Spider could be swift, decisive, deadly when the need arose.

People messed around with Ernie Tarantella at their peril. His assorted rap sheets listed two-score unsolved homicides in which he was suspected as the trigger or the guiding hand. In Pittsfield, Tarantella was the field commander of Girrardi's occupation force, but he had been restrained, so far, by Gino's disinclination to launch a bloodbath in the streets. With Manny Ingenito cooling in a drawer downtown, the Spider would now be gearing up for action.

As Bolan turned his rental toward the Tarantella homestead, he was looking forward to the meeting on Tarantella's home turf. It was too long since he had crushed a spider underneath his heel.

The Tarantella spread was old New England, with a dash of Modern Paranoid added by the latest tenant. The broken bottles mounted on the decorative wall were new, as were the TV cameras mounted at the gate. A human silhouette drifted in and out of sight behind the wrought-iron scrollwork of the gate, patrolling, and there would be others, Bolan knew.

After circling Tarantella's property—a corner lot with a narrow alleyway in back—Bolan parked the rental half a block beyond. He shed the slacks and jacket covering his blacksuit, buckled on his military webbing with the AutoMag, grenades and canvas pouches holding extra magazines. He slipped an Uzi submachine gun from its hiding place beneath the driver's seat and double-checked the load, then slipped the strap across his shoulder, ready to go EVA.

It would be simple to get over the wall, but he would have to be alert for roving sentries. From the vehicles in Tarantella's drive, the Executioner knew that Ernie had called his top lieutenants to a summit conference, doubtless laying out their strategy for dealing with a Bolan siege. The soldier smiled in sweet anticipation of providing Tarantella's shooters with a lesson in survival on the firing line. It was a lesson, Bolan thought, that some of them might not, in fact, survive.

The darkness swallowed him and carried him along toward confrontation with the enemy.

AL WEATHERBEE DECIDED he would pack it in at midnight. He was getting too damned old for cruising aimlessly around darkened streets in search of trouble, and he wasn't even getting paid for gas this time around. But in spite of the irritation and embarrassment, the former chief of homicide was running on his instinct, trusting a hunch.

He knew that Bolan was in town, as surely as he knew the soldier hadn't wasted Manny Ingenito. Pappas had summoned Weatherbee to the Pleasure Chest the night before, all scowls and sour temperament, predicting doomsday if the war expanded any further. Weatherbee had checked out the scene, examined Ingenito's Caddy and the rooftop sniper's nest. Something didn't ring true. He couldn't put his finger on it, couldn't sell John Pappas on his theory, but the ex-detective would have bet his life that Bolan had no part in smoking Manny or his pet gorilla.

Granted, it was Bolan's trademark, Bolan's weapon. It was almost Bolan's style. Almost. When he thought about it more, Weatherbee decided the timing made the difference. Bolan—or whoever—would have had to be in place before his targets left the Pleasure Chest. He would have had them squarely in his sights throughout their short walk to the alleyway that led to where Ingenito parked his Cadillac. Bolan would have taken them outside, on foot, Weatherbee was certain, although it was a feeling that he could never "prove" except by reference to past experience.

From the beginning, when he hit Frank Laurenti's crew at Triangle Finance, Bolan had preferred to execute his targets publicly. No stats were available, of course, but Weatherbee was betting that a count of Bolan's victims would reveal that a lion's share had met their maker on the streets. If the Executioner had been watching Manny Ingenito through a telescopic sight, with no one standing in the way, he would have popped the bastard in front of the Pleasure Chest, not waited for the target to stroll half a block and crawl inside a tank that might be armored fore and aft.

The technique the shooter actually used raised several possibilities. He might be short on experience with heavy weapons, fearing he might only wing a man on foot, or miss entirely, bag a passerby. Or the sniper might have had ample time—days, weeks—to study Ingenito and his operation, familiarize himself with the greasy thug's routine, make sure there would be no armor plating on the Cadillac.

If the gunner had been scoping Manny over several days or weeks, then the gunner wasn't Bolan. Q.E.D., you bet your ass. If the soldier had come to town one morning, studied Manny Ingenito in the afternoon and rubbed him out that night, he wouldn't have done it the way it had been done. No, it wouldn't play, no matter how you tried to make the pieces fit, and Pappas should have seen through all the bullshit trappings right up front.

Of course the current homicide chief was under heavy pressure to produce. The very rumor of a Bolan blitz had raised the roof on City Hall; Pappas would be feeling heat around the clock until the Executioner was in the ground or out of town. Unfortunately, pressure could sometimes blur the professional detective's senses, blinding him to subtle clues that might prove vital in the long run. Weatherbee, outside the pressure cooker, had a different perspective, tempered by his past experience with Bolan.

The ex-detective captain was under pressure of a sort, however, too. Alice, plainly disappointed by his eagerness to join the hunt, had treated him to stony silence after Pappas had called last night. The silence had continued over breakfast, thawing out toward lunch, returning with a vengeance when he mentioned going out tonight, just driving, nowhere in particular. He had said she was welcome to accompany him, but she had recognized the lie.

Of course he could not have her with him in the darkness, as he prowled in search of . . . what? Was he pursuing Bolan in the night, or was he chasing after youth, attempting to recapture moments that had passed him by forever?

In many ways, Mack Bolan *was* his past. The soldier's private war had made Al Weatherbee the premier "Bolan expert." His failure to collar the Executioner had ended his career. Never mind the platitudes mouthed by ranking officers to cover their embarrassment, Al Weatherbee was pressured to retire because he was a walking monument to failure. He was The Man Who Let Mack Bolan Get Away.

Beneath the dash, Weatherbee's scanner had been hissing out a string of routine calls, dispatching squad cars to investigate complaints about noisy parties, domestic squabbles, break-ins or suspected prowlers. Uninterested in the routine, he consciously listened to the radio only when the young dispatcher's voice took on an urgent, breathless tone.

"All South Hill units. Shots fired, the vicinity of 1327 Elmwood. See the woman. South Hill units. Shots fired, 1327 Elmwood Avenue."

Weatherbee heard the unit drivers acknowledging the run. He had no need of the city map in the glove compartment. He had learned the city as a young patrolman, had kept pace with its expansion as a homicide detective; the streets were indelibly emblazoned on his brain. He knew the South Hill district, where the houses were far beyond his means...and he was well aware of who resided just next door to 1327. Sure. It was a name and address that a former chief of homicide was damned unlikely to forget.

He cut a tight, illegal U-turn in the middle of the street, arresting traffic in both directions. Horns blared righteous anger in his ears, as he stood on the accelerator, daring any rookie traffic cop to pull him over.

He wouldn't have much time if there had been reports of gunfire on the property already. Ernie Tarantella had a small platoon of guns in residence around the clock—all duly licensed, strictly legal. Whoever planned to fumigate the Spider, whether Bolan or the slick imposter who had wasted Manny Ingenito, he was biting off a mouthful. Would it please him, he wondered, if the Executioner bit off more than he could chew, and choked to death on Tarantella's gunners? Would it make his day or ruin it?

When he couldn't find a ready answer to the question, the former chief of homicide was shaken. Still speeding, he fished one hand inside his jacket, withdrew the .38 revolver he had carried through the years of active service and laid it on the seat beside him, ready.

Bolan or the slick imposter. Either way, Al Weatherbee was in the game, and no one had to tell him he was gambling with his life.

THE HUNTER PARKED HIS CAR and killed the lights, surrounded instantly by darkness. South Hill streetlights were on strategic corners only, leaving tree-lined streets in shadow for the most part. The residents relied on patrols that were, perhaps, more frequent than the miniscule amount of local crime appeared to warrant. Money talked. Squad cars made their regular rounds in South Hill, even though districts with soaring crime rates were gravely understaffed.

Tonight, the locals would be thankful for the black-and-whites that usually were merely tolerated as a necessary eyesore. Tonight, they would be grateful for the men in uniform, with their flashing lights and creaking leather and guns. When the fireworks started going off at Ernie Tarantella's place, the neighbors would have welcomed tanks, if they had been available.

From where the hunter sat, the gunfire sounded strangely distant, muffled, though he knew ground zero was no more than half a block away. The intervening houses, trees and shrubbery deflected sound, served as baffles for the sharp, staccato fireworks.

He wanted to be part of Bolan's final moments, had been waiting for the call. He knew Bolan would be forced

to try for either Tarantella or Girrardi. The hunter would
have put his money on Girrardi, since he held the higher
rank, but undoubtedly Bolan had his reasons for deciding
on the Spider. Bolan always had his reasons, and so far his
strategy had always seen him through.

Until tonight.

South Hill was not the hunter's choice, but it would do,
if Bolan showed himself and offered an opportunity to
bring the curtain down. It wasn't perfect, granted, but if
Tarantella didn't tag the soldier, it would be enough to nail
him in the act of wreaking havoc on a peaceful, wealthy
neighborhood. The hunter would have preferred to put
Bolan through his paces himself and deliver him on
schedule to the chosen killing ground, but if it came to now
or never, he would be a fool to let this golden moment slip
away.

The hunter was no fool, by any means.

Beside him on the seat, his right hand rested on the Colt
Commando's telescopic butt. A cut-down version of the
classic M-16, the weapon had a ten-inch barrel that was
eleven inches shorter than that of the original assault rifle. With its telescoping stock collapsed, the lethal stutter
gun measured thirty-two inches overall, weighed less than
seven pounds. For all that, it had surrendered nothing of
the original M-16's firepower, maintaining the same cyclic
rate of 700 rounds per minute, spewing its 5.56 mm tumblers at a muzzle velocity of 2,974 feet per second.

The Commando was a devastating weapon, and the
hunter knew he would be needing it tonight. With Bolan
on a roll, already blooded by his contact with the Tarantella guns, he would be running hot and killing anything
that moved. The hunter might have milliseconds once he
spotted Bolan, and any wasted motion could be fatal to his
scheme. If Bolan showed himself—*when* Bolan showed

himself—there would only be time to hold down the trigger, let the Commando do its bloody work on automatic pilot.

It was a goddamned shame.

But it was better than no damned shot at all.

The hunter had no fear that Bolan would elude him, pass him by unseen. The Spider's house was on a corner lot selected for defensibility, which meant Bolan would be boxed when black-and-whites began arriving, mere seconds from now. The bastard couldn't leg it down the middle of the street with Tarantella's goons and half the uniforms in South Hill spraying bullets up his ass. He would be forced to seek another exit, down the narrow, darkened alleyway.

The hunter's car was parked across the street, downrange, where he could bring the alley under fire without emerging from the vehicle. He kept the engine running, ready to pursue if he missed, against all odds at such short range. *If* he missed, if Bolan went to ground, there would be time for a single strafing run, and that would do the trick. No doubt about it, the game was in the bag.

Except that he was sweating now. Despite the open windows and the cool night breeze. Despite the gooseflesh crawling on his arms and shoulders. The hunter was sweating like a rookie sneak thief, terrified of being collared, held up to the light of day. Exposed.

He took a breath and held it, willed the nervousness away. He picked up the Colt Commando and held it in his lap, the fingers of his right hand curled around the pistol grip, the stubby muzzle resting on the window ledge. He told himself the chance of a miss at such a range was negligible. Hours and hours of practice had prepared him for the worst.

Still, he could not be certain of the kill, and that uncertainty was gnawing at him, causing him to sweat. He swabbed a palm across his face and dried it quickly on his slacks, disgusted by the clammy moisture on his skin.

Tonight.

The Executioner would come to him as surely as water ran downhill. The hunter would be waiting for his quarry, primed and ready to erase the hatred of a lifetime in one searing blast of automatic fire.

Here.

Tonight.

In Pittsfield.

Near the scene of Bolan's original atrocities.

The Executioner was going to be executed, brought to justice by a man whose fearsome dedication matched the soldier's own.

He would not—*could not*—miss. He concentrated on success, the moment when his sights would settle on Mack Bolan's face, his finger tightening around the trigger, squeezing off.

Tonight. Right here.

And after it was finished, then perhaps the restless ghosts would leave him, let him rest in peace.

## 15

Bolan cut the gunner's legs from under him with a short, precision burst and watched him fall across the Uzi's line of fire. A second snort of parabellum manglers punched the straw man over on his back and left him sprawling on the patio, his vital fluids pooling, cooling, on the flagstones.

Other guns were yapping at Bolan, angry hornets buzzing overhead. It was time to move. He hit a flying shoulder roll and came up on his knees behind a hedge of juniper, momentarily secure from hostile eyes. The shrubbery wouldn't save him once they started in with probing fire, however, and the soldier hesitated only for a moment, gathering his strength before the next gymnastic lunge.

Three down, so far, and half a dozen others, minimum, returning fire from all around the patio. Other guns inside the house would be prepared to join the action, if he breached the Spider's first line of defense. How many more? No time to think about it now. This probe was swiftly going sour, like so much else over the past two days.

It should have been a relatively easy strike, despite the obvious alert of Tarantella's gunners after Manny Ingenito bought the farm downtown. Girrardi's number two was huddling with his lieutenants, the smoking deep-pit barbecue had not been cooking steaks for Ernie's button men—but they had moved to Tarantella's conference room before the Executioner arrived. It should have been so simple, with Girrardi's fighting brass assembled on the wide veranda, chowing down, but "simple" hadn't been the soldier's strong point lately.

Missing Tarantella's crew was bad enough, but setting off the infrared alarm had been a near disaster. Bent on his objective, he had overlooked the sensors buried in the undergrowth, and gunners were converging on him from left and right before he realized what was happening. He had been quick enough to drop the pointmen on either side, but then triangulated fire was snapping at his heels. Suddenly he was on the defensive, fighting for his life.

The gunners on the patio were feeling for him now, their well-spaced bullets slashing through the hedge at three-foot intervals. He hugged the grass and wriggled on his stomach, just below their line of fire, until he reached a spotty clearing in the foliage. Peering through, he marked their muzzle-flashes, counted seven guns, inched his way around until he could bring them under fire. He double-checked the Uzi's load by feel and poked the weapon's stubby muzzle through the scratchy undergrowth, juniper and rose thorns sharp against his bare hands.

It would be impossible to take them all at once, before they brought their guns around. If he could drop a couple of them, double back beneath the angry fire they would hurl in the direction of his muzzle-flash, then find another bracket in the hedge...

How long before police arrived?

Not long, in South Hill, Bolan knew. They would be close at hand, responsive to the shooting call. But he would hear their sirens approaching, if the gunfire didn't drown them out.

There might be time enough.

His finger curled around the Uzi's trigger, squeezed. Parabellum stingers marched across the wall of bricks downrange, exploding terra cotta flowerpots to find the sniper sheltering behind them. Bolan stitched a bloody pattern on his chest and let him find his own way down, already tracking on before the lifeless body toppled headlong to the flagstones.

Number five was good... but not quite good enough. The shooter saw his comrade fall, reacted swiftly and professionally, pivoting and swinging up the stubby riot gun he carried. Finger on the trigger, he was braced to fire when Bolan disemboweled him with a parabellum ripsaw, spilling all his secrets out as he toppled backward, triggering a blast of buckshot toward the stars.

And it was time to move, with five remaining gunners blasting Bolan, peppering the hedges with their rage and panic. Scuttling along on knees and elbows, he felt a lucky round trace fire across one hip, but he kept moving, gritting teeth against the pain.

He seemed to crawl for miles—though he knew it was no more than thirty feet—before he found another narrow firing port. A glance to fix the muzzle-flashes in his mind, then he let the Uzi go almost instinctively, his parabellums raking stone and brickwork, shattering windows, punching holes through trendy bits of furniture. He saw one adversary stumble, sprawl. Another. And another. They were breaking, caving in, retreating toward the house.

He dropped one runner—number nine—who wallowed on his stomach dying, while Bolan searched the kill zone for a final target. As if responding to his mental summons, number ten erupted from behind the barbecue, firing from the hip and making for the house, arms and legs pumping as he tried to outrun his doom.

The manglers overtook him squarely on the Spider's doorstep, hammering a lethal fist between his shoulder blades and driving him face foremost through the still-unbroken half of Tarantella's sliding doors. The sheet of glass resisted for a microsecond, finally yielded with a crack of brittle thunder, raining slick, transparent guillotines upon the dying soldier as he fell.

The way was open. All Bolan had to do was step inside. No sweat.

Except there were gunners waiting just inside the house, ready to blow his head off when he showed himself.

He fed the stutter gun a second magazine and eased a frag grenade from where it hung on his harness. Hooking one thumb through the pin, he worked it free, his fingers tightly wrapped around the egg, securing the safety spoon in place. The doomsday countdown wouldn't start until he let it fly, and after that, the Executioner would have five seconds before it blew.

He scrambled to his feet, the Uzi in his left hand, firing as he rose, the right arm cocked and sweeping forward with the pitch, his fingers opening. The lethal egg was airborne, wobbling toward its target through the semidarkness, disappearing through the shattered sliding doors. The housemen inside were unloading on him, giving everything they had, but Bolan's Uzi kept them down, prevented them from sighting carefully enough to make it count. Another second, then the Uzi emptied. It was time to dive for cover, hugging Mother Earth before the frag grenade exploded, spraying jagged shrapnel high and low around its kill zone.

Bolan felt the blast as much as he heard it, didn't need to see the remnants of the sliding doors as they were battered outward, hurled across the patio. Inside the house flames had taken root already, spreading to the drapes, the carpets. He could hear the wounded crying out their pain. He would help them, end their misery if there was time, but first . . .

The sirens stopped him halfway to his feet, distant still but drawing closer by the heartbeat, closing his options, telling him it was time to cut and run. No time to seek the Spider out, to teach him fear.

Perhaps the lesson had already reached him, traveling ahead of Bolan like the smell of battle smoke.

Perhaps.

But it was time to go. Bolan fed the Uzi as he ran, retreating from the house and homing on the alley that was his only means of exit from the killing ground. His rental lay beyond, and if he was quick enough he could make it yet, before the first patrol car cut him off.

Bolan scaled the fence, landing in a combat crouch outside, the submachine gun ready to answer any challenge with lethal fire. The silent shadows mocked him. He wasted no more time, backtracked toward the car.

He almost made it.

From the darkness, muzzle-flashes stabbed him, angry tumblers whined close behind his ears. Instinctively, the soldier feinted to the left, then hit a combat crouch and scuttled to his right, the Uzi rattling a sharp response to his assailants.

Make that singular. Bolan fixed the second flash, an ugly blossom flaring in the window of a dark sedan across the street. He went to ground, and none too soon, as half a dozen rounds sliced above his head, near enough to ruffle his hair.

It seemed impossible that any of the Spider's men had closed the door behind him. They were scrambling to save their asses in the house, and in another moment they would have the law to deal with, nasty questions to answer at the very least. For one or more of them to break away, predict his exit route and plant an ambuscade along his backtrack would require psychic powers. From Bolan's observations thus far, the Spider's crew did not possess the talent or the brains to pull it off.

Then who?

No matter now. The car was bearing down on him, tires screeching with the force of its acceleration from a standing start. Despite the darkness, he could see the muzzle of an automatic weapon jutting from the driver's window, leveled for the strafing run. Bolan knew it was time to move or die.

He moved, erupting in a single, fluid motion from his prone position, through a running crouch and on to stand erect. In his hands, the Uzi beat a sharp tattoo of challenge, peppering the charger as it closed the gap between them. He saw the dirty yellow flame explode from his adversary's weapon. He sidestepped, went down on one knee, the Uzi hammering its song of death.

Too late.

The first round bored in low on Bolan's side, deflected by a rib and tumbling before it ripped an exit wound above his hip. Round two punched through his thigh and ripped the leg from under him on impact. Bolan toppled, sprawling, and the third round drilled his shoulder, spinning him around to lie faceup beneath the stars.

He scarcely was aware of the other rounds that snapped and danced around him, chewing up the manicured lawn. As if from miles away, he heard the car accelerate out of range, retreating now, its job completed. He realized he had dropped the Uzi, lost it somewhere as he fell, and then darkness settled over Bolan like a blanket.

Like a shroud.

DISGUSTED WITH THE WAITING, almost ready to go after Bolan on his own, the hunter had been alerted by a sudden lull in the hostilities. When he heard the sirens he wondered if they might spook the Executioner, compel him to withdraw before he could crush the Spider.

Five more seconds, ten without a shot, and he was certain of it. The Executioner was pulling out the back way, breaking off from the enemy and sprinting through the darkness toward his rendezvous with death. Retreating from the frying pan into the hunter's line of fire.

There was a kind of poetry about it, he supposed, though he was not a man who spent much time on abstract thought. He had been longing for revenge since he had come of age, and now it was within his grasp. Another moment and he would have the soldier in his sights. Just one more time.

He raised the Colt Commando from his lap and braced it on his forearm, sighting down its barrel toward the alley's mouth. He had no fear of witnesses at this point. The patrol cars would be closing from the north, and any neighbor shaken from his sleep by the explosive fireworks would be homing in on Tarantella's shooting gallery, oblivious of one more car against the curb. If someone broke the odds and spotted him, they would be dealt with, swiftly and efficiently. He would not let some absurd accident deter him from fulfilling his appointed destiny.

A movement there, against the deeper shadows of the alley. He squinted down the rifle's barrel, intent on picking out the silhouette. If only he had access to a night scope... But it did no good to whine about deficiencies that could not be corrected. You did the best you could with what you had, and the Commando should be good enough.

The gliding shape detached itself from darker shadows in the alleyway, became a man edging across the nearest lawn with supple, catlike movements. Bolan! Rigged for doomsday, all in black, he was a wraith made flesh, the hunter's nemesis.

*Come and get it!*

He was squeezing off before the conscious thought had time to form, transmit itself along the network of his nervous system. The Commando rattled a warning burst, and before the final round was fired he could see that it was high, outside. Reacting with the swiftness of a jungle cat, the Executioner was dodging, feinting, seeking cover as the second burst screamed out across the blacktop, echoes battering against the houses opposite and ringing in the hunter's ears.

Another miss, but closer. He had seen the bastard jump that time.

The quarry triggered a searching burst from his abbreviated weapon. A single stinger drilled the car door, startling the hunter.

*Forget it! Make your move before the bastard's aim gets any better.*

He floored the accelerator. Steering with his left hand, holding the Colt Commando with his right, he veered across the narrow blacktop, straining toward his target as he closed the gap. Against the stucco backdrop of a sprawling ranch-style house, he saw the soldier rising to his feet, the submachine gun winking in defiance. He was standing up to fight, the bastard, knowing it would only get him killed; you could almost admire a guy like that, determined to take it on his feet.

The hunter held the Colt Commando's trigger down and emptied the banana clip in one hellish burst that swept the lawn and wall and everything before him. Then he twisted the wheel just a second before he jumped the curb. As it was, he scraped it, his hubcaps ringing off concrete as he veered away. For a microsecond he was eye-to-eye with Bolan, less than twenty feet away.

It was enough.

He saw the rounds strike home, his target toppling, spinning, folding as the tumblers ripped his flesh. The bastard was unconscious—maybe even dead—before he hit the grass—no doubt about it. If the bullets hadn't killed him outright, he would bleed to death in moments, well before police and paramedics strayed from Tarantella's slaughter pen downrange.

And it was done, all finished, just like that. He fought an urge to swing the car around, speed back and let the bastard have another clip...or hop the curb and flatten him beneath the tires. But extravagance accomplished nothing, invited danger to himself. He knew he should be satisfied with what he had.

But there was a sense of anticlimax to the killing, as if something had been missing from the final confrontation. He wished there had been time for him to face his quarry, let the soldier know why he had to die, and at whose hand. Perhaps a face-to-face would finally have purged the private demons that the hunter lived with day and night.

But all that would pass in time.

The hunter had succeeded where the FBI and other law enforcement agencies had failed. He had avenged his family, and all the other families left fatherless by Bolan's one-man war. This night's act would not retrieve the dead, but if there was a shred of justice latent in the universe, he knew they would be waiting for the Executioner in hell.

In time, the hunter thought, he might join them there.

But not tonight.

He had some details to attend to yet, before he could continue his normal life. His car had taken several hits from Bolan's submachine gun, and he would be forced to do the body work himself to avoid questions from mechanics or police. No problem there; he had the tools at home, or could acquire them inexpensively in Pittsfield.

He would have to ditch the weapons—some of them, at least—there were several he might hang on to for a while. You never knew when this or that illegal piece of armament might come in handy. He would not become another Executioner. But if the need for action should arise, then he should be prepared.

He found the irony of that intensely humorous, and hearty laughter bore the hunter home through darkness. Morning would be soon enough to go out searching for the light.

## 16

Pausing at a traffic light before he entered South Hill, Weatherbee had time to wonder if he had lost his mind. What did he expect to accomplish with his crazy cross-town dash? He was reacting like a fire horse that has been put out to pasture, but still responds blindly to the old alarms; he was endangering himself and hampering the men who had a job to do.

He felt ridiculous, yet that did not eliminate the strange compulsion that had brought him here, that drove him on. If Bolan had returned to run his razzle-dazzle on the home front one more time, Al Weatherbee would be there to see it. With any luck, the former chief of homicide might just get close enough to finish it.

The target would be Ernie Tarantella. The Elmwood address broadcast on the monitor had told him that much. Girrardi's place was farther out, on Whittier, secure for now unless the Executioner was setting records for the quarter mile.

Weatherbee cranked the window down. He could hear sirens now, still distant but approaching. Take it easy, boys, he chided silently. They had to know that Tarantella was the second biggest hemorrhoid in town—*the* biggest, if you counted reputation rather than rank within the brotherhood. The bastard had a list of priors stretching back to childhood, and you could forget about the shortage of convictions. If the Spider had been innocent of any given beef, Al Weatherbee was ready to believe in miracles.

The failure to convict the guy was thanks to methods of persuasion, gangland style. A simple bribe might open the negotiations, each side probing the strengths and weaknesses of the other. A witness who rejected money could be brought around by terrorism—threats against his property, his family, his life. If all else failed, the die-hards disappeared or were assassinated publicly, as a reminder to the populace at large. Weatherbee couldn't help but wonder if society might not be better served by letting Bolan take the Spider out, remove the cancer now before it spread.

And where the hell did *that* idea come from?

If Weatherbee subscribed to Bolan's methods, why in hell had he been losing sleep in pursuit of one more chance to break the soldier's chops?

The answer was simplicity itself. He didn't buy the soldier's method of dispensing justice by the round, but what battle-weary cop had not fantasized once or twice about a world where the enemy was readily identifiable, a bull's-eye painted on his back? Frustration was part of each policeman's life, beginning when he first pinned on the badge, and lasting till the day he died.

*Except you're not a cop,* the inner voice reminded him. He was not at all surprised that the voice reminded him of Alice's.

He was a civilian now, with all that term implied from the perspective of the man behind the badge. Outsider. Alien. Member of the crowd. At best, a nuisance...and at worst? The enemy.

He wondered how it was possible to miss a job so much when the pay was mediocre and the hours grueling, the risk of danger never far away. Instead of crying in his beer he should be glad the brass had put him out to pasture.

But in his heart and in his mind he *was* still a cop, goddammit! It didn't matter if they took his badge away. They couldn't take away its imprint on his soul. Like the veteran fire horse, he would answer those alarms until they put him in the ground.

That was what made his mixed emotions toward the Executioner so unsettling. As a cop—all right, *ex*-cop—he should have seen the soldier for the public menace he was, threatening the very fabric of society. But he had looked behind the warrior's graveyard eyes, had caught a glimpse of something warm and human, a vivid contrast to the primal rage that fueled his first vendetta, there in Pittsfield.

For a moment, Weatherbee wondered what he might find if he could look inside those eyes tonight. Would there be warmth, a vestige of humanity inside the killing machine? Or had it all been seared away, burned out of Bolan by the pain of waging endless war across the years?

No matter. The guy was bloody dangerous; motive only mattered if it helped you bring a perpetrator down. As long as the Executioner continued killing, making up his own rules as he went along, he was nothing but criminal to be eliminated, one way or another.

Fine.

Then why did Weatherbee feel such misgivings at the thought of taking down the man in black? Why was he so ambivalent about the guy?

No ready answer came to mind. Disgusted, the former homicide chief refused to think about it anymore. By now his mind was fully occupied, in any case, with beating the black-and-whites to Tarantella's.

He did not know the reason, but he was possessed by a sudden need to view the shooting scene before the uniforms arrived and SWAT teams hit the beach, destroying evidence in their aggressive zeal to bag the Executioner. If Manny Ingenito had been taken out by an imposter, which Weatherbee believed to be the case, Tarantella might be on that shooter's list, as well. Before he spent more precious time in pursuit of shadows, Weatherbee wanted to know if Bolan was in town or not.

He knew the patrol patterns in South Hill, knew the cruisers would close in from the north and east. He pushed the Buick through another light as it changed from amber to red, ticking off the names of cross streets that would bring him in behind the Spider's shooting gallery before the cavalry arrived.

He had to think like Bolan, sure, if such a feat was possible. If Bolan was at Tarantella's, if he was alive, he would hear the sirens, know the police were cutting off the major avenues of exit. He would try the back door first...and hopefully Al Weatherbee would be there waiting for him. Just like in the movies.

Driving with his left hand, Weatherbee reached across the seat to caress the Smith & Wesson. It gave him comfort, so close at hand. Aware that he was going up against an army toting automatic weapons, Weatherbee understood the danger that he faced. It was familiar, almost comfortable. But he could not suppress a little shiver of apprehension as he picked his cross street, turning east and homing on the wail of sirens.

He could die within the next few moments. Years of living with danger had not stripped it of its ability to frighten. Calling up the images of other firefights, Weatherbee was stricken with a sense of déjà vu that made his skin crawl. Still, there was a job to do.

Not your job, the Alice voice reminded him. But it was. The Bolan case had been his job from the beginning. It would be his job until the curtain fell on one or both of them.

Perhaps tonight.

A crackle like the sound of distant fireworks. He slowed the Buick, almost coasting for an instant, reached out to kill the volume on his monitor. Another burst of automatic fire, more distinct this time. Whoever it was who dropped in on Ernie Tarantella, he had come prepared for war.

And even as Weatherbee's car slowed, almost stopped, the fireworks faded, died away. As if a soundproof window had been closed, the night was silent now, except for sirens and the rhythmic panting of the Buick's engine.

*Think like Bolan, dammit.*

Bolan would have a set of wheels nearby. He would have anticipated the police reaction, would stay clear of major cross streets, keep to secondary streets and alleyways for his retreat. If he was able to retreat. If Tarantella's soldiers had not finished him already.

Weatherbee dismissed the thought. If this was a Bolan hit, the Spider's housemen didn't stand a chance. They might be the toughest muscle Boston or Manhattan had to offer, but they weren't soldiers. They were gorillas, *paid* to terrify the innocent and sometimes kill one another on command. Confronted with an enemy of Bolan's skill, they would be little more than cannon fodder.

Unless one of the bastards got lucky.

Weatherbee accelerated, his sense of urgency increasing with the absence of gunfire. If Bolan was withdrawing, there were seconds left, at most, before he cleared the scene. To intercept him, Weatherbee would have to get the lead out, get into position before it was too late.

He gunned the Buick down a curving, tree-lined avenue with darkened houses looming on either side. The neighbors here were obviously unaware of World War III erupting in their own backyard.

Weatherbee was close and closing in when he heard automatic weapon fire again. This time it was near enough to make him wince and duck involuntarily. No muzzle-flash, but he recognized the sharp reports of two weapons now—a submachine gun and an automatic rifle. They were just around the corner. In another instant . . .

As Weatherbee reached for his Smith & Wesson, a sleek Camaro roared around the corner just in front of him with rubber smoking, high beams lancing his eyes. In a flash the driver passed him and was gone. No time to catch the Camaro's plates, but he had glimpsed the driver's profile, blurred with motion. He was not the Executioner. Weatherbee might not recognize the driver if they met face-to-face in daylight, but he would know Mack Bolan anywhere, day or night. The guy was in his blood, and he could no more rid himself of Bolan's image than he could forget the features of his wife, the son whom they had lost to Vietnam.

He took the corner cautiously, the Magnum in his lap, one finger taut around the trigger. The Camaro's driver wasn't Bolan, but he was certainly a shooter. His target might be Bolan. One of Tarantella's goons, perhaps . . . or someone else.

At once, he remembered the hit on Manny Ingenito, wondered if the blurry profile might belong to the hypothetical imposter. Before he could decide to swing his car around to give chase, his headlights settled on a crumpled figure, clad in black. He caught a flash of crimson—Jesus, so much blood—and then he brought the Buick to a sliding halt, scrambled out on legs that felt like rubber.

He held the Magnum out in front of him, prepared to fire at once if Bolan made a sudden move. But by the time he reached the curb, the former chief of homicide could see the soldier wasn't going anywhere. He was alive but badly wounded; shock, loss of blood, might finish him before the black-and-whites arrived. A cautious man, Al Weatherbee stepped wide around the prostrate form and snared the Uzi Bolan had obviously been firing when he was hit.

A streetlight on the corner, some yards distant, gave only faint illumination, but Weatherbee would have known the soldier anywhere. This was the face that he had seen in Texas. Altered by cosmetic surgery until Bolan's mother wouldn't have known him, the face retained all the strength and character Weatherbee had noted in their first encounter, years before.

The soldier's breathing was a labored rattle. The thought occurred to Weatherbee that he should end it here. A single round between the eyes would do it, end the hold that Bolan had on him. And it would be a kindness to the man himself, a mercy kill.

When the uniforms discovered Bolan, as they were sure to do, they would call out the paramedics to save his life. What then? Would the man survive another prison cell? Another trial? What kind of death was waiting for him in the bowels of the "justice" system? Wouldn't he prefer to die as he had lived, in combat?

Sighting down the four-inch barrel of his Smith & Wesson, Weatherbee was still debating with himself when Bolan shifted slightly, moaned...and his eyes snapped open. Something sparked between them, officer and fugitive, a pulsing current that was more than recognition, nothing like enmity. Before he even thought about it, Weatherbee lowered the Magnum, tucked it inside his shoulder holster, crouched to inspect the soldier's wounds.

He might survive, at that. There was less blood than Weatherbee had first imagined. The wounds he could see were clear of vital organs. If he got the soldier to a hospital in time...

Now where the hell had *that* come from? It was not his intention to support the Executioner, to assist him in escaping from the law. Besides, the doctors at emergency receiving would report his wounds, as they were legally required to do, and Bolan would be slapped in irons as soon as he was wheeled out of surgery.

No doctors then.

*Goddammit, knock that off!* He was beginning to hallucinate, to imagine that the soldier's health was his responsibility.

Then, in a sudden flash of insight, Weatherbee grasped the answer to his problem. When he looked at Bolan, part of him was seeing Tommy, flattened by a VC mortar round outside Pleiku. The man who lay before him was a decade older than Weatherbee's son would have been if he had lived, and there was no physical resemblance...but he felt it, all the same. A kinship, deeper than mere understanding of the soldier's motives. Incredibly he felt a sort of bond with Bolan. The former homicide detective realized that the bond had been there all along.

It explained the mixed emotions, certainly, the way he was torn between his duty and a sudden urge to help the Executioner escape. But how in hell could Bolan flee, anyway, when he was unable to stand?

The soldier's lips were moving, forming soundless words Weatherbee couldn't understand. He wrote it off to Bolan's pain, the near-delirium of shock after massive injury. The words didn't matter, anyway. The former chief of homicide had already made up his mind.

"You take it easy," Weatherbee commanded, moving briskly toward the Buick, conscious of the strength returning to his legs with every step. He dropped the Uzi on the floor behind the driver's seat, and doubled back for Bolan, glancing at his watch and guessing at an ETA for the approaching black-and-whites.

They would converge on Tarantella's house first, of course, unless a resident in one of the surrounding homes had phoned another call to headquarters about the later shooting, thereby alerting dispatch to the shifting nature of the battle. If he was lucky, he had time to get the soldier on his feet and into the Buick, to make a break before reinforcements closed the door behind him.

Sure.

*If* he could get the soldier on his feet. If Bolan didn't hemorrhage and die from the exertion of the move.

And when he got him into the car, what then?

Home. Of course.

He couldn't take the soldier to a hospital, any more than he could leave him where he was to be discovered by the uniforms and carted off in irons. When Weatherbee considered all his options, he knew he really had no choice. No choice at all.

He didn't want to think about how Alice would react. Time enough for that when—*if*—he got Bolan home. There was a chance he would be stopped, the Buick searched, before he cleared the neighborhood. In that event, the game was up, and he could kiss his freedom goodbye forever. They could fit him for a set of prison grays while Bolan trundled off to maximum security with both doctors and detectives at his bedside.

Weatherbee stood above the fallen soldier for a moment, hesitating on the brink of an action that would change his life forever. Two blocks over, sirens made his mind up for him. He stooped to slide his hands beneath the other's arms, knowing that any sudden movement could be lethal but that they had no time to waste.

"You've got to help me now," he whispered, not knowing if his words got through the soldier's fog of pain. They must have, because Bolan was responding, weakly but determinedly, rolling over, pushing with his good arm at the blood-slick grass beneath him.

When Bolan was on his feet, one arm wrapped around the shoulders of his former nemesis, they started for the Buick. Bolan dragged one leg slightly, leaned heavily on Weatherbee, his blood already dampening the former detective's shirt. By the time they reached the car, Al Weatherbee was soaked with Bolan's blood, his clothing clammy, plastered to his skin. It was another bond between them, and he was amazed to find he didn't mind at all.

The Buick was a four-door. He put the Executioner in back, let him stretch out on the seat as best he could. Later he would have to swab the vinyl clean of bloodstains, but for now the soldier would be out of sight of any passing cruiser on the street. When Weatherbee got in behind the wheel, he stared at his hands a moment, amazed that they were steady, firm.

That proved he was insane. A psycho had the strength of his convictions, and his mania kept him from feeling fear. Al Weatherbee was crazy, by God. And he would not have had it any other way.

He fired up the Buick and cut a tight 180 in the middle of the street as the sirens grumbled into silence two blocks over. He could hear the reinforcements in the distance, but the early uniforms were on the scene now, closing in on Tarantella's place. With luck, they would be there long enough for him to slip away.

With luck.

But he had used up all his luck already, and he was spinning out his life on borrowed time from this point on. No matter how you tried to talk your way around it, his passenger was sheer catastrophe.

Weatherbee was not worried that Bolan would retrieve his Uzi from the floor and slam a burst between his ears. That was not the soldier's style, and in any case, he was too far gone to fight. The trouble would come later, from police . . . and possibly from elsewhere. Members of the local family would be out for Bolan's head and would spare no effort, no expense, to track him down. What made the former chief of homicide believe that he could shelter Bolan from the best—and worst—each side could muster.

Never mind. His immediate problem was to get the soldier safely home and tend his wounds. He would need a story for his wife, to explain why he was risking everything they had together, risking life itself to help a wanted criminal escape from the police.

She would not understand, of course, any more than Weatherbee himself completely understood. But she would stand beside him.

She was his strength . . . and she could be his weakness, too. He was endangering her life by taking Bolan home, and yet . . .

He had no choice. It all came back to that.

His destiny was intertwined with Bolan's now, and there was nothing he could do to free himself. Whatever happened, they were in the shit together, all the way.

# 17

The jungle stretched forever, thick, impenetrable. Overhead, the sun was shining on the treetops, but its light was filtered, muted into twilight in the forest world below. In a few more hours, it would be too dark for human eyes. Already some nocturnal predators were stirring from their daytime slumber, yawning, stretching muscles, making ready for the nightly hunt.

Mack Bolan knew the jungle by its sights, its sounds, its smells. The steamy forest was familiar to him from a hundred sorties against the Cong and countless penetrations to gather intelligence. The daytime darkness did not frighten him, and he paid no heed to the stirrings of the evening predators. His eyes were accustomed to the jungle darkness, and he would find his way by touch if necessary, pressing on until his mission was fulfilled.

As he had so many times before, the Executioner was hunting human prey. It troubled Bolan that he could not remember the target; left with only fleeting mental images, he wondered if it would be possible to make the strike on schedule, without endangering the innocent. But something in his gut told him he would know when he found his prey. It troubled him, also, that he could not identify the jungle. It was not Vietnam, he knew that, although the heat and the density of the tangled undergrowth equaled the worst that Asia had to offer. South America, perhaps? Or Africa?

Strangest of all, he was naked, his pale skin vulnerable to thorns and biting insects. With that realization the soldier knew he must be dreaming. How else would he embark on a mission that was clearly suicidal, seeking unknown prey in unknown territory? It was the stuff of nightmares, but the jungle fighter could not wake himself. He might be hunting for the government—whose government?—or on his own behalf, but either way, his enemy would be the same.

Mack Bolan recognized the spoor of savage man, his track in primal mud, his unmistakable aroma clinging to the undergrowth. He would track him to the farthest corners of the earth to complete his mission.

Bolan moved along the trail, heedless of the vines that tangled underfoot and thorny branches reaching out to stroke him, leeches dropping from the foliage overhead to fasten on his naked flesh and gorge themselves with blood. No time to stop and pick them off. His prey was closer now. Any moment and . . .

Bolan froze, sensing something on the trail behind him. Turning swiftly, he squinted through the gloom, unable to detect the maker of a sound that had been scarcely audible. The Executioner was sure there had been movement, and the way his skin was crawling told him he was being scrutinized by hostile eyes.

*A dream. It's just a dream.*

No matter, Bolan braced himself for the assault. After several seconds, he wondered why the enemy had not made a move. Bolan was defenseless, save for hands and feet. His adversaries might not find a better time to take him.

But they waited, biding time, lurking invisible in the shadows of the forest. Taunting Bolan with their presence. Forcing him either to turn his naked, unprotected back, or let his own quarry slip away.

Bolan let them see his back as he continued following the trail, expecting the hunters to strike with bullet, blade or claw. When he had covered fifty yards, he knew they meant to follow him instead, prolong the game and see if they could cheat him of his quarry.

Fair enough. The Executioner had played that game before, and he was still alive. Or was he?

Concentrating on his quarry, Bolan did his best to purge the lurking apprehension from his mind. If he was being stalked, the predators would choose a time and place to show themselves. He would be ready for them when they came, or he would die. It was that simple.

Sure.

Unless, of course, he was already dead.

The jungle cleared a little in front of Bolan, and he heard rushing water just ahead—a river, by the sound of it. He wriggled through the clinging undergrowth, aware of creeping things, rodents or reptiles, scuttling away on either side. The trees gave way to muddy slopes, and Bolan stood on the riverbank.

No ordinary river, this. The water was a swirl of reddish-brown as if from mud or silt. Bolan had to look twice to realize that it was blood. From where he stood, the Executioner could see bloody footprints on the opposite bank, leading away toward the trees.

The bloody current was not swift, but too murky to judge its depth. A careless wader might be overwhelmed before he made it halfway to the other shore. He did not know if he could ford the channel of blood . . . but someone had done so and was not far ahead of him. The crimson footprints were not yet dry.

He stepped into the sanguine current, clinging to an overhanging branch, unmindful of the thorns that pierced his palm. The blood was thick and warm, like gravy. Letting go the branch, he took a cautious stride, the river bottom slick and treacherous. Beneath the ooze, he felt a layer of rounded stones. Or were they skulls, embedded in the sludge of centuries?

The blood was rising past his knees now, lapping at his groin. It felt like a thousand sticky fingers tugging his body, urging him to let the current have its way and carry him downstream. It would be easy to relax, accept the warmth and simply float until the last of conscious thought deserted him and he was swept away, insensible, along the jungle's pulsing lifeline. Easy...but the memory of his mission made the Executioner resist.

He felt the hostile eyes again and turned too quickly, almost lost his footing. Unbalanced for an instant, Bolan missed the chance to see his nemesis. The silent jungle mocked him with its shadows.

So near, and yet...

He almost screamed as something brushed his thigh. Turning more cautiously this time, he saw the floating shape—a log?—drift out of reach and out of sight around the nearest bend. A glance upstream revealed other shapes carried lazily on the current toward him. Bolan waited there, midstream, tepid blood around his hips, and let the floating shadows overtake him.

The nearest almost passed him when he caught it, tangling his fingers in a growth that felt like Spanish moss, and pulled it close. The shape was hauntingly familiar. Part of Bolan's mind cried out to him to let it go before he learned the secret. Stolidly the soldier forged ahead, both hands immersed in blood as he rolled over the piece of flotsam to reveal a human face. The eyes were open, filmed with blood.

The thing he had snared was his father's face.

The soldier cried out and staggered as he lost his balance and went down on one knee. The blood swirled up around his chest, spattering his face and shoulders as he struck about him with his hands, attempting to dispel the image of his father's gaping face, awash in crimson. Closing on him now, propelled by a swifter current, the other human-shaped logs revealed faces from his childhood, from his endless war. The soldier recognized a gathering flotilla of his enemies: Gambella, Frenchi, Marinello and Matilda. Nightmare faces, yawning at him, struggling to speak, their voices strangled, full of blood.

A rumbling upstream, as if the floodgates had been opened, and he felt the current gathering momentum. Bolan saw the river choked with corpses, packed together like a human logjam, twisted faces pointing skyward. Something in him snapped. He scrambled to his feet, unmindful of the treacherous footing, the blood around him, as he thrashed toward the bank and sanctuary.

With a dozen strides remaining, Bolan fell headlong, and was immersed in blood. The stuff was in his eyes and ears; he dared not take a breath for fear that he would swallow some of it, and thereby swallow part of *them*. A skull collided with his hip, another butted against his ribs, and suddenly the lifeless hands were clutching him, struggling to hold him under, drown him in the river of blood.

Again, for one eternal instant, Mack Bolan wondered if he had the right to turn away from death. It would be easy to find a place among the dead and let them carry him along...

The soldier's mission called him, and he broke the surface, gasping, beating the hands that tried to pull him down. His fingers found a purchase on the river bottom, digging into empty eye sockets, clinging to the polished skulls, using them to drag himself toward shore. As Bolan reached the muddy bank, he wriggled forward, calling up the desperate reserves of energy that had occasionally served him in the past. A few more yards, a few more moments, and he would be clear.

Dead hands gripped his ankles, talons digging in and reaching higher, for his calves, his thighs. He twisted over onto his back, tried to dislodge the creature with a kick, but his legs were immobilized. The man-thing's head and shoulders were above the surface, the face leering at him, features too far gone for recognition. It was crawling slowly, painfully ashore, using Bolan's naked body as a ladder, snapping yellow, twisted teeth, the raisin eyes intently focused on his groin.

Bolan's blindly groping fingers found a tree root, worked it free of earth and brought it crashing down across the skull of his cadaverous assailant. In the microsecond prior to impact, Bolan saw his bludgeon was not wood after all, but bone. It was the femur from a human skeleton.

Brutally he smashed the long bone down across the head and face of his attacker. Again, and yet again. The bone splintered in his hands, and still he hammered his enemy until the clutching fingers gradually lost their grip, the twisted form retreated, yielding to the bloody current, and was gone.

Bolan lay for several moments on the bank, a livid scarecrow painted crimson head to toe. Then, exhausted, he struggled to his feet and turned to face the jungle. Suddenly a human figure emerged from the shadow of the trees. Startled, he took a backward step, caught himself before he came too near the bloody river. The shadowy figure spoke to him, and Bolan was surprised to find he understood the language.

"I've been waiting for you."

One more step, and he could see the figure's face. It was important to him to see it, for something in the voice had touched a tender chord of recognition. Something...

One more step, and Bolan recognized the face of April Rose.

He moved to wrap his arms around her, and she stopped him with an outstretched hand. He recognized the old, familiar hunger in her eyes, but there was something about her attitude, a distance or reserve, with which the Executioner was not familiar.

"April." It was all he could think of, all he could say.

"You shouldn't be here yet," she told him almost sadly. "Mack, it isn't time."

"I'm here," he answered, trusting in the obvious to make her understand.

The lady shook her head, implacable. "Not yet."

"I've missed you," Bolan said.

"People leave. You can't hang on."

"I can."

She smiled and shook her head again. "Let go."

"Goddammit, April—"

Bolan took a step in her direction, reached for her. Again she raised her hand, palm outward, pressed against his chest. She did not strike him, but the Executioner was staggered by a sudden hammer blow beneath his heart. He toppled backward, sprawling, felt his consciousness fade.

From somewhere high above him, bending to touch him like a specter from a fever dream, the figure that was and wasn't April traced the outline of his cheek with one soft hand.

"Goodbye."

And she was gone.

The soldier had no sense of passing time to know how long he lay there on the muddy riverbank, but he was conscious, suddenly, of a noisy splashing in the river behind him. Reluctantly he struggled to his knees and faced the bloody torrent, found that it had slowed again, the jam of bodies cleared away.

A solitary shape had surfaced and was floundering toward shore. A man this time, instead of animated carrion, with dark hair plastered to his skull by blood, his naked chest and shoulders streaming crimson rivulets. The soldier knew his adversary, smelled him from a distance, rose to his feet before the enemy.

His adversary reached the riverbank and came ashore on hands and knees, remaining on all fours just long enough to shake himself like a dog, before he rose. The words he spoke were April's, but the voice was something else entirely.

"I've been waiting for you."

Sure. Bolan recognized the truth of that immediately, even as he recognized the bloody face.

The face that was his own.

## 18

Bolan sat bolt upright in bed, or tried to, but the pain defeated him. He lay back, eyes and teeth clenched tightly for a moment, waiting for the first debilitating wave to pass. The worst of it was in his side and shoulder, but a separate white-hot brand was pressed against his thigh an inch or two above the knee.

With pain came clarity of thought, and Bolan pushed away the hazy residue of fever dreams to concentrate on here and now. He knew the source of his discomfort, vividly recalled the hostile gunner's strafing run, the bullets snapping all around him, ripping through his flesh. Somehow, against the odds, he was alive...but countless questions were still unanswered in his mind.

For openers, where was he? Survival meant that someone must have found him, scooped him up and carried him away. He had a fleeting memory of being helped to stand, of leaning on another, with his arm around broad shoulders, but the images were fragmentary and disjointed. He must have been discovered by police, for the soldiers of his adversary would have killed him on the spot. And yet the room in which he found himself bore no resemblance to the prison ward of a hospital.

Despite the semidarkness, Bolan could see paintings on the walls, a window opposite his bed with curtains drawn. The bedroom furniture was solid, homey, not institutional. The sheets that covered him to his waist were a cheery floral print, and the bedspread was embroidered, possibly by hand. As Bolan turned his head toward the door to seek the source of filtered light, he noticed carpeting on the floor.

No hospital featured such accommodations; the soldier knew he must be in a private home. The knowledge did not put his mind at ease, by any means. While Bolan's unknown hosts had plainly saved his life, controlled his bleeding, bound his wounds, he had no way of judging what the future held. If he had not been captured by the Tarantella forces, then there was a wild card in the game, and wild cards could be the deadliest of all.

His dream came back to him in bits and pieces, gradually making the progression into conscious memory. The soldier thought of April, as she had appeared within his nightmare, and instinctive, painful loss was tempered by an unaccustomed feeling of relief. He felt almost as if an ancient wound was healed at last, familiar pain remembered now instead of reexperienced with each new day.

It wasn't Bolan's time to die, not yet. Survival was a privilege rather than a curse, and if the Executioner intended to survive, he had to start immediately, with the problems that confronted him. He must meet his hosts and take their measure, read their intentions, and respond accordingly. If there was danger here, he would be forced to stall for time until his strength returned and he had mastered the pain. Aside from being injured, he was naked, in no condition to assert himself. A break, if one was called for, had to wait.

He began by taking stock of his condition, sorting out the trivial discomforts from the pain of battle wounds, evaluating his ability to fight at need. Reclining in the bed, he tensed each arm and leg in turn, surrendering reluctantly when thigh and shoulder wounds demanded to be left alone. The pain in his side had settled to steady, rhythmic throbbing, keeping time with his accelerated pulse.

The bandage on his shoulder looked professional. He pried one corner loose to glimpse the damaged flesh beneath. Someone had cleaned the wound and stitched it, swabbing the area with bright merthiolate to halt infection. Bolan recognized the sutures as commercial thread and knew there would be more pain when they were pulled. But he had lived with worse before and would doubtless live through worse again.

He didn't need to check the wounds of side and thigh; they would be cleaned and sewn identically. A cautious probing with the fingers of his good hand told him the slugs had found their own way out, or else had been removed while he was unconscious. Given his surroundings, so unlike a clinic or a doctor's office, Bolan now was doubly curious about his host's identity.

As if in answer to his thoughts, the soldier overheard voices from what he supposed must be another room or corridor outside his bedroom door. Two voices, by the sound. While he could not understand their words, he marked the different tones of male and female. They might be arguing—he sensed an undertone of anger in the woman's voice, at least—but they were careful to speak softly, probably thinking he was still unconscious.

He glanced again around the darkened room, searching for an object that might serve as a weapon if necessary, finding nothing to fill the bill. His hosts had either taken care to check the room, or else had never kept lethal objects there. Bolan didn't know which thought bothered him the most—being held a prisoner, or being at the mercy of a good Samaritan whose kindness might destroy them all.

Once before he had been rescued, badly wounded, from a shoot-out in Pittsfield. Val Querente had been his angel then, and his intrusion on her life had placed her in grave danger. The Executioner had inadvertently repaid her loving kindness with a curse of fear, and his sense of guilt was not alleviated by the fact that Val had found sanctuary with a federal officer who loved her dearly, had raised his precious brother Johnny as her own. So many decent lives, on intersecting Bolan's, had been brutally snuffed out. He wondered for a moment if imprisonment by enemies might not be preferable.

At least when Bolan dealt with enemies he knew precisely what to do, the steps to take to eliminate the danger, neutralize the threat. His problem came in dealing with the friends and allies who, from time to time, attached themselves to his war. He was an albatross around their necks, bringing them suffering, untimely death.

A sound of footsteps drew closer to the bedroom door. Relaxing on the pillow, Bolan closed his eyes, watched through the slits of narrowed eyelids as a slender woman opened the door. She was in her fifties, aging gracefully, from all appearances still fit despite her years. He had never seen her before.

She was staring at him, frowning. Her manner radiated disapproval, tempered with a grudging sympathy she was unable to suppress. He guessed she did not want him in her home but had grudgingly agreed to the intrusion, granting sanctuary to a man who carried danger with him like a plague bacillus in his blood. He wondered if the lady knew how perilous this exercise in mercy could prove to be.

There was only one way to resolve the riddle in his mind. Bolan opened his eyes. The lady didn't flinch, although she looked embarrassed for a second when he seemed to catch her watching him. Instead of speaking to the Executioner directly, she retreated through the doorway, turning back to glance over her shoulder.

"He's awake."

A muffled answer—male—from somewhere in the other room, and heavy footsteps over carpeting. A taller, broader shadow momentarily blocked the light, circling around the lady, one hand feeling for the light switch beside the door. A blaze of artificial brilliance made the soldier wince, but there was nothing wrong with his eyes. He would have recognized the new arrival anywhere.

Al Weatherbee.

The craggy face called up a host of jumbled memories, some painful, some almost amusing. Weatherbee was the first detective to encounter Bolan at the outset of his private war; he had tried to warn the soldier off before the feud got out of hand. He hadn't known—could not have known—that it had gone too far the moment Bolan's father took his old revolver from the closet shelf. Before the echoes of that fateful fusillade had died away, before the neighbors got up nerve enough to telephone for the police, Mack Bolan's fate was sealed. The war had been inevitable; only its longevity had come as a surprise.

The soldier's mind was racing now, trying to untangle all the possibilities suggested by his presence in the home of a detective working homicide. He clearly was not under house arrest; the captain would not push his luck that far, exceeding any vestige of legitimate authority. That meant Weatherbee was covering Bolan's presence here for reasons of his own. Bolan could not even start to look inside the other's mind.

"Long time," the captain said, and let it go at that.

"I meant to say hello in Texas," Bolan told him, "but I never got a chance."

"No sweat. I noticed you were otherwise engaged."

He dragged a straight chair over to the soldier's bedside and reversed it, straddling the seat with both arms folded on the top.

"So what brings you home?"

"Would you believe I'm on vacation?"

"Not unless your travel agent's Ernie Tarantella."

Bolan glanced around him at the furnishings once more. Illuminated now, the room felt dated, as if time was frozen here. Behind Al Weatherbee, a young man in his teens or early twenties smiled at Bolan from inside a picture frame. The young man seemed to be in uniform.

"Should I be asking for a lawyer?"

The homicide detective frowned and spread his hands. "What for? Were you expecting an arrest?"

"It crossed my mind."

"Forget about it. I'm retired."

The soldier arched an eyebrow. "Oh? Since when?"

"Since eighteen months ago."

That was well before the firestorm in McLary County, Texas. A picture had begun to form in Bolan's mind, and it was not entirely reassuring. If the former chief of homicide was not involved professionally in Bolan's case, then he was pursuing it on his own time, at his own expense, for reasons of his own. Those reasons might be totally innocuous—and then again, something in the ex-captain's psyche might compel him to continue the pursuit. He might be dangerous to Bolan, to his war, especially while the Executioner was helpless, under his control. If he was working out some twisted scheme of vengeance...

As soon as the suggestion surfaced, Bolan put it out of mind. There was no fire of animosity in the former homicide detective's eyes, no hint of madness in his voice or attitude. If he wanted Bolan dead, why had he taken in a hunted fugitive and stitched his wounds? Why had he not left Bolan to be captured or to die?

The captain might have something working in his mind, but it was not a murder plot—the Executioner was sure of that.

"What brings you back?" Weatherbee asked again, his voice intruding on the soldier's thoughts.

A simple lie might be enough to put him off, but instinct told the Executioner to play it straight with Weatherbee. The man had saved his life.

"I got an invitation."

"Oh?"

Bolan laid it out for Weatherbee, plain and simple, from Hartford and the Giulianno-Petrosina conflict, through the cul-de-sac encounter and the destruction of his safe house, to the business card from TIF, and the recent events in Pittsfield. When he was finished, Weatherbee said nothing for a moment, mulling over all that he had heard, his face contorted in a frown.

"You figure someone's out to settle old scores?" he asked at last.

The soldier tried to shrug, thought better of it when his wounded shoulder screamed in protest. "It's a possibility. There aren't too many of the old crew still around."

"Damned few. The ones you left have mostly moved away. I hear a couple of them even got religion."

Bolan smiled, surprised to find himself enjoying Weatherbee's company. "There must have been some family."

"Oh, sure. You want to figure in the widows, orphans, all the aunts and uncles and second cousins, you could probably fill a phone book."

"Any one of them could have a motive. Some of them are bound to have connections, opportunities."

The captain's frown became a full-blown scowl. "That's too much ground to cover. We could never find 'em all."

The soldier was surprised to hear his former adversary speaking in terms of mutual cooperation. Cautiously he left the ball in play.

"I think it's possible to narrow down the field."

"How's that?"

"The business card," he said. "I'd look for a connection back to TIF."

"Laurenti's outfit? Could be something there, I guess. I'd have to tap some files to get information on survivors."

"Can you do that?"

"I'm retired, not excommunicated," Weatherbee replied. "I've still got some connections on the job."

"Why bother?" Bolan asked, no longer able to restrain his curiosity.

The captain looked confused. "Why not?"

"You know the risks involved. You're way out on a limb, already, harboring a fugitive. I'm curious about your reasons."

"Maybe I'm pissed off because the brass hats put me out to pasture," Weatherbee responded. "Maybe I can help you show 'em up."

The soldier shook his head. "It doesn't wash."

The former chief of homicide was silent for another moment, staring at his hands. When he spoke, his voice was thoughtful.

"No, I guess it doesn't," Weatherbee replied. "Let's say I've had some time to think about the system, how it works—and how it sometimes doesn't work. The system didn't work for you, your family, and it didn't work for me. I know that sounds like sour grapes, but I'm so far beyond that now, it doesn't matter anymore.

"While I was working seven days a week to clean the streets, the whole establishment I was working for got turned around somehow, twisted up and tied in knots. I don't believe it's all corrupt...but the system needs an enema. It doesn't take a Ph.D. to figure that much out."

Weatherbee laughed out loud, but with a trace of bitterness. "Maybe the brass hats thought they were doing me a favor when they cut me loose. Who wants to spend his whole life paddling against the tide, for God's sake? But the job gets in your blood, like a disease. You can't just take it off and hang it in the closet with your uniform." The captain hesitated, frowned again. "I don't know if I'm making any sense, but that's the way I feel. That's why you're here."

And Bolan read the message, five-by-five. The guy was talking dedication, not to an assignment or a uniform, but to an ideal. Justice. Law and order. Duty. He was making perfect sense from where the soldier sat. For all of his disguises and charades, the Executioner had never really taken off the uniform he'd worn in Vietnam.

The smiling face behind Al Weatherbee caught Bolan's eye again. He nodded toward the photograph.

"Your boy?"

The ex-captain didn't have to turn around and check. He simply nodded once. "Marines. He caught a VC mortar outside Pleiku."

"A lot of good men bought it in the Nam."

Weatherbee rose and returned the chair near the window where it belonged, lingering a moment by the photo of his son. He stretched out a hand toward the picture, hesitated short of contact, finally withdrew.

"You need your rest," he said. He sounded as if there was something in his throat. "You've lost a lot of blood. I wasn't sure you'd come around."

"Who did the needlework?"

"That's Alice," Weatherbee responded, nodding toward the open doorway and whatever lay beyond. "Used to be a nurse before . . . well, anyway, she's kept her hand in."

"Thank her for me."

"You can thank her for yourself. She isn't thrilled to have you here, I'll tell you that. We had some words about it, then we had *no* words about it, if you get my drift. She'll come around. Just give her time."

"How much time do I have?"

"I'd say a week at least, all things considered. Maybe more."

Too long. The soldier frowned and kept his reservations to himself. His host was in the doorway now, reaching for the light switch that would return him to the shadow world of sleep and bloody dreams.

"I'll try you on some dinner by and by. You get some sleep now, build your strength up. You'll be needing it before you're through."

"I owe you one."

"We'll talk about it later."

Darkness, as the door swung shut. Exhausted by the conversation, Bolan felt as if his conscious thoughts had been connected somehow to the light switch, blurring now and fading into shadows. There was time to recognize a certain feeling of security, and time enough to realize that it was false. He was not safe with Weatherbee; the captain and his wife were not safe while Bolan was beneath their roof. His presence was a curse upon the house, an omen of disaster.

But Weatherbee had recognized the risks, had plainly weighed them before he made his move. For now, conditionally, he was on Mack Bolan's side. Whatever his eventual intentions, Weatherbee would not betray the soldier to police, or to his enemies outside the law.

That was enough for now; it would have to do.

Relaxing with a conscious effort, Bolan focused on the inner darkness, let it carry him away to jungles where the rivers ran with blood, and every shadow that pursued him was his own.

## 19

"He really let 'em have it."

"This is nothing," Pappas answered. "If the cruisers hadn't interrupted him, he would've brought the house down."

Lawrence watched the paramedics haul another body through what remained of the shattered sliding doors that opened onto Ernie Tarantella's patio. The line of shrouded forms was growing: eight already, and there might be others still inside, or scattered around the property. They would be checking the grounds more thoroughly when Pappas got the extra uniforms he had requested. In the meantime, they would have to work the house. And wait.

"You'd think that after Ingenito, they'd have been ready for him," Lawrence said.

"They were. Hell, they *thought* they were." John Pappas took another disgusted glance along the line of corpses. "How do you prepare for Bolan?"

Lawrence shook his head and turned to stare across the sloping lawn, in the direction of some trees that marked the line of Tarantella's property. The alley was invisible from where he stood, but Lawrence had it firmly fixed in mind, knew it intersected with adjoining streets.

"I'd say he came across the grounds from that direction, on their flank." He pointed toward the trees. "First sound of sirens, he was out of here and back the way he came. He could have parked his car on any one of half a dozen streets back there, within an easy sixty-second run.''

The captain nodded wearily. "It fits.''

"I've got a team from traffic checking, just in case. So far, they've turned a rental that the neighbors can't account for, one block over, but some families are not at home. We won't be sure of anything until we talk to everybody, check the rental through records at the agency.''

"Keep on it," Pappas said. "It's slim, but we've got nothing else." He turned to peer at Lawrence, squinting in the morning light. "What makes you think our boy might be on foot?''

The sergeant shrugged. "I don't . . . not really . . . but we had a telephone report of automatic weapons fire from neighbors over where the alley empties out on Fisher. It's a long shot, granted, but if Tarantella had some gunners running grids around the neighborhood, they might have spotted Bolan on the fly and cut him off before he made it to his wheels.''

"More likely, those earwitnesses were listening to Ernie's Waterloo right here.''

"No, sir, they swear it was machine guns, loud, like in their own front yard. The other fireworks didn't even wake them up.''

John Pappas scowled and shook his head. "We couldn't get that lucky. Hell, if our boy's on foot, where is he? You don't lose a one-man army in a neighborhood like this.''

"We're working on it," Lawrence told him. "As I said, the traffic team has run across some vacancies, and Bolan might be hiding out in one of those. Your average person here keeps banker's hours, and they don't start running sweeps around their property first thing in the morning.''

"Today, I wish to hell they did.''

"We'll find him, if he's here. But first, we need more uniforms."

"They're on the way." The captain thought of something else and turned toward Lawrence, brightening. "Why don't you see if you can get hold of Weatherbee? I'd like to have him take a look around here while everything's still fresh."

The sergeant had to work at hiding his contempt, the instant irritation welling up inside. "You figure he can tell you something that the lab boys can't?"

"I wouldn't be surprised." The captain noticed his incredulity and let it pass. "He knows how Bolan thinks, the way he looks at things. If Bolan had to leave his wheels behind, the way you think he might've, Al might have a jump on where the guy would go to ground."

"I said it was a long shot."

"It's a shot, all right? And it's a damned sight better than the pocketful of nothing we've been holding up to now. I want him here while there's something left to see."

"What is this guy, some kind of psychic?"

"No," the captain answered stonily, "he's just a copy with damned near thirty years' experience who knows our perpetrator inside out."

"He didn't know the bastard well enough to bag him when he had the chance." Frank Lawrence felt his irritation grow into sudden anger, knew he should rein it in before he went too far. "We've got Al Weatherbee to thank for everything Bolan's done since he was here the last time."

Pappas bristled. "Sergeant, don't mistake my order for an invitation to debate the issue. Make the call, and do it now."

"Yes, sir."

Goddammit, Lawrence asked himself, when will you be smart enough to keep your opinions to yourself?

He turned away from Pappas, fuming inwardly, determined not to jeopardize his position any further by showing his disgust. If the captain wanted Weatherbee, it wouldn't hurt to roust the old man out of bed and let him do his thing. Forensic would be finished by the time he got there, anyway, unless more bodies turned up on the property. A civilian couldn't damage the investigation if the captain kept him in his place.

It galled Frank Lawrence, all the same. Al Weatherbee had let the Executioner escape him once. He had been called on as a Bolan expert by other jurisdictions, all without result. Each time he offered sage advice, the bastard waltzed away without a scratch, to kill and kill again.

In business and in pro sports, losers were eliminated. In government, the sorry specimens were voted out of office. But in law enforcement, they were often enshrined on pedestals, revered as experts, even though their vaunted expertise resulted in embarrassment and failure. Has-beens seemed to hang around forever, peddling their "knowledge" to the brass, congressional committees and the media, and the public ate it up, never seemed to realize they were being taken for a ride.

The brass had waited too damned long to pull the plug on Weatherbee. Now that he was out, the idiots were sniffing after him again, soliciting opinions from the failure who had shamed them to begin with. It was stupid, suicidal. But the brass had not requested Lawrence's opinion—and they wouldn't, not while he was wearing sergeant's stripes.

When all the bullshit had been swept away, it would be Sergeant Lawrence who stopped the Executioner, brought him down and put an end to his private war. Lawrence owed it to the citizens who paid his salary, and to the stupid bastards at the top who wouldn't listen when they had the chance. Most of all, he owed it to himself.

To Frank Laurenti, Jr.

He changed his name before he joined the Corps, for reasons of security. A friend of young Francesco's father had a way with documents, and was sympathetic to the boy's predicament. A military background couldn't hurt, no matter what the young man's goal in life, but paperwork—birth certificate, driver's license, this and that—could ruin him before he got a decent start. It took a member of the brotherhood to understand how vindictive some members of the government and media could be. If they were looking into Frank Laurenti's business dealings, they would soon be looking at his family, examining their lives under a microscope in search of any blemish.

Francesco's mother had been through a lot, but when the old man had bought it, right out there in public, she had reached her limit. The light behind her eyes had flickered, died. For the final eighteen months she had walked in a kind of dreamworld, never really there at all. Sometimes she would sit and stare at nothing, trembling, whispering to herself. The cabbie swore she was talking to herself the afternoon she wandered in front of his cab in heavy midtown traffic. Frank believed him, and let the cabbie live.

The Corps had taught young Laurenti to kill in a hundred different ways, and had given him the opportunity to practice what he'd learned in Vietnam. Newborn at seventeen, the phony signatures of missing parents scarcely dry on his enlistment papers, Frankie Lawrence took to combat as a fish to water, savoring the sights and sounds and smells of violent death like a necrophiliac gourmet. The young man recognized that he was passing through a phase, eradicating some of the aggression and frustration that had dogged him since his father's death, but at the same time he was learning, preparing for the mission of his life.

He meant to kill Mack Bolan. Not because his father was innocent—he'd known the truth by then—but rather as a debt of honor to his family...but there was more. He had to stop the Executioner because the man's existence was an affront to justice. Every day that Bolan lived, law and order were injured and humiliated. The failure of law enforcement agencies to bring him down was a disgrace.

Frank Lawrence didn't even want to think about the rumors that his quarry had been working for the government, a licensed killer in the service of his country. Such things happened, certainly...but Bolan? It was preposterous. The man had murdered thousands, and if none of them had been precisely pure at heart, what difference did it make? The man had set himself above the law, above society. He had become a rogue. A menace to be hunted down, eradicated.

In the hunter's own good time.

Before they brought him home from Vietnam, Frank Lawrence knew what he had to do. He needed work, a job where he could be useful, while simultaneously keeping track of Bolan, waiting for the time when he could make his move and bring the curtain down. With his experience, he settled easily on a career in law enforcement, drawn by the paramilitary trappings of the job, the opportunities to strike a blow for justice while he bided his time. The Pittsfield force maintained an open file on Bolan, adding evidence from here and there as it became available. The file became Lawrence's bible. He memorized it, front to back, ingesting every detail of the soldier's life. Sometimes he thought he knew Mack Bolan better than the bastard knew himself.

He knew enough, for instance, to realize he would never trap the soldier through routine. The Executioner was unpredictable, appearing yesterday in Florida, today in Washington, tomorrow in Timbuktu. The failure of police and mafiosi, Lawrence knew, had been a failure of technique. Both sides had dogged Bolan's footsteps here and there around the globe; they were always just behind him, crashing in the front door as their prey slipped out the back. Yet despite repeated failures, they had never changed their methods. Lawrence knew it would take an accident for either group to bring the soldier down.

You couldn't stalk a man like Bolan; it was a waste of time. Instead, you had to manufacture situations that the man could not resist, put out your lures and wait for the Executioner to come to you. It might take years—it *had* taken years—but in the end, a patient hunter would be rewarded for his persistence.

Throughout the years of Bolan's private war, Frank Lawrence had collected clippings, law enforcement circulars and rumors from the underground. When Bolan "died" in Central Park, the fledgling homicide detective had been stricken, suddenly deprived of purpose. He had taken sick leave, driven to New York and started an investigation of his own. The Pittsfield badge had opened doors and files that would otherwise have been closed to Lawrence, and he had emerged with a conviction that the Executioner was still alive.

He kept the theory to himself. There were times in the next few years when Lawrence thought he was going crazy, playing mind games, keeping his longtime enemy alive to give his own life some meaning. But there were other times when Lawrence knew that he was right, his vision corrob-

orated by events abroad: the execution of a ranking ter-
rorist, frustration of a plan to slaughter some minority, a
strike against scattered remnants of the Mafia. And in the
end, with Bolan's sudden and mysterious return from nowhere, Lawrence had been proved right.

Beyond a certain academic interest, Lawrence didn't
care where Bolan had been hiding. He was back, beyond
the shadow of a doubt, and that was good enough. More
years might pass before the hunter could perfect his plans,
but Lawrence had the strength and will to wait. He had his
hate to keep him warm.

Lawrence hated Bolan for many reasons. First, for
murdering his father, though the crime was understand-
able in terms of the vendetta, the repaying of a debt that
sprang from blood. The men of Triangle Finance had
brought destruction on themselves, but just as Bolan had
avenged the deaths of his father, mother, sister, so Lawrence felt compelled to do the same.

For he hated Bolan for the murder of his mother, also.
Never mind the talk about an accident, the cabbie's sworn
description of a demented woman who had missed the
crosswalk by fifty feet. Cecile Laurenti had begun to die
the moment she heard the news from Commerce Street,
and Bolan might as well have made it six for six. It took a
while for her to die, but she was one of his victims, all the
same.

Above all else, he hated Bolan for compelling him, while
still a child, to face the truth about his father's "business," Frank Laurenti's crimes and underworld connections. How long might Lawrence have lived in blissful
ignorance, before the old man was indicted or some hungry journalist got wind of something rotten down at TIF?
If he had been allowed to cherish some illusions through
adolescence, to worship his father as a young man should,

instead of being forced to hide his face in shame, how different his life would have been.

The Executioner had robbed Lawrence of his family name, his birthright. This was the loss, above all others, that Lawrence would never forgive. He could have looked the other way as Bolan kicked the shit out of the brotherhood, terrorists...but he could never forget, never forgive, the crime against himself, his family honor.

After years of planning, years of waiting, the opportunity had opened up in Hartford. Bolan had been close, in Jersey, mopping up what was left of the Marinello empire; a shooting war so close would be irresistible to him. And so it had been. Bolan showed himself in Hartford, took the hunter's bait and followed him to Pittsfield.

The first surprise, for Lawrence, had been Bolan's disappearance from the lawn on Fisher Drive. He had seen with his own eyes that the guy was hit. No doubt about the range, the blood, the way he had collapsed on impact, loose and tumbling like a shattered mannequin. The cruisers should have found him lying there, but had found nothing.

Wounded as he must have been, the Executioner had disappeared. It made no difference to the hunter that he had left his rental car behind. In fact, if Bolan had escaped on foot, the mystery was even deeper. He should have left a bloody trail that any child could follow. His corpse should have been found by now, stretched out beneath some hedgerow.

Except they hadn't found him yet...which meant he had been assisted from the scene. The bastard had an ally somewhere, who had taken pity on him—or who might have been there waiting for him all along.

How thoroughly had Homicide checked out the Bolan family connections in the early days? Was there a second cousin stashed away somewhere in the vicinity, prepared to offer aid and comfort in the soldier's time of need? A friend, perhaps, who still remembered Bolan's parents from the good old days?

The bastard had a brother who had disappeared, Frank Lawrence knew. There was speculation that the younger Bolan helped his brother to escape a guarded courtroom out in Texas. Still, there were a hundred different stories coming out of Texas, and the sheriff had been less than helpful when it came to spelling out what had happened in his one-horse town.

If Bolan's brother was alive and kicking, someone ought to know about it. If he was in Pittsfield, someone could discover him and rout him out. The hunter really didn't think he was dealing with a pair of Bolans now, but he could not afford to leave any stone unturned.

Whatever Lawrence had to do, whatever sacrifice he had to make, he was prepared to go the limit. Bolan had eluded him this time, but Lawrence would never rest until he stood above the soldier's broken body, took the bastard's pulse himself and verified his death. It was all that he had lived for, everything he cared about in life.

If calling out Al Weatherbee could help—or if it just gave Lawrence breathing room, away from Pappas and his watchful eye—then it was worth the aggravation. Maybe the old man could teach him something, after all. If nothing else, he might be useful as a bad example; Lawrence could avoid the same old, tired mistakes that Weatherbee's investigations made. It might even be fun to watch the has-been go through his paces, frowning down his nose and acting like God's gift to law enforcement.

Just as long as Weatherbee did not intrude upon the hunter's mission, try to block him from achieving his life-long goal. If the old man became an obstacle, then he would have to be removed, effectively, permanently.

Nothing could stand in Frank Lawrence's way now. His honor and his life were on the line. He had to find Mack Bolan now, before some other cop lucked in with the collar of a lifetime. It was his destiny.

## 20

Bolan took the push-ups slowly, favoring his injured shoulder at the outset, gradually picking up the pace until he reached the limits of endurance. Teeth clenched tight against the pain, his torso slick with sweat, Bolan pushed those limits, forced the tender muscles to respond on cue. When he began to weaken, he changed positions, rolled over on his back and started doing sit-ups to improve the tone of the muscles on his injured side.

Ten days had passed since Bolan awoke in Weatherbee's spare bedroom, three days since Alice Weatherbee removed his stitches. The process had been painful, and the woman had faltered early on, when Bolan's leg wound started bleeding. When he'd offered to complete the job himself, she'd got angry with him. Impatiently, she had pushed his hands away, finishing the process with grim determination. When all his dressings had been changed and she'd prepared to leave, the soldier was surprised to see a cautious smile on her face. But she was stern in her demand that he rest and give the tender flesh some time to heal.

He had begun to exercise next morning, knowing she would be annoyed if she knew, knowing also that he was running short of time. He could not shelter with the Weatherbees forever. His war was waiting for him in the streets; his enemy was waiting for the Executioner to show himself.

Al Weatherbee had saved his life. The soldier cherished no illusions that he could have survived the Tarantella ambush on his own. If Weatherbee had not arrived, Bolan's options would have been reduced to death or prison, which both came out the same. He would have been a dead man; his enemies would have won.

He had been granted a reprieve, no more, no less. His mission had not changed. The hunter who had stalked him from Connecticut to Pittsfield was still out there, watching for the prey to show himself. In Bolan's gut, he knew the hunter would be waiting for him if he stayed in hiding for a year, a decade. Instinct told him that his nemesis was motivated not by greed or simple anger, but by something much more vital, much more personal.

The hunter was conducting a vendetta, and he probably was acting on his own. The kind of slick, precision planning that the Executioner had witnessed up to now was rarely achieved by groups. If a dozen men were chosen for a mission, their commander faced a dozen opportunities for error. But a single, dedicated man could work apparent miracles if he had done his homework, gathered the necessary equipment.

That was the secret of the Executioner's success, and the method should work just as well for his determined adversary. The enemy was one man, dedicated to his mission, motivated by some inner rage that Bolan could appreciate from his own experience.

At first he had believed the gunner in the dark Camaro must be one of Tarantella's men, a mobile sentry running the perimeter, but Bolan had revised his thinking lately. If the hunter had been able to predict Bolan's moves in Hartford, wire his safe house with explosives, direct the soldier to a different battlefield, then he should be equally capable of dogging Bolan's tracks in Pittsfield. As he recuperated swiftly, Bolan had become convinced that his brush with death was engineered not by a lowly Tarantella gunsel, but by that same mysterious antagonist.

It all made sense. Manny Ingenito, hit by a slick imposter who wanted Bolan's name in headlines and on APBs before he made his final move. The gunner had parked on the track of Bolan's retreat from Tarantella's shooting gallery, ready to take him down as soon as he showed himself.

The hunter wanted Bolan dead, for sure. But more important, he wanted Bolan dead in Pittsfield, for symbolic reasons or to exorcise some private demons of his own. Somehow it all tied in to TIF, but there were still some pieces missing from the puzzle.

The soldier had not seen his guns since waking from a fever dream ten days before. He knew he had been armed when Weatherbee found him, and there had been backup weapons in his rental car. By now detectives surely would have used the car to try to identify the driver. In time, he would be forced to ask Weatherbee about his guns.

In time.

The sit-ups had exhausted Bolan. He realized painfully how far he had to go before he would be ready to confront his enemy. The hunter would be waiting for him, as would Homicide investigators, patrolmen, Girrardi's soldiers, maybe mob reinforcements out of Boston or New York. An army against one man. And he would take those odds, because he had no choice.

In time.

But not today. Not yet.

A sound of footsteps, muffled by the carpeting outside the door. Bolan lay immobile, listening. It would be

Weatherbee or Alice, listening to find out if he was up and working out. Despite the recent thaw, some cracks in her facade of disapproval, Bolan knew the woman would be glad to see him go. As for Al Weatherbee…he did not have a fix on that one yet.

Determined not to let them find him slacking, Bolan began another set of sit-ups, grimacing against the pain. The healing flesh was holding, and he knew that it would see him through.

He would survive until they killed him, right. Bolan almost laughed aloud at the irony of his condition. He was being nursed to health by strangers, in the certain knowledge that he would be going out to risk his life again as soon as he was able. Bolan was reminded of the medical attention lavished on some death row prisoners, maintaining them in perfect health for their date with the executioner.

It would be Bolan's turn to face his judgment soon, and he intended to be fit for the appointment. If he fumbled, failed, it would not be through careless lack of preparation. If he lost it all, he would have done his best.

In his heart, he was already looking forward to his final confrontation with the hunter. He was eager for the one-on-one that would resolve their private war.

In time.

When he was ready.

Soon.

OUTSIDE THE BEDROOM DOOR, Al Weatherbee stood listening. He heard the soldier's heavy breathing, knew that he was working out to regain the strength and stamina sapped by days in bed. Bolan would soon be ready to continue his war. Weatherbee could feel his injured houseguest chafing at the bit to avenge himself against the enemy who had come so close to killing him.

The sounds of strenuous exertion ceased. Weatherbee moved on along the corridor, embarrassed at having overheard. It was his house, after all.... But Bolan raised a wall of privacy around himself, despite the extraordinary circumstances, and attempts to penetrate that wall made Weatherbee feel he was encroaching on the warrior's soul.

There had been time for conversation in the past few days, between naps and meals and bouts of exercise. In Tommy's room. The former homicide detective knew that some of his confused feelings came from having that room occupied again, however briefly. It was almost tempting to pretend that Tommy had returned, that he had walked away from that barrage of mortar fire outside Pleiku. But Tommy wasn't ever coming home, and it was foolish to use Mack Bolan as a surrogate.

So much about the soldier spoke to Weatherbee of bygone days—the war in Vietnam, the violence that had shaken Pittsfield during Bolan's blitz, the sudden shift in Weatherbee's career—that he was suddenly oppressed by déjà vu. It was incredible, the way those intervening years seemed to be stripped away.

He paused before a decorative mirror in the hallway, stared at his face, his hair, and knew at once the past could never be recaptured. History was carved in stone. He could no more resurrect his son or his career than Bolan could regain the murdered members of his family. Whatever might be waiting for them in the future, neither of them could do a goddamned thing about yesterday.

He made a wry face at his reflection in the mirror and continued toward the kitchen, following the smell of eggs and bacon to its source. As always, Alice heard him coming, turned to offer him the quizzical expression that had recently replaced her smile.

"Is he awake?"

"He's working out. I don't know how the hell he does it."

Alice frowned and shook her head. "He should be careful. He could hurt himself again."

Weatherbee could not resist a smile; he knew her attitude toward Bolan had been changing. His presence in the house still concerned Alice deeply, but Weatherbee could sense her slowly warming to the patient, seeing Bolan in a different, if not entirely sympathetic, light. She would be glad to see him safely gone, and yet . . .

"I don't suppose there's any chance they'll just forget about him?"

"No."

He didn't have to ask who "they" might be. The soldier had enough attention focused on him at the moment to satisfy the most conceited of celebrities. After ten days with no new developments the local press was speculating that Bolan might have slipped away, but the detectives under Pappas remained on full alert. The members of Girrardi's family were ready, too, to move in force the moment Bolan showed himself. There was not the remotest chance that either side would let the soldier slip their minds.

Even so, it wasn't cops or mafiosi that concerned the former homicide detective. Although his houseguest had been silent on the subject, Weatherbee was convinced that someone else was stalking Bolan, someone independent of both the law and the mob. Uncertain how to raise the subject with Bolan, Weatherbee was waiting for something to suggest itself. And time was slipping through his fingers.

"What will you do?"

The question had been there, unvoiced, for the past ten days, and still it took him by surprise. He stared at Alice for a moment, frowning, knowing he should have an answer, a solution to the problem thrust into their lives through no fault of hers. The burden rested squarely on his shoulders, and he had had ample time to think it over, but . .

"I don't know yet," he told her honestly.

She did not scold him for his indecision, but her voice was sad as she removed their breakfast from the stove.

"He'll need to leave us soon."

It took a moment, but he finally realized she was speaking for the soldier's sake rather than her own. She understood the urgency of his mission, his need to carry on.

"I know."

It was the only answer he could think of, and it wasn't good enough. There should be something else he could say.

"There should be some way . . . something we could do to help him."

Alice's unexpected words struck Weatherbee silent. Despite the thaw in her reserve, he had not understood how deeply Bolan's plight had moved her. The sudden knowledge left him speechless for a minute.

"I could ask around," he said at last, afraid of overstepping hidden bounds and shattering her mood. "I might pick up some information he could use."

She faced him squarely, and her voice quavered as she responded. "Just as long as you protect yourself."

"Of course."

"It must be very dangerous."

"I guess so." Weatherbee was shamed by the attempt to casually dismiss her fears. "It is."

"Be careful."

"Yes."

She put her arms around him and held him tightly for a moment, then turned away to serve the eggs and bacon.

"Will you call him for breakfast?"

"Yes."

He detoured through the master bedroom, reaching up to lift a lumpy O.D. bundle down from overhead. The duffel bag was heavy; its contents clanked as he held it in his arms. It held the Uzi submachine gun, sidearms, webbing and other military gear Bolan had been wearing when the former chief of homicide half carried him across the threshold of his home. Bolan would be asking after his weapons soon enough. It would not hurt to let him have them now.

The heavy duffel dragged one shoulder down as Weatherbee walked on to Tommy's room. To Bolan's room. He knocked and waited for an answer before entering. The soldier faced him, sitting upright on the bed, his back against the wall.

Weatherbee crossed the room and set the duffel bag at Bolan's feet.

"I thought you might be needing these," he said.

TEN DAYS, AND LAWRENCE KNEW that if the bastard didn't surface soon, the chances of a satisfactory conclusion to his hunt were slim. Or nil. Already, sarcastic newspaper editorials were announcing that Bolan had escaped again, that once more the authorities had failed to do their job. No matter that the bastard couldn't possibly have cleared the city limits; no one but Lawrence knew that he was wounded, and Lawrence could not reveal his knowledge without coming under suspicion himself.

He knew Bolan must have gone to ground somewhere in Pittsfield, but the questions still remained: if Bolan was alive, where was he? If he was dead, why had his body not been found?

Too many questions. If Lawrence didn't find some answers soon, he would be up shit creek, for real.

The local mafiosi didn't have the Executioner, that was certain. They were still on full alert, their operations buttoned down while soldiers stood a wary watch around Girrardi's properties and Tarantella's street concessions. For the moment, mob expansion had been brought to a standstill, and the authorities owed the bastard for that, at least.

But it was not the mob that worried the sergeant. He could deal with members of the brotherhood, as he had dealt with them in Hartford, as he had dealt with Manny Ingenito and his hardman. Once the Executioner had been disposed of, Lawrence looked forward to performing his duty as a lawman with no distractions, driving savages and scumbags off the streets of Pittsfield.

But until he had an answer to the Bolan riddle, he could think of nothing else. The bastard's disappearance had him worried. He had no handle on the problem, no damned way around the mental block that had been plaguing him for days.

There was an outside chance that Bolan might have crawled away to die. One family on Fisher Drive was in Europe, their house, one block from the location of the shoot-out, was locked up tight. While Frank Lawrence didn't think the soldier could have traveled half that distance unassisted, it was possible. With no evidence to back the theory up, a warrant could not be obtained; a search would have to wait until the travelers returned.

But Lawrence knew in his gut that Bolan wasn't rotting in the vacationers' living room. The bastard was still out there, somewhere, alive. Lawrence was certain that Bolan was still in Pittsfield, healing, waiting till he was fit to face his adversary one-on-one again.

If Lawrence was right, then he had a chance to nail the Executioner yet. But where? How? If Bolan had not been arrested, had not been caught and killed by the mob, had not escaped on foot, then where the hell was he?

Lawrence thought often about the car he had passed as he sped from the scene of the shooting, certain that Bolan lay dead or dying behind him. A Buick four-door, he remembered, but could not visualize the style, or pinpoint the year, or the color. He had been anxious to keep his face turned, to prevent the other motorist from making even a tentative ID, and so he had not glimpsed the other driver's face.

Had Bolan been picked up by the driver of the Buick? Would anyone in Pittsfield knowingly help him escape? Would anyone pick up a bloody stranger from the roadside?

Certainly.

The sergeant knew enough of Bolan's story to know the bastard had been sheltered by civilians more than once. Right there in Pittsfield, in the early days of his campaign, a lonely woman had adopted Bolan, offered him her home and who could say what else for the duration of his war. Whatever happened once could happen twice, and there was every chance that Bolan had met another good Samaritan.

But who?

His wounds had been serious, Lawrence knew. His savior would be equipped to deal with major bullet wounds and blood loss, only if the nosy fucker was a nurse or doctor. That was something to pursue. But however Bolan had got clear of the battlefield, Lawrence's major concern now was driving him out from under cover.

Perhaps if Lawrence turned the heat up, made the press and public think Bolan was renewing his offensive, he could force the soldier's hand. If nothing else, it would prevent Girrardi's mob from growing so confident that they reopened their operations prematurely. And if Bolan took the bait, well, that would be one hell of a bonus. If he didn't, Lawrence would have to devise another plan.

But he had time. He had been waiting half a lifetime, and he could wait another, if it came to that, for one more shot at Bolan. One more opportunity to bag the man who'd killed Lawrence's father, destroyed his mother, ruined his life.

The sergeant could afford to wait till hell froze over.

And if hell froze over, he could wait some more.

For Bolan. For the opportunity to watch him die.

## 21

"That done enough to suit you?"

Bolan did not have to check the slab of beef. Its rich aroma had been taunting him throughout the afternoon, since Alice Weatherbee had slipped it in the oven.

"Perfect."

"I prefer it rare, myself, but Alice raises hell about cholesterol and such. You'd think she wanted me to live forever."

Bolan smiled. "It might be worth a try."

"Like hell."

He was alone with Weatherbee. The captain's wife had gone to a committee meeting, occupied with what her husband called "some kind of civic folderol." It was the Executioner's first chance for a totally private conversation with the man who had witnessed his war's beginning.

It was not that Weatherbee had been avoiding Bolan. Rather, he had been busy with errands on behalf of Alice, the police department and his houseguest. Detectives on the Bolan watch had called for Weatherbee three times in the past four days, inviting him to study crime scenes, look at bodies, ponder evidence. Each time, the former chief of homicide came home distracted, uncommunicative.

The time had come for talk. When they had finished eating, when the plates were cleared away and they were

settled over coffee spiked with Irish whiskey, Bolan knew
that he could wait no longer for some answers.

"I still don't understand why you took me in."

The gray-haired ex-captain of detectives settled back and
sipped his coffee, groping for words to explain.

"I don't know if I've got an answer for you," Weatherbee replied finally. "It wasn't planned, I'll tell you that.
Somebody got a squeal that you were coming back, and
when they called me for advice it sounded easy. Looks like
I was wrong."

Bolan heard alarm bells going off inside his head. "You
knew I was coming?"

"Someone knew."

It did no good to worry that one for the moment. Obviously calling in the police was part of the elusive adversary's plan.

"You could have left me where I was, or turned me in.
You could have ended it."

"I thought about it, sure. Both ways. It would have been
the easy thing, the safe thing. Hell, I could have been a
hero for a couple of days, but who needs heroes anymore?"

The former chief of homicide was covering, but the soldier let it go. He didn't need to analyze the motives of his
host and savior. There were other problems on his mind.

"Somebody's turning up the heat," he said.

"Somebody, yeah. The PD and the papers think it's
you."

"How do the hits stack up?"

"Professional. Precise. Our shooter does his homework and he doesn't miss." The captain glanced across his
coffee cup to grin at Bolan. "Usually."

"Could it be a family beef?"

"What family? Girrardi's on his own, with sanctions from New York and Boston. He's been having problems with the boys from Bogotá, but this is definitely not their style. Too subtle. If the Indians were opening hostilities, I'd look for bigger body counts, plenty of civilian casualties."

"It wouldn't be the first time someone tried to scam his way around the local capo," Bolan said.

"Agreed, but Tarantella is the only candidate, and he's been covered since you hit his place in South Hill. He's not even bitching over the surveillance."

"Wild cards?"

"Nothing on the grapevine. If the Spider's got an ace, he's being cool about it, and they've been in touch since you were hit."

Bolan had anticipated Weatherbee's response, expected him to answer as he had, dispelling the alternatives, but it did not relieve the soldier's mind.

"That makes it personal."

"I'd say so."

"No matter how I try to turn this thing around, it still comes back to TIF."

"The business card?"

"It's all I've got, so far. Our shooter could have staged a dozen different incidents to hook me, once he knew I was in Hartford. When he played his hole card, he was feeling for a special nerve."

"I'd say he found it."

"Maybe." Bolan didn't want to think about his family now, this close to home, with so much riding on the line. "I need to get a handle on the Triangle survivors."

"It should all be in the files," his host replied. "I'll run it down this afternoon and get a readout we can work from."

"You're exposed already," he reminded Weatherbee unnecessarily. "It's my war now."

"Okay." The ex-captain spread his hands. "I don't suppose they'll notice you at headquarters. Hell, they probably won't even glance at the Wanted posters hanging on their walls."

Weatherbee had a point, of course. The jailhouse photographs of Bolan in Texas had been destroyed, thanks to Hal Brognola's sleight of hand, but there were sketches now, Ident-i-Kits, and some of them were too damned close for comfort. There had been no opportunity for facial alternations since then. Surgeons who performed such miracles illicitly were bankrolled by the syndicate, and Bolan dared not place his life, his war, in any doctor's hands. If he survived the anesthesia, he would wake in jail...or worse.

"What did you have in mind?"

The captain shrugged. "They want advice from me, so I'll need to double-check some background information. I can nose around the files, make up a list of brothers, cousins, this and that."

"It isn't much to go on."

"Maybe not, but it's the only theory yet that seems to have a snowball's chance of proving out."

The silence stretched between them for a moment. Bolan knew exactly what he had to ask, but knowing didn't make it any easier. At last, unable to devise a smooth approach, he plunged ahead.

"How long ago did you retire?"

"Two years come October. Why?"

"Just curious."

"My ass. You're wondering if you had anything to do with it. You think somebody finally got around to dumping me because I let you get away."

"It crossed my mind."

"Well, in a way you're right... but not the way you think. We all caught hell when you blew up Don Sergio and walked away without a scratch, but there was no suggestion of a purge, no prejudicial transfers like the old days."

"So what happened?"

"Me. *I* happened. Hell, I couldn't let it go. I studied up on every move you made, in case I got a second crack. I guess you'd say I was obsessive. Other jurisdictions started calling me the 'Bolan expert,' and I ate it up. They called me in to look at bodies, listened to my words of wisdom, and I loved it. Somewhere along the way I lost direction, though... or maybe I just lost my faith. Who knows? Whatever, I began to wonder if it would do any good to stop you, if I even had the right to try."

"You had a job to do."

"It's not enough," the former homicide detective told him flatly. "Even so, it wasn't doubts that finally did me in. I could have covered that, if I'd been smart enough to keep my mouth shut. Toward the end, when they came asking for opinions, I began to tell them what I really thought... or hint around it, anyway. It wasn't long before the brass began suggesting that I might be happier as a civilian."

Bolan sensed the bitterness, disguised by jocularity, and knew that Weatherbee had done enough—perhaps too much—for him already. The detective's midstream change of heart did not especially surprise him. All those years ago, he had recognized an undertone of sympathy in Weatherbee's demeanor, hidden well beneath the homicide investigator's rough exterior. He had explained it to himself as the cop's sadness at the massacre of Bolan's family. He had not seen the captain as a future convert to his cause then, and now he was not entirely comfortable with the thought. Allies of the Executioner had a way of dying off before their time, and Bolan had no wish to see the Weatherbees struck down.

"You've done enough," he said. "I couldn't ask—"

"You haven't asked," his host responded, almost angrily. "I'm offering, and if you tell me no, I'll go ahead and do it, anyway. More Irish?"

"Just a touch."

Bolan still didn't know what to make of Weatherbee, but his reservations had evaporated. If the ex-captain had intended to betray him, for some reasons of his own, he had missed his chance. With the return of Bolan's weaponry, his gradual recuperation, it would be more difficult for enemies to take him by surprise.

No, it was not Weatherbee's sincerity that worried Bolan now, it was his survival. The "Bolan expert" might be able to recite from memory the dates and body counts of every Executioner campaign, but he had never really seen the inside Mack Bolan's war. As a detective, he had always been once removed from Bolan's struggle, picking up the pieces, dealing with survivors, the residue of violent death. The years of grim experience with pimps and child molesters, stickup men and contract killers might have left him unprepared for Bolan's brand of unrestricted, no-holds-barred guerrilla warfare.

But the guy was signing on in spite of that, in spite of age and something like diminished confidence that lingered just beneath the surface. He was signing on because he saw no other way to go, and Bolan could not fault him there.

Instead he just said, "Thank you."

PAPPAS HAD BEEN WAITING for him when he reached the station house, and Weatherbee had cursed him silently, reminded for the umpteenth time that nothing ever came easily these days.

"What brings you in so early, Al?"

"I'm boning up a little, and I want to double-check some files for old times' sake."

"What have you got?"

"A lot of nothing, at the moment. I was hoping that a stroll down memory lane might jar the cobwebs loose."

John Pappas stared at him with frank suspicion, dark eyes probing Weatherbee's as if he might pick out some vestige of deception, seize on it like a weapon and convert it to his own devices. When he came up empty, Pappas seemed disgruntled.

"Anything that I should hear about?"

"Not yet." It wouldn't hurt to prod him just a little. "If I break the case, you'll be the first to know."

"I hope so, Al. I really do."

"You know me, John."

"Uh-huh."

A pretty woman wearing navy blue and sergeant's stripes was hovering around them now, afraid to interrupt the chief of homicide, but urgently desiring his attention. Pappas turned to face her grudgingly, defeated in the staring contest.

"Yes?"

"Your call from Hartford, Captain."

"'Kay." He shot a cautious parting glance at Weatherbee. "You'll keep me posted?"

"That's a big ten-four."

The files he needed had been formally retired, like Weatherbee himself, and Bolan's second coming had apparently not required their resurrection from the basement archives. Weatherbee was guided through the ranks of filing cabinets by a clerk with too much hair. The clerk apologized profusely, explaining that the files would be computerized "as soon as possible"—which, in the department's lexicon, might be a synonym for "never."

When the several bulging files had been retrieved, and he had been instructed how to pursue cross-references, he was conducted to a solitary table fitted out with straight-backed chair and gooseneck lamp. The clerk excused himself, with more apologies, and disappeared.

The Bolan files were like a dusty time machine for Weatherbee. With vivid clarity they took him back to younger days, many of the crime reports were terminated with his own inimitable scrawl. He browsed for several moments, letting the old emotions reassert themselves before he turned his full attention to his task.

Five men had fallen outside Triangle Finance on the afternoon of August 22. Frank Laurenti had been the man in charge, and he had been the first to die. He'd left behind a widow—now deceased, according to the files—and a son, Francesco, Jr., whereabouts unknown. The TIF accountant, Pete Rodriguez, had been a bachelor when he'd died; his parents were deceased, but he had two brothers in the Pittsfield area, and a married sister in Los Angeles. Eddie Brokaw had been office manager, divorced, three daughters living with their mother and her boyfriend in Miami when the hit had gone down. The driver, Tommy Erwin, had left a wife and a girlfriend, both of whom professed to love him madly up until the moment of their meeting at his funeral. The button, Vinnie Janus, had been sighted by informants in a string of local gay bars, seemingly in search of a companion. Vinnie had left no heirs.

It could have been a great deal worse, and Weatherbee resigned himself to checking out the several possibilities. Of the Rodriguez brothers, one had been eliminated during Bolan's blitz; the other had escaped to Michigan, where he was sitting out a term of twenty-five to life for aggravated sexual assault. The sister in Los Angeles had not thought enough of Pete to send him flowers, let alone pursue his killer through the years.

The Brokaw girls—or two of them, at any rate—were settled happily in Florida, with no apparent interest in obtaining vengeance for the man who'd battered and abused their mother on a nightly basis prior to the divorce that set them free. The eldest daughter, Marilyn, had never quite recovered from the family rift. A teenage alcoholic, she had not felt a thing the night her V-8 graduation present married with a semi on the highway south of Lauderdale.

That left Laurenti's boy. Weatherbee felt a nagging apprehension when the files refused to yield the usual information on Francesco, Jr. He had graduated high school at the age of seventeen...and dropped from sight. No forwarding address, no move to live with relatives when his mother died—no anything. From all appearances, the earth had swallowed Frank Laurenti's only son, as it had swallowed countless others through the years. Except...

As an ex-policeman—Weatherbee was familiar with the stats on missing persons. More than 150,000 persons vanished every year across America, but the numbers were misleading. The majority of missing persons vanished voluntarily, escaping from their parents, bad marriages, debts, the law. Many reappeared, unharmed, within a relatively short time. A few were murder victims, lost forever while their killers were at large and unsuspected. A very few went missing under mysterious circumstances.

Young Frank Laurenti, Jr., might have been a runaway, but something in his gut told Al Weatherbee that Frank belonged with the mysterious minority. If the boy had vanished voluntarily, he had covered his tracks like a pro. If not . . .

Indeed.

If not, then where the hell was Frank Laurenti, Jr.?

It was a long shot, but he made a note before returning the files to their respective drawers. There might be other avenues worth following, a few more bureaucratic trails he could pursue before he gave the effort up as wasted. If the kid had entered military service, if he had been arrested anywhere across America, if he had changed his name or gone to jail, there had to be a record of him somewhere. All it took was time—the one commodity that Weatherbee did not possess.

The Executioner was getting edgy, anxious to confront his faceless enemy. His wounds were nearly healed; in a few more days, there would be nothing to prevent him from embarking on a new blitz of his own, to rock the town in hopes of shaking something loose. Committed as he was to helping Bolan now, the former chief of homicide wanted to avoid a bloodbath in the streets. It went against the grain for him to help to prepare for a massacre.

He didn't see John Pappas on his way back through Homicide, relieved that he would not be forced to face another inquisition. Pappas couldn't break him—Weatherbee had been around too long for that—but the chief could become suspicious enough to put surveillance on his former boss. A stakeout on Weatherbee's house would lead to Bolan, and he didn't even want to think about the consequences—to himself, to Alice, to the Executioner.

The sudden sunlight stung his eyes, and for a moment Weatherbee was nearly blinded. As it was, he almost missed Frank Lawrence, just emerging from a dark Camaro parked with its front against the whitewashed cinder-block wall. Weatherbee raised a hand in noncommittal greeting, and the sergeant nodded, brushing past him as he headed for the double doors.

Sergeant Lawrence didn't like him much, a fact that ranked somewhere below the falling value of the peso on a list of Weatherbee's concerns. He glanced at the sergeant's car, admiring how he kept it up, wondering what sort of accident had led him to replace a fender on the driver's side. The paint would pass a casual inspection, fooling nine out of ten would-be purchasers, but as he studied it more closely Weatherbee detected subtle differences in color, in the luster of the paint itself. The fender was a new addition, not a simple touch-up job; there was no sign of bodywork beneath the paint, no rippling of damaged steel restored to something less than its original condition.

Weatherbee pondered the problem as he slid behind the wheel of the Buick. Why should Lawrence's Camaro or its damaged fender matter to him, anyway? With all the other problems pressing in on him now, why should he care if Lawrence came to work by rickshaw, with a grinning coolie in the lead?

The answer was, it didn't make a goddamned bit of difference. He had the world's most wanted fugitive at home, a city that he loved was about to blow up in his face, and he was playing amateur detective like a schoolboy on vacation. It was time to get his damned priorities in order before he lost it all.

He owed the Executioner his full attention. And in his gut, he knew he owed the guy a great deal more than that.

## 22

It had taken time for Lawrence to assemble all the pieces in his mind, but now he had them, and they fitted. It was incredible that no one else had put the thing together. It was so damned obvious, when you considered all the details... but then again, nobody else possessed his knowledge. No one knew it all except Frank Lawrence.

Something had been nagging at him from the moment he reached the station house, demanding his attention, though he couldn't put his finger on it. Meeting Weatherbee first thing was bad enough. It put the sergeant in a sour mood, reminding him that Pappas and the rest were still relying on a has-been failure to protect their asses. Lawrence would not be surprised if they consulted psychics next, the way things had been going. He could almost picture Pappas with a crystal ball and tarot cards spread out on his desk, attempting to discover Bolan's aura by communing with the dear departed.

John would get a shock if he connected with the ghosts of Manny Ingenito and his driver, or the others who had fallen to the hunter's guns. Eight bodies in the past six days. Pappas was convinced that Bolan still stalked the streets of Pittsfield, picking off his targets with the cold precision of a murderous machine. It was just what Frank Lawrence wanted Pappas and the rest of them to think; if they believed the soldier was among them, kicking ass all over town, his final execution "by the mob" would come as no surprise, would be accepted as the natural conclusion of a one-man war against the odds.

Except that Lawrence would know better. As would Bolan, while he sweated out the final microseconds of his wasted life.

No sooner was Lawrence through the double doors of the station house than Pappas made a beeline for him, brandishing a sheaf of telephone reports. So far that morning they had received sixty calls, most of them from residents convinced that they had sighted Bolan driving, walking, shopping, even lounging by a motel swimming pool, all at different points around the city. One hysterical old biddy thought her son-in-law might be Mack Bolan; he was on the road a lot, and she had never really liked him, anyway. They were a waste of time, but each and every call had to be checked out, eliminated, added to the growing "loony file" of false alarms, dead ends and mistaken identity.

Somebody had to check out the loonies, and Lawrence didn't mind. It gave him some time to think, some time alone, without the captain breathing down his neck. He knew there was something lurking just below the conscious level of his mind that might ensure his victory, the Executioner's defeat. If only he could focus, pick it out of all the jumbled thoughts and images collected in his memory...

It came to him at lunch with such astounding clarity that Lawrence nearly choked on his salami sandwich. In a sudden flash of recognition, brighter than the sun, he had the answer, knew there could be no mistake. The pieces fitted, and Lawrence didn't even have to force them. The solution had been waiting for him all along.

Al Weatherbee.

The bastard had been loitering around the station more and more the past few days, until it almost seemed he had been restored to active duty. Asking questions, rifling the files...in search of what? He was supposed to be the frigging "Bolan expert," but he acted like a rookie starved for information on his first big case. Whenever Pappas asked for an opinion, Weatherbee would chew his lip and scratch his head awhile before producing dip-shit noncommittal answers that were worse than useless. If the old man meant to help them, he was failing miserably. But if he wanted information for himself or someone else—if he was helping Bolan—then it all made sense.

The Buick finally clinched it for him, and he recognized at last that elusive "something" that had haunted him all morning. It was the glimpse of Weatherbee's sedan, no different from a million others, that had started Lawrence thinking. It resembled the four-door that had passed him, eastbound, on the night he'd shot Mack Bolan. Never mind that there might be a thousand four-door Buicks in the city, plus a few more thousand imitators, similar enough to pass at night when you were trying to avert your eyes, prevent yourself from being made. Car and driver, Weatherbee's obsession with the Bolan case, his sudden interest in collecting scuttlebutt around the station house—they added up to more than mere coincidence.

A driveby banished any latent doubts. The former chief of homicide was home, his Buick in the driveway. Lawrence knew that he was right, knew what must be done.

Weatherbee was in the phone book, and Lawrence called him from a booth at a service station three blocks over. He recognized the old man's voice immediately, and did not bother to disguise his own.

"Hello?"

"I've got a message for your houseguest."

"What?" Suspicion in the tone, and caution now. "Who is this?"

"Never mind. Just put him on."

"There must be some mistake."

"You made it, Al. Don't make it any worse. I'm waiting."

"If you'd tell me who you're calling for..."

"I'm calling for the goddamned fugitive that you've been hiding, Al. Now I can take my story to the cops, or I can drop a pound of C-4 down your fucking chimney...but I'd rather talk to Bolan. Will you put him on?"

He could almost see the old man thinking that one over, weighing odds and options. When he spoke again, there was a weary resignation in his voice.

"Hold on."

He had the bastard. Lawrence felt it in his bones. But he was not prepared for the electric tingling in his stomach when another, deeper voice came on the line.

"I've been expecting you," the bastard said.

DEAD AIR, FOR JUST A MOMENT, and Bolan thought the caller might have hung up, satisfied to know that he was staying with the Weatherbees. If he had broken off, they could expect a raid—by gunners or police—at any moment. Either way it played, it would be worse for Al and Alice Weatherbee than for the Executioner.

But he could hear the caller breathing now, as if afraid to speak. He tried to visualize the hunter, then gave it up as hopeless, concentrating on the open line.

"You knew I'd call?"

"It stood to reason."

Bolan did not recognize the voice, but that meant nothing. The caller knew him well enough to trace his hiding place, as he had done in Hartford with the safe house. This time he was calling, rather than implanting high explosives, and the soldier knew that could only mean one thing.

"You got my card," the caller said.

"You didn't leave a forwarding address."

"It was an oversight. I'd like to make it up to you."

"I thought you'd never ask."

"We didn't have much time to talk the other night."

"I caught the gist of what you had to say."

"I owe you one—you know that."

"No time like the present."

"Midnight's better."

"Suits me fine."

"I hope you're feeling well."

"I can't complain."

"The old man saved your bacon, guy."

"He's been a friend."

"I ought to blow his ass away for meddling in things he doesn't understand."

"You'll have to get through me."

"I'm looking forward to it, Slick."

"So name the place."

"Let's take it from the top. Remember Commerce Street?"

"It sounds familiar."

"Yeah, I'll bet. You got your start there, didn't you?"

"It was as good a place as any."

"What about the names? Do you remember any of them? Did you even know the fucking names?"

"I'd like to know your name."

The caller chuckled wickedly. "Don't worry, Slick. You'll know my name, all right. I'm gonna carve it on your chest before you get your ticket punched."

"We'll see."

"You're dead already, man. You're just too god-damned stupid to lie down."

"Tonight."

"You'll come alone?"

"I wouldn't miss it for the world."

He cradled the receiver, beating the caller to it, turned back to face Al Weatherbee. Alice was out, and Bolan felt a pang of apprehension for her, but he shook it off. The caller would have gloated over a hostage, delighted in the opportunity to terrorize his prey. Alice would be safe, at least until the midnight meeting was completed. Later, if the caller was alive, he might turn to the elimination of potential witnesses.

"Our boy?"

The gray-haired ex-captain's frown was dark as thunder. Bolan nodded silent confirmation.

"Dammit, how'd the bastard get this number?"

"Never mind. He won't be using it again."

"You set a meet."

It didn't sound like a question, and the soldier did not answer.

"I'd appreciate a lift," he said.

"Damned right. Between us, we can squeeze the little scumbag like a tube of toothpaste. By the time we're finished with him—"

Bolan stopped the captain with his eyes. "I'm solo this time out," he told Al Weatherbee. "I need to find a rental agency and get myself some wheels."

"Take mine."

The soldier shook his head. "No good. If anything goes wrong, the trace would bring it home to you."

"Goddammit!"

Bolan understood the older man's frustration, but he would not further jeopardize the Weatherbees. Already, by saving Bolan's life, they had invited mortal danger, flirting with disaster that had not yet been averted, only postponed. If he failed to meet his adversary, if he let the hunter slip away, the Weatherbees might pay the price of Bolan's failure with their lives.

"I'll get my things together."

"Are you up to this?"

"No choice," he said. "There may not be a second chance."

"I'll leave a note for Alice."

"Tell her you'll be home within the hour."

"Sure."

He left the captain standing in the kitchen, scowling, and retreated toward the bedroom. There were preparations to be made before he faced his nameless enemy. He knew the killing ground, surmised the hunter's motive, but he would not have the final answer, right, until he looked his adversary in the eye.

At midnight.


THE CALL HAD RATTLED Weatherbee. He was listed in the telephone directory, unlike a host of other cops who jealously guarded their domestic privacy, but his caller had not found Mack Bolan listed there. Hell, no. The cryptic caller had Weatherbee's number in more ways than one, and it would be enough to rattle anybody.

In law enforcement, information was a prized commodity. The more you knew about a man, the easier it was to deal with him from strength. If you knew enough, you held his future in your hands. Like now. The caller was a big one-up on Weatherbee, possessed information that could land the former chief of homicide in jail, or worse. It was the alternative to jail that worried him the most.

If his secret had been discovered somehow by another cop, he would have expected a direct approach. The raiders would descend on his house with riot guns and warrants, or at the very least a former colleague would meet him somewhere after hours, offering sage advice for Weatherbee to put his act in order. Either way, there would have been no cryptic phone calls, no demands to speak with Bolan. If the Feds or the local force were on to Weatherbee, he would be sitting in a cell right now, praying that a second mortgage on the house would cover bail.

The Mafia would not have talked to him at all. If Tarantella's shooters knew about his guest, they would surround his tract house with steel, and slaughter every living thing inside before the neighbors had a chance to call for help. According to mythology, the mob could reach you anywhere, anytime, and if the legends weren't entirely factual, the truth was close enough.

So it was not police, and not the mob. That left the wild cards, and Weatherbee didn't even want to think about the implications there. If someone had been stalking Bolan all the way from Hartford and beyond, he might have traced him to the Weatherbees in any one of several ways. He scanned the recent past, trying to discover the error that had placed them all in mortal jeopardy, but came up empty. Bolan had not ventured from the house in fifteen days; there had been no careless conversations on the telephone. Weatherbee was convinced he had acted normally around John Pappas and the other homicide investigators. As for the neighbors, Weatherbee could count his friends on the fingers of one hand, and none had come to call these past two weeks.

He thought of Alice briefly, knew at once that she would not betray him, consciously or otherwise. She had become accustomed to keeping secrets while he worked in Homicide, and would not have failed him now. Unless...

His heart was in his throat, immediately threatening to strangle him. If Bolan's enemies had gotten to her somehow, if they had made her talk...

The sheer illogic of it stopped him cold. The bastards could not have suspected him, could not have turned on Alice, without knowing the soldier's whereabouts beforehand. Likewise, if they knew where Bolan was, they had no need to drag information from Alice. But Weatherbee derived small consolation from the knowledge that his fears were groundless.

If the enemy had not seized Alice yet, why not tonight, tomorrow? If the plan to lure Bolan was unsuccessful, or if Bolan let a member of the hostile force escape, what form of retribution might they fix on?

He had to help out the soldier, however much his houseguest might resist. He was no match for Bolan on the firing line, but there must be something he could do, some contribution he could make.

The answer came to him in bits and pieces, nagging at him, skittering around the corners of his mind while he tried to catch it. A memory, unpleasant in itself, but more significant than he had first imagined. If he could only put his finger on it...

The Camaro.

Why was it important?

Bodywork.

So what?

"Sweet Jesus."

As he stood in the kitchen, an icy chill raced along Weatherbee's spine and raised the short hairs on his neck. He saw Frank Lawrence on the memory's screen, the dark

Camaro just behind him, gleaming brightly, the left rear fender oh-so-slightly different from the rest.

The Executioner had fired on his assailant before being wounded. He had missed the man . . . but what about the car?

Frank Lawrence.

Frank Laurenti.

Frank Laurenti, *Jr.*

"Jesus Christ."

This time, the captain knew that he was losing it. He didn't like the sergeant, never had. He was letting animosity create illusions in his mind. Frank Lawrence couldn't be any more than thirty-three years old, Weatherbee figured. When Bolan dropped his hammer on the scum at TIF, the sergeant would have been . . .

About fifteen.

Removed from the routine of life around the station, Weatherbee had no way to check the sergeant's movements, but if Lawrence had taken any kind of leave around the time Bolan was in Hartford, there would be a record of it. Weatherbee would have to pull some strings. Glancing at his watch, he knew that time was short. In about four hours the Executioner was scheduled to confront his nemesis, and in the meantime, Weatherbee didn't know if any friends he trusted were working the night shift.

Still, he had to try.

If there was any way on earth to prove his theory—or prove it wrong—he had to find the necessary strings and pull them, hard. He only prayed that enough time remained. Enough time for him to rip away the traitor's mask, or prove himself a fool.

Right or wrong, he wasn't looking forward to the answer. In many ways, it would be better *not* to know. Except that Bolan would be counting on him, trusting in him, and he could not let the soldier down. Not after letting Bolan touch his life so intimately, changing it, perhaps forever.

Until he knew for sure, however, he could not afford to share his vague suspicions with the Executioner. It was a dirty job. He would have to do it on his own.

Tonight.

Before Mack Bolan laid his life on the line.

Weatherbee would have to find the answer for himself and he was running out of time. Whichever way it went, the shit was sure to hit the fan. Tonight.

## 23

The shops and offices on Commerce Street were closed by six o'clock. Custodians and overtime personnel were gone by eight. At twenty past eleven, Bolan had the district to himself.

Almost.

There would be someone waiting for him, in or near the former offices of Triangle Industrial Finance. Someone with an ax to grind, a grudge that would not go away until it was expunged with blood. The soldier meant to find his faceless adversary here, and soon, to close the old, unfinished chapter of his life.

He circled twice around the block, eyes scanning darkened offices, shops with lights left on inside to help security patrols. He drove past windows filled with strutting mannequins and displays of furniture, a gun shop with steely shutters that looked like a giant cage. The space once occupied by Triangle Finance was shabby in comparison, the faded signs on door and windows wearily proclaiming that it was available For Sale or Lease.

The rental car was cramped, but it had been the best available when Weatherbee dropped Bolan at the agency. The soldier didn't mind; the wheels were transportation, nothing more. They would take him where he had to go...if he was still in shape to travel once his business was completed there on Commerce Street. It had been difficult persuading Weatherbee to let him come alone, but he had finally secured a promise that his host would wait at home with Alice. He trusted Weatherbee, but only to a point, so he had not mentioned where the midnight rendezvous was to occur.

Throughout the crosstown drive, the Executioner had doubled back repeatedly, to avoid being followed. It had cost him precious time, but he had reached the target zone without a tail.

The district was patrolled sporadically, and Bolan knew that any effort to conceal his vehicle would excite suspicion. Opting for audacity instead, he parked the rental curbside, half a block from the abandoned premises of TIF. The car might belong to anyone: a night clerk working overtime, a customer with engine trouble, a custodian employed by one of several nearby shops where lights had been left on. If anyone was interested enough to check it out, a call downtown would trace it to the rental agency, where Bolan had obtained the wheels with false ID. He would be on about his business with the enemy before the phony driver's license could be double-checked through records in the capital.

Beneath the trench coat, Bolan was in blacksuit, his military harness buckled into place. He made a point of tuning out the pain where the webbing chafed against his injured shoulder. There might be worse in store, before the night was over. With the Uzi submachine gun loaded and secured in its rigging underneath his arm, the soldier was prepared to make his move.

He locked the rental, turned away and crossed the empty street without a backward glance. If police were waiting for him later—if he ever came back out—time enough then to face the problem. For now, he was eager to gain entry to the offices of TIF, to seek out the man who had stalked him across two states.

He had discussed the field of suspects with Al Weatherbee, concurring in the captain's hunch that his assailant might be Frank Laurenti's son. They might be wrong, of course, and it didn't really matter now who the enemy was. They were light-years beyond the point of compromise, and Bolan had no alternatives. He must destroy his enemy or be himself destroyed.

Once the name of Frank Laurenti had conjured up a seething hatred in the soldier's gut, compelling him to seek revenge against the monsters who had destroyed his family. The hatred had been exorcised by fire—gunfire—and the Executioner had come away from Frank Laurenti's death a different man.

His act of vengeance, carried out so long ago on Commerce Street, had shown him that the enemy was not a single man or group of men. The evil did not wear a static face, but spread through society like a pervasive cancer, gnawing on the vitals of the body politic. The execution of Laurenti and his gunners had treated the symptoms, rather than striking a blow against the root of the disease. From TIF, the soldier had gone on to making war on the sickness where it lived. Laurenti's death had been an education, the lesson etched in blood.

For others, for Laurenti's family, the man's death would have seemed a tragic murder, plain and simple. Bolan sometimes thought about the women who were widowed, children who were orphaned by his private war. He sympathized with them, recognized that they were victims—not of his crusade, but of the malignancy he fought against, victims of savages who thought so little of their families that they brought death and misery upon them all. The savage fathers' sins rebounded into future generations, wreaking havoc on the innocent. That was a pity, sure...but it did not weaken his commitment to his cause.

If Frank Laurenti's son was waiting in the dusty, dark offices for Bolan, he would have to take his chances like the rest. He must know by now what kind of man his father was, and why he'd died. If anger and lust for vengeance overrode his common sense, and if he was driven by a need to even up an ancient score, then Bolan would accommodate him.

In the narrow alleyway, he found a metal ladder bolted to the wall. Memory told him there had been a skylight on the roof that would provide the perfect means of entry, if it was still there. He shed the trench coat and scrambled up the ladder, ignoring stabs of pain in his shoulder, side and thigh. His still-mending body would perform because it had to. Bolan would accept no failure, brook no compromise.

His destiny was waiting for him inside the deserted building, and the soldier would not keep it waiting any longer.

FRANK LAWRENCE HAD BEEN WAITING in the dark since nine o'clock. He knew enough of Bolan's tactics, to know the Executioner would show up early, looking for any advantage he could find. He would not be this early, though, and once again the hunter's knowledge of his prey had served him well. Now Lawrence had the high ground, and he meant to use it.

He did not know from what direction the Executioner would come, but he covered all his bets as far as possible. From his position in the central office that had once been his father's, he would hear any attempts to enter through the doors at front or back. The front was locked, and Lawrence doubted that Bolan would be rash enough to make his entry from the street. The back door, through which Lawrence had gained access hours earlier, was closed, but he had made a point of leaving it unlocked. It was so obvious that the soldier just might try it; if he didn't, Lawrence had the other means of entry covered.

The frosted glass windows in the rest rooms at the rear were painted shut. If Bolan wasted half the night, he might be able to remove enough rust and paint to open the windows, but the task would be noisy and time-consuming, not his sort of move at all. The skylight above the lobby, where Lawrence's father's secretaries used to sit and type, was another possible, all right. He would have to keep it covered, too, while he waited for his quarry. If the Executioner thought himself to be the first to arrive, he might relax his guard enough for Frank to make it quick and easy, like stepping on an ant.

But no, he did not want it to be quick and easy. In the nightmares of his youth, Bolan had been slow to die, his end protracted, painful. There was no justice in a bullet whistling through the darkness, snuffing out the bastard's life before he knew who was killing him and why.

Frank Lawrence cared about justice, however corny or old-fashioned that might sound to some people. His father's murderer deserved to die, but first, he had to realize he was being executed for his crimes. If Bolan died believing his enemy was just another greasy thug from Little Italy, all the time and preparation would have been wasted. The hunter needed to observe a certain ritual, preserve the symbolism of his deed.

The Colt Commando seemed to weigh a ton. He felt nervous, jumpy, now that he was on the verge of achieving something that had been his goal since he was a child. If anything interfered to rob him of his moment . . .

No.

Defeatist thinking might become a self-fulfilling prophecy. In Vietnam and, later, on the streets, he had observed the soldiers and policemen who became their own worst enemies. The moment a soldier lost his confidence, he was as good as dead.

He would not be cheated of his moment. If the Executioner surrendered, gave up his life without a fight, he would be disappointed. The bastard must not cheat him now, when he had come so far and risked so much.

With something less than ninety minutes till midnight, he heard the enemy approaching. It was not the wind, did not sound like a rat, although the old, deserted office building had its share of vermin. Standing in the darkness, trembling with anticipation, Lawrence sought to pinpoint the direction of the sound. It had seemed to come from everywhere at once, and for an instant he was terrified that the acoustics of the office building might betray him, rob him of the advantage of surprise.

The hunter held his breath and waited for the sound to be repeated. Just when his lungs were close to bursting and he knew that he would have to breathe or else lose consciousness, he heard another sound, different from the first, more readily identifiable.

Someone opening the skylight.

Lawrence recognized the first sound now, in retrospect; it had been Bolan snapping off an ancient hasp that held the skylight shut. Rusty hinges squealed now, briefly, and Lawrence was already moving toward the lobby, homing on the sounds that had betrayed his enemy and brought the Executioner into his hands.

The office windows had been painted over, and the lobby was a cavern shrouded in darkness. It took another moment for his eyes to adjust, before he could detect a gleam of starlight through the open portal in the ceiling twelve feet above. Underneath the skylight, the darkness varied in degrees. For just an instant, Lawrence almost thought he could see the secretaries, still typing and erasing at their desks.

But there was nothing in the lobby now, of course, not even a stick of furniture. And a rope was snaking downward through the open skylight, stopping a foot or so above the concrete floor.

He had the rotten bastard now! Let Bolan try to wriggle out of this one. A burst to shatter kneecaps, once the guy was safely through the skylight, and it would be time to let some light in on the subject, sit down with the corpse-to-be and have a chat.

He flicked the Colt Commando's safety off and brought the rifle to his shoulder, sighting on the skylight. When Bolan's shadow blocked the starlight, he would have seconds to correct his aim, allow for Bolan to descend a yard or so, make doubly sure the bastard couldn't scramble up the rope and out again before the shock of losing both his legs brought him down.

Atop the roof a shadow shifted, moved. Lawrence watched the stars wink out, eclipsed by Bolan's silhouette as he lowered himself through the opening. Seconds now. The hunter's hands were moist and clammy on his weapon.

*Now!*

He squeezed the trigger, let the flashing muzzle sweep for half an inch from left to right and back again. He heard tumblers smacking into fabric, ripping through and peppering the naked wall beyond. Half blinded by the muzzle-flash, he caught a fleeting image of the soldier as he fell; there was something fluid, almost batlike in the swift descent.

He listened for the heavy impact of flesh and bone, but heard only a rustle, like tent flaps in the wind. The short hairs on his neck stood up, his finger tightening around the Colt Commando's trigger as he scanned the darkness, desperate to know what the hell was happening.

Before he moved, the skylight came alive with winking flame. Lawrence had been suckered. Even as the parabellum rounds came slicing in above his head, before he heard the submachine gun's rattle, he was cursing Bolan's ingenuity, his own reckless hunger that had prompted him to waste his first and all-important rounds on a decoy.

Lawrence fired a burst in the direction of the skylight, but the stars were beaming at him now. His prey had made the drop while he was scrambling for cover, and now he was alone there, in the darkness, with the Executioner. He knew that only one of them could leave the place alive. For the first time in a life devoted to revenge, Frank Lawrence wondered whether he was equal to the challenge.

BOLAN WAS PREPARED when automatic fire erupted from the dark interior of the deserted offices and snatched the trench coat from his nylon line. He had retrieved the garment on a hunch, lowering it ahead of him after he'd opened the skylight. Now, with darkness on his side, he spied the hostile muzzle-flash at once and rattled off a string of parabellums from the Uzi in response. He would not take the gunner out that easily, but the fire would keep his head down for a moment, and a moment might be all the soldier needed.

He slithered down the line, a moving target, vulnerable for the second it took to reach the floor. His adversary reacted, but too slowly; the gunner's second burst sliced through empty air a foot above Bolan's head.

The office was deserted, stripped of furniture and devoid of cover. Bolan hugged the concrete floor, his Uzi cracking out another burst in answer to the probing automatic rifle fire. Downrange, he heard the bullets slapping into plaster, knew that he had missed his target once again.

It would be suicidal to remain in place, but where was he to go? From memory he resurrected floor plans of the TIF establishment, which he had visited the morning after burying his family. He knew that he was in the lobby, separated from the office proper by a waist-high railing. The four working offices of TIF, were just ahead of him, two doors on either side of a bisecting corridor. Beyond lay rest rooms, storage space, an exit leading to the narrow alleyway in back.

As far as Bolan could determine, his assailant was in the doorway of the nearest office on the left. Bolan wriggled along the floor, his Uzi still directed toward the deeper darkness of the doorway, just distinguishable now that his eyes were starting to adjust. If he could clear the gunner's line of fire, just long enough to close the gap between them...

In the pitch-black office, Bolan's adversary had also been weighing odds and angles, revising strategy to fit the changing situation. Bolan was about to make his move when sudden fire erupted from the open doorway, sweeping left to right across the lobby, forcing him to hug the floor. He heard the pounding footsteps of his enemy, was standing to chase him with a string of parabellums, when a spherical metallic object struck the floor a yard in front of him. The soldier could not see it clearly, but he recognized the telltale sound as the hand grenade began to wobble toward him.

Frantically he twisted to his left and scuttled off on hands and knees, putting space between himself and the explosive charge before it detonated. His assailant loosed a random, searching burst that rattled over Bolan's head, but bullets were his least concern. If the grenade contained a high explosive or incendiary charge, if it was fragmentation, he would not have time to clear its killing radius. He might be fried, or pulverized or riddled . . . but he would certainly be dead.

It was a concussion grenade, meant to stun, to immobilize without inflicting mortal wounds—although a man on the receiving end might pray for the relief of death. Bolan's back was turned to the initial, blinding flash, but its reflection off the barren walls was sharp and painful to his narrowed eyes. The shock wave struck him like a giant boot and lifted him off the floor, propelled him with jarring impact into the nearest wall. His ears were ringing, deafened by the blast, and for an instant, as he fought to breathe, the Executioner thought he was dying. In another moment he would feel the burning pain of shrapnel, fading with the massive loss of blood. . . . But when the moment passed and he was still alive, his addled mind quickly put the fractured pieces back in place.

And his aching eyes were not on fire after all; the lights had come on above him, and in the offices and corridor beyond the wooden railing. His assailant obviously had had electric power restored to the premises in preparation for their showdown. It had been his secret ace, and he had played it wisely.

Bolan felt the presence of another in the lobby, realized that he was not alone before he ever saw his enemy. The Colt Commando leveled at his chest was a familiar point of reference, but he did not recognize the face above the rifle. Bolan's enemy was watching him from twenty feet away, the weapon braced against his hip, one-handed, casual. He made no move to interfere as Bolan struggled to his knees, slouched back into a seated posture with his shoulders pressed against the wall. Before the move had been completed, Bolan realized he had lost the Uzi. Both his sidearms were in place, secured in their rigging, but his adversary did not seem to be concerned.

"I guess I ought to introduce myself," the gunner said at last. "No, don't get up. We're casual here. The name's Laurenti. Frank Laurenti. It was 'Junior,' but you know how these things go."

The shooter's voice hardened as he finished, but his words did not surprise the Executioner. Al Weatherbee's suspicion had proved, but Bolan would never have a chance to tell the former homicide chief that he had solved another mystery.

Laurenti stepped closer. A flash of gold drew Bolan's eyes away from the Commando's muzzle to his adversary's belt. The bright detective's shield winked back at Bolan like a solitary, mocking eye.

"Surprised? I guess you wouldn't think a loan shark's son could make the grade." Bolan's captor made no effort to disguise the anger and contempt he felt. His free hand rose to stroke the shiny metal of his badge. "It put me on the inside track, you know? This opens doors that don't exist for John Q. Citizen."

"That's smart." The words were sand in Bolan's aching throat. "How long have you been tracking me?"

Laurenti's voice went hard. "How long have you been on the road? You had me worried once or twice, I don't mind telling you. That business in New York was cute. You could've pulled it off if you'd had sense enough to let it go."

"No choice," he told the steely eyes.

Laurenti's mocking smile was gone, and the expression on his face had altered slightly, turning introspective. "Same with me," he said at last. "No choice, no options. I've been waiting for you all my life, and here we are."

The rifle didn't waver as he took another cautious stride toward Bolan. There was something else he had to say, or Bolan would have been dead already.

From the beginning of his private war, the Executioner had clung to his firm refusal to fire on a badge, no matter how the man behind it might have shamed himself, his oath of office. He knew he could not kill Laurenti now, not if it meant his life...but if the gunner took a few more steps, if he had a chance to slip beneath Laurenti's guard and grab the Colt Commando...

As if he had read Bolan's mind, Laurenti hesitated, still too far away for any attempt to reach his weapon.

"I wanted you to know why you were dying," Frank Laurenti said. "When it came, I wanted you to know who pulled the trigger. I owe you that much...and I owe it to myself." He grimaced, as if he had tasted something sour, and he said, "I owe it to my father."

"Not tonight, Laurenti!"

Bolan's captor didn't bat an eye or hesitate. He swiveled toward the unexpected voice, his automatic rifle gripped in both hands now and rattling before he verified his target. Bolan squinted past Laurenti, glimpsed Al Weatherbee beyond the office railing, both hands leveling a stainless steel revolver.

Bolan saw Laurenti's tumblers tracking, chewing up the wall and closing in on Weatherbee. He recognized the Magnum by its report. Bullets ripped through Frank Laurenti's jacket; Laurenti's blood sprayed in Bolan's face.

The impact lifted Laurenti off his feet and hurled him backward, ripped the Colt Commando from his hands. He slithered on the blood-slick floor, came to rest against the soldier's knees, his head in Bolan's lap. The upturned eyes stared into Bolan's, fading fast, and Bolan saw the life flicker out of them, the jaw go slack before Laurenti could speak.

Another moment, and the former chief of homicide stood over Bolan, frowning.

"I finally put two and two together. Better late than never, I guess."

"I guess," the soldier answered. He used one hand to close Laurenti's sightless eyes.

# Epilogue

"It was the car that made me take a look at Lawrence...er, Laurenti. After that, I had to pull some strings and wake some people up, but there was still a record of the legal name change. Lucky break, I guess. If they'd been on the ball, it would have been destroyed years ago."

"And he'd been waiting all this time."

"Apparently." The ex-detective put his Buick through another turn and shade trees closed above them, blotting out the sun. "I never cared for Lawrence much—we never hit it off. But from appearances, he was a fair detective when his mind was on the job."

"There must have been some sticky questions."

"What, the brass? No sweat. I've got them all believing that I sniffed Laurenti out with great detective work."

"No arguments on that."

Al Weatherbee suppressed a grin of satisfaction.

"I'll admit there were some doubting Thomases, but I convinced them that Laurenti led me straight to you...and you escaped while we were squaring off. As far as anybody knows, you're miles away by now."

"I wouldn't want to disappoint them."

Weatherbee was silent for the balance of their drive. He steered the Buick through the arching gates with wrought-iron angels overhead, and took the first turn on their left.

He drove with confidence, and Bolan was surprised that his companion found the place without directions.

"Well, we're here," the driver said, and noticed Bolan staring at him thoughtfully. "I guess I might've stopped by here a couple of times before."

Bolan placed one hand upon the driver's shoulder, pressed it warmly for a moment, finally went EVA. The cemetery was deserted. He figured even devoted mourners generally visited on weekends or holidays. He and Weatherbee had the graveyard to themselves . . . but somehow, Bolan knew they were not alone.

Three headstones, pressed as close as the family had been in life. He knelt before them, read the clean inscriptions to himself, although he could easily have quoted them from memory. Husband and father. Loving wife. Beloved daughter. All the names were his. Something of Mack Bolan had been buried here when three-fourths of his family was laid to rest.

His war had come full circle. The warrior knew, as he had never known before, that it was time for him to let the old, familiar ghosts lie down to sleep. So many ghosts, from Pittsfield to the Blue Ridge Mountains of Virginia and beyond. If any of them traveled with him in the future, they would have to travel on their own; he could not let them hold him back.

On Commerce Street, his war had changed again. Laurenti's death had reaffirmed the understanding gained in Bolan's first campaign: his war could not be strictly personal if he intended to survive. The enemy was far too numerous, far too diverse, for any soldier to approach the hostile camp with blinders on.

He thought about Brognola's latest offer from the Oval Office. If he took Brognola up on it, he would retain personal autonomy, the freedom to select his targets free of interference from above. From time to time, he would be offered "sensitive" assignments, which would not detract in any way from the direction or the conduct of his private war.

It was an offer worth considering, and for the moment, warrior Bolan was not closing any doors.

He spent another moment in communion with the friendly dead, then rose and started back toward where Al Weatherbee was waiting in the Buick. Wherever home might be, it did not lie in Pittsfield any longer. Bolan wondered if he still had time enough to find it, time enough to see his duty done before a bullet dropped him in the company of strangers, and his life ran out on foreign soil.

No matter.

There was time for looking, time for fighting, and if time ran out tomorrow, he would still have beaten the odds. It was the best he could hope for, living as he was on borrowed time.

But he had not forgotten how to dream.

For a lonely soldier, ever on the firing line, dreams could be enough.

## SuperBolan #8

# ROGUE FORCE

## AN EAGLE FOR THE KILLING

A covert clique within the U.S. military is set to launch an all-out war in Central America. This secret cabal of generals believes the American people are being betrayed by a soft U.S. government. Their idea is to stage another "Vietnam." But this time on America's doorstep.

There's only one way that Washington can neutralize these superpatriots: pit it's supersoldier against the very men who trained him!

SB8

# 4 FREE BOOKS
# 1 FREE GIFT
## NO RISK
## NO OBLIGATION
# NO KIDDING

# TAKE 'EM NOW

## FOLDING SUNGLASSES FROM GOLD EAGLE

Mean up your act with these tough, street-smart shades. Practical, too, because they fold 3 times into a handy, zip-up polyurethane pouch that fits neatly into your pocket. Rugged metal frame. Scratch-resistant acrylic lenses. Best of all, they can be yours for only $6.99. **MAIL ORDER TODAY.**

Send your name, address, and zip code, along with a check or money order for just $6.99 + .75¢ for postage and handling (for a total of $7.74) payable to Gold Eagle Reader Service, a division of Worldwide Library. New York and Arizona residents please add applicable sales tax.

Remove from pouch...

unfold once...

**GOLD EAGLE**

Gold Eagle Reader Service
901 Fuhrmann Blvd.
P.O. Box 1325
Buffalo, N.Y. 14240-1325

unfold twice...

and they're ready to wear.

GES1–RRR

*Offer not available in Canada.*